A Calf for Venus

A Calf for Venus

Norah Lofts

LARGE PRINT

Oxford

First published in Great Britain 1949
by
Michael Joseph Ltd.

Published in Large Print 2008 by ISIS Publishing Ltd.,
7 Centremead, Osney Mead, Oxford OX2 0ES
by arrangement with
the Author's Estate

British Library Cataloguing in Publication Data
Lofts, Norah, 1904–1983
    A calf for Venus. – Large print ed.
    1. Historical fiction
    2. Large type books
    I. Title
    823.9'.14 [F]

ISBN 978–0–7531–7944–4 (hb)
ISBN 978–0–7531–7945–1 (pb)

Printed and bound in Great Britain by
T. J. International Ltd., Padstow, Cornwall

Towards the end of the year 1800 the Lady Venus looked down from Mount Olympus and saw that the Century of Reason was about to give way to the Century of Steel; and she was sad, and said wistfully to Jupiter that her altars had been cold and bare for a hundred years, and that if she read the signs aright they would, for another hundred, remain so, though Bacchus and Mars received sacrifices every day. Jupiter was sorry for her and said, "I will send you a calf."

And so, on an afternoon in November, 1800 . . .

CHAPTER
ONE

At Newmarket the coach halted for fifteen minutes and all but two of the passengers alighted with the haste and urgency of prisoners suddenly faced with a chance of freedom, and began to push their way into the inn parlour where a great leaping log fire promised comfort for nipped fingers and noses, and a table laden with food and drink, specially prepared for hasty consumption, offered sustenance for the rest of the journey.

Of the pair who resisted the inn's enticement on this raw November afternoon, one was a girl who remained in her seat in the coach, huddled in such apathy that she appeared to be oblivious to her surroundings: the other, more lively, was a young man who got down with the rest, but who proceeded to walk rapidly about the inn yard, stamping his feet and beating his arms across his chest and occasionally glancing from the small, white-wrapped parcel in his hand to the figure of the girl within the coach.

He was very young, only just emerging from boyhood, his long, loose, powerful limbs still capable of awkwardness, his features, which later might harden into an austere handsomeness, still ill-assorted and indecisive. There was, at first sight, something a little countrified about him, but the bucolic suggestion was contradicted by his clothes, by his long, sensitive, well-kept hands, fine prominent nose and lively observant eyes. When he ceased stamping his feet and beating his arms his bearing took on a prodigious slightly ridiculous dignity which would, in time, when it ceased to be conscious and assumed, be very impressive. In fact something of his history could be read into his physical being. He was the product of a forty-acre farm, a boy whose mother had recognised his potential abilities and slaved and half-starved herself to give him an education. He was within two months of his twenty-first birthday, and if, at the coming Midsummer he passed his examination — as there seemed no doubt he would do — would be a qualified medical man. At the moment he was a doctor's apprentice, but the people of the small town where he lived already called him the young doctor or Doctor Shadbolt. On this particular afternoon he was on his way home from Cambridge, whither, during the past two years, he had gone at intervals to attend certain courses of lectures. This great and unusual privilege had been achieved for him by his master who not only thought highly of his promise, but was also aware that his own theoretical knowledge had grown rusty during forty years of practice.

The girl inside the coach bore the name of Letitia Rowan and she was four years his junior. They were destined to affect one another's lives in no uncertain manner. They had travelled in close proximity from

Cambridge to Newmarket, but they had not yet spoken a word.

He had noticed her, even as he edged himself into the spare seat by her side, and his first thought had a professional flavour. He had seldom, he thought, seen anyone, in bed or out of it, who looked so pale and fragile, so ill-conditioned to undertake a long journey upon an inclement day. Yet she had borne the cold and the lurching of the coach without any sign of distress, and when a jolt which one might have thought would have shaken her to pieces, threw her, now against the side of the coach, now against Humphrey's arm, she gathered herself together again, self-contained and silent, and renewed her grip upon the clumsy, badly wrapped parcel which she held in her lap. He decided that she was just a bad case of anaemia, and for a moment or two, with the young disciple's inordinate interest in his chosen profession, amused himself by pretending that she was his patient and that he was prescribing a tonic for her.

And then, all at once, and for no reason, since he often amused himself that way, there seemed to be something subtly indecent about his imaginary relationship. She wasn't his patient and she had as much right to her privacy as any other passenger. So he diverted his attention and exercised his mind and excused his lapse by brooding over the difference between doctors and other men in a general sort of way. What a feeling of detachment not to mention superiority, could be derived, for example, from seeing, in a man in a flaming temper, not an intimidating force, but an over-blooded body badly in need of phlebotomy.

When he had explored this line of thought for a time he reverted to the girl again, this time with a determination to confine his interest to external things. She was — or would be, in a more favourable state of health — extremely pretty, he thought. Even her greenish pallor and hollow cheeks could not rob her face of a curious sorrowful beauty. Everything about her looked so soft, so very vulnerable. Her hair was brown, a soft, genuine brown with nothing of red or gold in it, and it hung, heavy, untidy, from under a battered little hat. Her nose was like a child's, flattened in a sweet curve between the eyes and blunt at the tip. Of her mouth the top lip was full and protruded a little, the lower drooped above a slightly receding chin. Save for the eyes it might easily have been the face of a twelve-year-old; and in everything save their expression the eyes, too, had a look of youth. The brows and lashes were the same brown as her hair and the lashes were incredibly long, so that with each lowering of the lids they met and interlaced and then disentangled themselves, perceptibly, almost with difficulty. But when once, during his unobtrusive scrutiny, her eyes met his, although he looked away in confusion, as though caught in the act of spying, he saw that the eyes themselves were not those of a child; they were old and full of a sorrow that he found disturbing. It was not a bereaved look — he was familiar with that, and did not jump hastily to the conclusion that she was on her way to a funeral — nor was a look of active unhappiness. In

4

a more mature face, perhaps, that expression of experience, of disillusionment, of remoteness, would not have been noticeable; but set in that small, pale, childish face it sent a stab to the heart.

For the rest she looked poor. Her cloak and the gown which showed beneath it were both of black, rusty with age, and skimpy and threadbare, inadequate for a winter journey. Her white cotton stockings were cobbled and her shoes were derelict, a mass of patches and the patches in places worn away again. She had no gloves, and though from time to time she changed hands, tucking one away into the poor shelter of her cloak, one was always exposed, clutching at the parcel in her lap. They were thin hands, with little knuckly fingers, blue veined, and whiter than one might have expected in a poor girl, but the first finger of her left hand explained that, the top joint was calloused with needle-pricks. She was evidently a little sempstress.

At last he had learnt all that his eyes could tell him about her; but he kept glancing at her, feeling the pull of some extraordinary fascination. Then he wondered if she were hungry, if indeed her frailty and apathy resulted from prolonged underfeeding. He was familiar with poverty, both in its ordinary and genteel forms, and knew all too many cases when a bowl of beef tea or a good egg custard wheedled from his master's housekeeper had been more effective than any physic.

He was by this time healthily hungry himself, for in order to catch the coach he had missed his dinner, but the good woman in whose house he lodged during his Cambridge visits had put him up what he still called by the country term of "stay-piece" and the food, wrapped in a clean napkin, was just inside his valise. He would eat it during the halt at Newmarket, as was his custom.

As they neared the town he became extremely conscious of the parcel of food. When the coach stopped he found himself hoping that the girl would descend with the others and go into the inn and take her share of the pies and pasties, the ham rolls, the slabs of cheese which were laid out ready to be snatched by such as could afford to pay for them. But when the moment came she remained in her place, showing no sign of movement or even of interest. So he alighted and from the yard watched to see whether she, like himself, short of pocket-money but otherwise well-provided for, had a private store of food. He circled the yard twice, the parcel weighing heavy and heavier in his hand, his pulses quickening from indecision and a premonition of embarrassment. She had nothing. She sat as he had left her, one hand clutching the parcel, one sheltering in the cloak, her gaze fixed, remote and sorrowful.

There was something outrageous in the thought of a young man addressing a young woman in such circumstances and the offer of food invited a snub. He had often experienced the extremely touchy pride of the very poor. On the other hand he knew that if he ate his food alone, without offering her a share, the thought of the lonely, hungry child sitting there while everyone else had some refreshment would haunt him for a long time. Even a snub was preferable. So he walked back to the coach and said,

"You're not getting down?"

It seemed that she came back from vast distance in order to answer him.

"This is Newmarket, isn't it? I heard the man say Newmarket. I don't get out here."

Her voice was low and hoarse, a little nasal, not very pleasing. But it was gentle; and there was a touching simplicity about the words.

"You don't have to get out, of course. But most people do. You see, it takes nearly two hours to get to Bury."

"That's right. That's where I'm going."

"I meant — most people like to get something to eat. Wouldn't you?"

A faint flicker of interest crossed her face. Then she hunched one shoulder in a gesture of resignation.

"I'm all right. Don't you worry about me."

That decided him. He climbed quickly back into the seat beside her.

"I can't afford to patronise inns," he said, opening the napkin and spreading out its contents, "but I'm well provided for. In fact I have far more than I need. Won't you share with me?"

He saw that he had been right. She was hungry. Her eyes brightened and her lips grew moist at the sight of the food.

"If you're sure you can spare it," she said hesitantly. "I don't want to be greedy but I didn't get any breakfast."

"No breakfast?" he said, and looked down at the food which had been packed for him because he had missed his dinner, and thought of the supper which would await him. "You *must* be hungry. Look, have the pasty. I had an enormous breakfast: the roll will be quite enough for me."

"Well," she said, "thank you very much." Her voice and manner were still hesitant, but as soon as she had the food in hand she bit into it avidly. A crumb of the crust broke off and lodged on her chin and she retrieved it with a flick of a little pink tongue. She ate half the solid pasty before she spoke again. Then she said,

"You see, I couldn't get to Bury last night and had to find a lodging. It was sixpence to sleep and sixpence for breakfast and I'd only got ninepence after paying my fare."

It was altogether too revealing and confidential and heart-breaking. Better not to take any notice.

"And you're going to Bury?"

"Yes. I'm going to live with my aunt." The words came out very casually, but he was left with the impression that the arrangement was not altogether of her choosing. So he said nothing and the girl bit into the pasty again. He had seldom seen so solid a piece of food disappear so quickly. As unobtrusively as possible he broke the roll which he was holding into halves and laid one back on the napkin beside the piece of cheese. When his half was eaten he went through as many of the gestures of repletion as a man might who had no plate to push away, no chair to ease from the table. And as soon as the last crumb of the pasty had gone he said, "Do finish this. I've had my fill, honestly."

She looked at him again, and now her gaze was neither impersonal, nor remote, nor sorrowful. The long lashes disentangled themselves and revealed a swimming look of gratitude, almost of adoration. As he met it something seemed to turn over inside him. Absurd as he knew the fancy to be, it felt as though his heart or his diaphragm had shifted and in shifting sent a bubble of excitement through his blood. At the same time a feeling of responsibility laid hold upon him. She mustn't ever be hungry again.

As though he could prevent it! As though hundreds of people didn't suffer hunger every day!

The other passengers came back, wiping mouths and fingers, munching a last mouthful, one even clutching a remnant of food. The sight of them made him thankful that he had allowed impulse to oust convention. It also brought to his mind the knowledge that the little interlude was ended. As the coach left the yard and rumbled upon its way he settled into his place and fixed his eyes on the flat countryside, over which the threat of the early winter twilight was already brooding. The sudden intimacy must not be advertised, nor taken advantage of. He resigned himself to the thought that she might not speak to him again, that at the journey's end she would disappear into some poor part of the town and that it was very likely that he would never see her again.

But after a long time, when only a few miles remained to be covered, the girl turned slightly in her seat and said:

"Do you know this place where I'm going?"

"Bury? Oh yes. I live there myself. I've lived there, on and off, for the last eight years."

"What's it like?"

"It's a nice town. It's the nicest place I know. But I don't know many others, so perhaps I'm no judge. I think most people would agree that it's a pleasant place."

"I've been fighting off coming to it for two years. Not because of the *place*." She brooded for a moment and then seemed to decide upon confidence. "I was beat in the end. I got ill and when I rose from my bed I could see it was either the New Cut or Bury for me. So I chose Bury."

He had never heard of the New Cut or the drab wrecked women who walked it, so he had no idea of the extent to which she was confiding in him, or the significance of the alternative. He said:

"I thought you looked ill." She looked at him astonished.

"Oh, I'm all right now. I was dead, nearly." She spoke with detachment. "But somebody took the trouble to set me on my legs again. I s'pose I should be grateful." She laughed, unmirthfully. "If it's a small town p'raps you know my aunt, Mrs. Rowan. She says she has a Coffee House right in the centre of the town."

He could only hope that his face did not betray the consternation which this piece of news roused in him. He reminded himself that he was a professional man, schooled in control. He must behave as he would if a patient mentioned some significant, ominous symptom.

10

And immediately his voice and manner became imbued with his master's blustering geniality.

"Mrs. Rowan? Why yes. Yes, of course. I know of her. Everyone in Bury knows Mrs. Rowan and her Coffee House. I've never been in it myself. I've no time. But it's very well known."

"What's it like?"

"Well, it's . . . it's a Coffee House, you know. Very much like the rest of them I should imagine. But as I say I've never been in it, so I can't tell you very much about it."

He could feel, with some suddenly developed extra sense that the girl beside him was bracing herself to ask another question. Hesitating, because of its implications, and determined, because of its importance.

"Is it . . . a respectable place, would you say?"

His natural instinct was to blurt out "No, and you must on no account go there!" But as the words ranged themselves in his mind he realised that he hadn't a single piece of evidence to bring in defence of such denunciation. People had been gossiping for years about Mrs. Rowan, her daughters, the other young women who appeared and disappeared, but anyone who had attempted to take the gossip seriously had inevitably been put to confusion. Humphrey remembered that about twelve months earlier rumours had become so rife and so virulent that the town authorities had combined with those of the Church — upon whose property the Coffee House stood — in an attempt to close the place. An informal inquiry had been held. Doctor Coppard as a near neighbour and a responsible citizen had attended several meetings. But nothing had happened. No sound, unshakable evidence that the place was other than it seemed to be had ever been brought forward. All the rumours, it seemed, had been based upon hearsay, or malice: and Mrs. Rowan, when her turn came, had produced many reputable citizens to say that they regularly frequented her house to drink, to meet one another, and to read the papers and periodicals. "Naturally," Doctor Coppard had said in his dry way; "no man came forward to say that he'd been there for any other purpose; and I'm afraid that unless the Reverend Mr. Pollinger goes himself and provides it, he'll never get the evidence that he needs." Mrs. Rowan had endured the inquiry with a tolerant good humour which did little to help her detractors; but she had dealt a blow or two. "You can any of you come in at any time, gentlemen, and if you see anything that shocks *you* I shall be the first to be surprised": and "It is a poor reflection upon the probity of gentlemen to suggest that because we are three females without male protection we automatically become the recipients of dishonourable suggestions." Doctor Coppard, who had never entered either the front or back door of the establishment, had enjoyed the proceedings, even Mrs. Rowan's thrusts, but it was said that there were others who, forced into a false position by their own hypocrisy, had been at pains to confuse the issue and bring the inquiry to a close. Mrs. Rowan still flourished and people still gossiped about her.

But such matters could hardly be spoken of to Mrs. Rowan's niece in the middle of a coachful of people.

And suppose they were, and suppose the girl took heed of the hinted warning, where else could she go? On her own admission she had turned to her aunt as a refuge against destitution, and with the best will in the world he could not suggest an alternative.

"It always looks very nice," he said, and knew that his words were feeble and the question still unanswered. Or perhaps he had answered her.

"All I know is my aunt always wrote to me very kindly," she said, with a trace of defiance in her voice. "I didn't always answer, even, but over and over again she wrote that I could come any time."

There'd been some gossip about another niece, Humphrey seemed to recall; but he hadn't been much interested in the bits of gossip which Doctor Coppard had relayed to him over the meal table and he couldn't remember exactly what was said to have happened. Now he wished he had listened more attentively. The only scrap which came back to him clearly was irrelevant. The bell-ringer of St. James' church had at one time lodged with Mrs. Rowan and since the bell-tower adjoined the house, the idle fellow had made a hole in the wall and arranged the rope so that he could pull the bell without getting out of his bed. That had been one of Mr. Pollinger's grievances, but as Doctor Coppard had pointed out, it wasn't a reflection upon Mrs. Rowan's moral character.

It wasn't that kind of thing which the girl wanted to know. But then, who could answer her question quite fairly? Who knew?

He took refuge in a remark which would show his interest and commit him to nothing.

"Mrs. Rowan has daughters of her own, I believe. I've seen them going in and out. I live almost opposite, you know."

"Yes. Cathy and Susan." He felt her centre of interest change and saw her look down at the hem of her skirt and the broken shoes that showed beneath it. "So you know them . . . by sight I mean? Are they very fine?" He was again aware of pity. Evidently she was nervous of meeting her cousins.

"They always look very nice. But they aren't as pretty as you are."

She gave him one of her fluttering glances, but it was completely innocent of coquetry. She said flatly:

"I was prettier before I was ill. Not that I mind. Being pretty doesn't do a girl much good, if she's poor and on her own."

The frankness embarrassed him afresh. At the same time his mind raced away, wondering what her experience had been to have taught her that, so young.

They did not speak again until the coach turned in at the yard of the Angel Inn and stopped. He alighted quickly and helped the girl down.

"Have you any other luggage?"

"Yes, a bundle. That one there. Oh, thank you. And thank you again for the food. And for talking to me. It's taken my mind off for a bit."

"Perhaps someone is meeting you," he said, looking round for Mrs. Rowan or one of her daughters or for the old hunch-backed man who did odd jobs about the

Coffee House. "If not I can show you the way. It's hardly a step."

"Oh, nobody'll meet me. My aunt has been inviting me for these last two years, ever since my father died. She said come any time, and yesterday I knew it was now or never, so I just got on the coach to Cambridge. I hope it'll be all right. She *said* any time."

So she wasn't expected! He found himself wishing that the big red house just beyond the inn were his own, that he were like Doctor Coppard, established, independent, with no one to criticise his actions. If he were he would say to her now, "Don't go to the Coffee House. Come home with me and I'll tell you something about it and give you time to think over your decision." But he wasn't Doctor Coppard; he was only an apprentice, with not an inch in the world he could call his own. So he could only say soothingly, "I'm sure it will be all right. I'll walk over with you. It's this way."

They struck out diagonally across the open space between the Inn and the old gateway to the vanished Abbey. At the far corner loomed the dark bulk of a church and next to it, crouching between it and the tall grey tower which was another relic of the past was a prim neat house with a heavy swinging sign over its door. The windows to the left of the door were lighted, but the curtains were drawn and only a dim rosy light showed through them. The house had a secret, withdrawn look.

They halted just between the window and the door and now that they had arrived Humphrey knew a moment of panic. If a half, or even a quarter of the things — if just one single thing — that he had heard about this place were true it was the last place at which to leave so young and innocent and confiding a girl. But what could he do? Where else could she go? And really what reason could he give for making any other suggestion? And what business was it of his? He'd just met a girl on the coach and shared his stay-piece with her and carried a bit of luggage from the coach stop to the house for which she was bound, her aunt's house, to which she had been invited. One must be reasonable, sensible.

"Well," he said, "here we are. This is the house."

She looked up at it in the dusk. "It isn't much like I expected."

She freed one hand from the bundle she carried and moved one step towards the door. But she did so reluctantly and hesitantly, and he realised that he had just one moment in which to say . . . what was it that must be said?

"Look," he blurted out, "my name's Humphrey Shadbolt. I live over there. D'you see that big red house just past where the coach stopped. If you . . . if you ever want anything come across there for me. I mean if anything went . . . er went wrong . . . or you needed a friend. D'you understand? Shadbolt, just across the road. Will you remember that?"

"Oh, I will," she said. "You have been kind. I never thought I'd meet anybody so kind. Thank you again and again." Her manner changed abruptly. "Now I'd better ring the bell hadn't I?"

16

She reached out and tugged at the iron bell handle. As he turned away he heard, deep within the house, the sound of the bell. And it had, because of his unspoken suspicion, and his impotence, and his new-found feeling of responsibility, the sound of doom.

CHAPTER
TWO

After each of his visits to Cambridge Humphrey dutifully reported everything that he had seen and done and learned. The recountal gave him pleasure, and was a test of memory; besides it was no more than Doctor Coppard's due, for the old man had taken pains to arrange this extra, almost luxurious course of training, and was paying for it. The boy had never noticed that Doctor Coppard's interest in his account was merely perfunctory and polite or that he sat passively, letting the flow of enthusiastic talk wash over him until it came to an end and he could bob up with some bit of town gossip or news about a patient. The old man's attitude towards his profession was beautifully simple. Forty years ago he had mastered certain principles, learned to be skilful with certain tools, and in these and perhaps a dozen drugs he put his faith. He had no interest in speculations or discoveries or new methods of treatment. He knew very well that there were conditions which defeated his skill and defied his medicine, but he viewed them philosophically, with the private conviction that they would have defeated anyone else.

Against this hide-bound complacency Humphrey's enthusiastic discourse had broken ineffectually several times during the past two years, but he had never noticed it until tonight when, for the first time, his own interest was divided. Now, as one part of his mind devoted itself to a meticulous, academic report, another part wandered off into memories and speculations about the girl; and yet a third part observed dispassionately that his listener was far more interested in his supper than in what he was hearing.

"But I'm boring you, sir," he said at last.

"Boring me? No, no, my boy. Go on. It's very nice to hear talk; and nicer still to have you back again. You know, Humphrey, I've been thinking this time while you've been away, I'm getting old. I've missed you. I seem to get tired. Last evening d'you know, I came straight in and sat down and when Mrs. Gamble brought in the supper damn me I was sound asleep. But you were saying . . ."

"I think I've told you practically everything now, sir."

"Well, well, it all sounds very interesting, I'm sure. I think I'll have another piece of that pie. Isn't it wonderful what a difference a slice of quince makes to the flavour of apple pie?"

Humphrey rose and went to the side table and replenished both their plates. As he did so he thought again of the girl, of her being so hungry — "you see it was sixpence for sleeping and sixpence for breakfast and I'd only got ninepence" — well, at least she would be in no danger from hunger at the Coffee House; but she might suffer worse things.

He said, almost without thinking, as he carried the plates back to the table, "There was a girl on the coach this afternoon . . ." Instantly Doctor Coppard's attention focused sharply.

"A girl eh? Pretty?"

"I thought so. But it wasn't that so much . . ." He launched into the story of her hunger and of her destination.

He had the old man by both ears now.

"Oh, so Madam performs an act of sweet charity and augments her staff at the same time. Another niece, eh? There was one there, some years back, a little black-haired thing. Had a baby and died. There was a lot of talk at the time, but I must say Madam buried her decently and the girl's name *was* Rowan . . . began with T . . . Thomasina, that's it. This might be a sister. Did she tell you her name?"

"No."

"Not that it signifies. If Madam says she's a niece who can deny it? She's clever, you know. All in the family. Technically that's not running a whore-house."

"Do you honestly believe that it *is* that, sir? That's been bothering me ever since the girl told me where she was going. Is it a fact, or is it only rumour? Is the girl in any danger?"

"She's in danger of changing those clothes for a lot of flounces and flummery. Moral danger?" He thrust out his lower lip. "Depends upon the girl. Judging from her behaviour on the coach I shouldn't say she'd much to learn."

A faint annunciatory pang of dislike for the man who had been his benefactor, mentor and friend made itself felt in Humphrey's heart.

"She was hungry. She only accepted what was offered her. I don't see any harm in that."

"No. But a disposition to take what strange gentlemen offer should ease her way in Mrs. Rowan's house," said the old man, laughing at his own wit.

There had been a time when he had curbed his tongue in the presence of his apprentice, but that time was passed. The boy was full grown, older than his years in many ways; and they had lived and worked together in such close harmony that Doctor Coppard had grown blind to the gulf which lay between their ages and their experiences. He had no notion that by a single sentence he had affronted Humphrey, hurt him, and worst of all silenced him. When, after a short interval, Humphrey asked in a normal voice:

"And how is Mrs. Naylor, sir?" he was as ready to turn his flippant tongue upon the eccentricities of the demented, miserly old woman who was always terrified that she would die in the night, as he had been to joke about Mrs. Rowan's niece. He saw no difference. Humphrey, he had found, was inclined to be sentimental about women, even when they were dirty and crazy like Mrs. Naylor. That, Doctor Coppard thought, was due to his upbringing. A woman like Hagar Shadbolt could hardly avoid impressing her children with the superiority of her sex. Doctor Coppard had only met Hagar twice and each meeting had been brief; but in his early days Humphrey had talked a good deal about his mother and it was plain that the boy owed his education and his chance to get away from the forty-acre farm entirely to his mother's energy and determination. It was right that he should realise and appreciate that fact. But when it came to the point where his own personal background inclined a young medical apprentice to take women's ailments over-seriously, and to waste time in listening to their tales of woe it was time to apply a little astringent treatment. This Doctor Coppard was able and willing to do. Brought face to face with genuine distress he was profoundly kind-hearted, but his general attitude of mind and turn of speech were cynical, almost misanthropic. His remark about the girl who had gone into Mrs. Rowan's house was entirely characteristic and if it had been spoken about any other person Humphrey would not have given it another thought. But the suggestion — even if it were made in fun — that anyone so innocent and trustful and young would take kindly to loose living simply because she had accepted a bite of food when she was practically starving, shocked him a great deal. He thought of it several times during the course of the evening and each time its importance grew. It had made a little breach in the wall of gratitude and admiration which had hitherto stood firm between him and the slightest criticism of his master. It seemed not only possible, but likely that a man who could make so mistaken and insensitive a judgment might not be as infallible as he had hitherto seemed.

CHAPTER
THREE

During the next forty-eight hours he thought about the girl and the Coffee House whenever his attention was not actively engaged with his work. It was as though a chain had been fastened between his mind and Mrs. Rowan's house and as soon as his thoughts were idle the chain tugged, drawing them in that direction. He had left the girl at the door on Saturday afternoon and all through Sunday and Monday he was obliged to resist the idea of stepping across to the place and seeing if he could learn anything of her.

Diffidence was the main element in his resistance. He had never been into the Coffee House and his mental concept of it swung like a pendulum between the two aspects of it revealed by the inquiry, details of which he had had from Doctor Coppard; a place of drunkenness and vice, a place where sedate citizens and gentlemen and rather dashing young dandies foregathered. Both aspects were intimidating to the inexperienced young countryman who still lurked, at times ill-concealed, behind the rather pompous professional manner which was half conscious dignity of his calling and half imitation of his master. Called to a case of sickness in the Coffee House he could have entered it with ease and assurance; to enter it for the first time as a customer was far harder. But all through the Sunday and the Monday he knew, in the depths of his mind, that it was the only thing to do, the thing he wanted to do, the thing he would do, finally. By the time when he sat down to supper on the Monday evening he had made up his mind.

Immediately a fresh problem, first of many, presented itself. In the past four years he had very seldom gone out in the evening, and never without saying where he was going. He had come into Doctor Coppard's household straight from school, a boy of seventeen, accustomed to control and supervision. It had seemed natural enough to settle down to his books after supper, or to say, "I would like to take a walk, sir. Do you mind?" Quite imperceptibly this pattern of master-and-apprentice had changed into a kind of partnership. During the last year since Humphrey had been judged competent to go to a case alone, he had considered that he was, as it were, on duty during the evening and through the night. Any late call — unless it came from a known and valued patient — was more likely than not to be answered by "the young doctor", though Doctor Coppard would sometimes from his easy chair — or his bed if the call was really late — conduct a preliminary inquisition and suggest or hint at a procedure.

So habit and a sense of duty alike forebade that on this Monday evening he should suddenly walk out of the house without announcing his destination.

He could simply have said, "I'm going over to the Coffee House for an hour." He did not suppose that Doctor Coppard would object or forbid it; but he would wonder, and he would connect this sudden decision with the girl on the coach; and he would joke. Everything — dignity, sensibility, discretion militated against making such an open announcement. At the end of the meal he said as casually as he could, "I think I shall go for a walk. I'll be back in less than an hour."

"Do you a world of good," said the old man, moving away from the table to the comfortable chair by the fire. His slippers were already on his feet, his pipe and tobacco and a decanter of port wine were set ready on a little table, his Blackwood's Magazine lay upon the arm of the chair. As he sat down he cast a thought upon the abounding energy of youth which could set a young man walking for pleasure through a cold November night; but age had its compensations, no doubt of that. An appreciation of comfort was one of them — if you could cater for it; and thank God he could. He took out the stopper of the decanter, poured himself a glass of wine and found the page in his Magazine. He did not give his apprentice another thought.

The door of the Coffee House was ajar and swung open at a touch. Inside was a long dim passage, but a lamp burned on a table near the door and it was possible to read the words "Coffee Room" on a door half way down the left hand side of the passage. Rather hot in the face and feeling taller and more angular than usual Humphrey pushed at this door and stepped into a warm, brightly-lit room of moderate size, austerely furnished with tables, upright oak chairs and high-backed settles. There was nobody in the room at all.

The walls were panelled in dark wood and heavy beams ran across the ceiling. From the centre beam a lamp hung and immediately below was a large round table upon which papers and magazines were laid out in orderly fashion. Around the room were smaller tables, each bearing a candlestick, a snuffer tray and a brass bell. Some of the tables had chairs by them, some were almost enclosed by having a settle on either side. He remembered that several men had said that they went to Mrs. Rowan's to do business, and one could imagine quite confidential talk going on in such little enclosures.

On the side of the room opposite the door was a wide hearth, very neatly kept, upon which a great log fire was burning. One bright coloured rug lay before it and another was spread under the central table. To the extreme right of the room a wide counter stood, mid-way along the wall and just behind it was a door. The room reflected something of the primness of the house front. It was extremely tidy and specklessly clean. Humphrey's first reaction was surprised relief. He did not know what he had expected to find, but not this well-polished, orderly, rather severe apartment. Looking at it made it very easy to believe that men did come here to drink and talk business and read the papers. Perhaps it was all right after all. He was glad that he had entered the place, because now — in all probability

— he would see the girl and learn that everything was all right; then he could go away and not worry any more.

He chose a settle in the corner and was just wondering whether to ring the bell upon the table or to wait for a minute, when a wave of cold air announced the opening of the street door and after a second or two old Duffle, the apothecary, shambled in and went straight to the fire, holding out his hands to the blaze. Having warmed them and his face, he turned and exposed his back to the heat, saw Humphrey in his corner and took on an expression of interest and curiosity.

"Very cold for the time of the year," he began, conversationally.

"Very cold," Humphrey said shortly. He found himself resenting the old man's presence. He was a busybody and his shop a clearing house for gossip. By tomorrow noon everyone in the town — including Doctor Coppard — would know of this visit to the Coffee House. Not that it mattered; not that it was anybody's business what he did in his free time; not that he hadn't as much right here as anybody else.

"It isn't often I see you in here, Doctor Shadbolt," said the old apothecary, giving Humphrey his courtesy title.

"It's my first visit," Humphrey said, even more shortly, repressing a desire to add — and damn well you know it.

"Well, it won't be your last, or I'm mistaken. Very comfortable, cheerful place. And as good as a club.

You'd be astonished at the amount of business done within these four walls." He gave a little, old man's titter of laughter and added slyly, "It's a champion place so long as the street door's open. After that I don't know. Too old to find out now." He let his rheumy eye dwell upon Humphrey in a way that made him awkwardly conscious of his youth. Then he leaned over and rang the bell on the table nearest the fire.

Immediately the door behind the counter opened and one of Mrs. Rowan's daughters appeared in the doorway. She was the younger of the two girls whom Humphrey had seen together on infrequent occasions in the streets of the town, and indoors she looked more attractive, less flamboyant and aggressive. She was rather plump — too plump for Humphrey's taste — but her fair pink and white skin, glossy fair hair and bright brown eyes had all a look of health and well-being which was pleasing.

"Come along, come along, Susie," said old Duffle in a familiar, half-teasing, half-testy way. "Just because I'm old and regular you think you can neglect me. But you see it's not me alone you're neglecting. Here's young Doctor Shadbolt on his very first visit. What'll he think of the service, eh?"

The name meant something to her. That was made plain by the look, one of startled recognition, which she shot towards Humphrey's corner. Then she turned back to the old man and said:

"Your usual, Mr. Duffle?" in a calm, amiable way. "*And* I won't forget the brown sugar. Last night was a mistake you know. But Letty's new to the job. You'll have to forgive her."

Letty. That must be the girl on the coach. Letty. It was suitable. An endearing little name.

He gave his order. Just coffee. No, nothing else.

As Susie whisked away through the door in the panelling three more men entered from the street. One was the Town Clerk, another one of the Grammar School masters whom Humphrey recognised, the third was unknown to him. They went towards the fire and Mr. Duffle fastened upon the Town Clerk, demanding to know whether anything was ever to be done to the shocking great hole in the road in Looms Lane just opposite his shop. "Full of water," he said crossly, "and this morning there was a dead cat in it, with other abominations. It's a disgrace."

"I should have thought that would stimulate the sale of rose water and smelling salts! I wish I had a shop," said the school master, as the Town Clerk began to explain the difficulties of finding labour and material for road mending.

Then Humphrey ceased to pay the group any attention, for the inner door opened again and Susie Rowan entered, carrying a tray which she deposited on Mr. Duffle's table, and just behind her was the girl — Letty, with another tray; and she was coming across to Humphrey's corner. He felt his face go hot and his heart begin to beat in great heavy throbs, high up his throat. And in the space of a minute he realised, with a mingling of sharp perception and stunned incredulity that his concern for her had only been a fretting surface symptom of something else. He knew then that he was in love with her. He knew it by the violent turmoil into which his blood, his nerves, his every sense was thrown by the mere sight of her. Knew it by the sudden revelation of the fact that he had not come here because he was curious or anxious — though he had been both, genuinely enough — but because he had wanted to see her again. Knew it by the impact of what was, for him, the very epitome of beauty; and by the feeling of contentment, of accomplishment with which he greeted her approach.

She set the tray rather clumsily upon the table.

"Hullo," she said. "I didn't really believe Susie when she said it was you. I thought you didn't come here."

"I . . . I . . . just thought I'd look in and see how you were getting on."

"Oh, I'm quite all right. They didn't mind a bit that I came unexpected. They made me *very* welcome." The long lashes disentangled themselves and revealed a clear-eyed happiness, like that of a child who has dreaded some ordeal and then found it no ordeal at all.

"I am glad of that."

He could think of nothing further to say, although there were a dozen things he wanted to ask her. So he sat and looked at her, feasting a sense which he knew was insatiable. She looked better, her hair was brushed smoothly to the top of her head where it was tied with a blue ribbon and then allowed to escape confinement in a cascade of curls. Her gown was blue too, with a demure little collar of frilled muslin, matching the little apron which protected the front of her skirt and which, with its tight band and great bunching bow of strings at the back emphasised the extreme slenderness of her waist.

But even as he looked at her he saw that fleeting look of astonished happiness die out of her eyes, leaving that peculiar look of settled sorrow. And now he recognised it. It was an animal look, the very expression which, seen in the eyes of an intelligent dog, made one say "What is it, old fellow? What are you trying to tell me?" and set one's mind speculating about the mystery of speech and whether animals were conscious of their vast deprivation. Why then should it be there in the eyes — beautiful eyes, blue tonight above the blue gown — of a girl who possessed the ordinary means of communication?

Before he had found even a hint of answer to this question, or bit upon the kind of casual, friendly remark which was needed to hold Letty in conversation by his table Susie Rowan called from across the room. The place was filling up now, growing loud with male voices, hazy with tobacco smoke. Letty turned hastily and began to make her way back to the counter.

"Come back," Humphrey said. She smiled without saying anything.

He drank his coffee and watched the room. He saw Cathy Rowan, taller, less plump, darker than her sister, moving about among the tables. She was genuinely beautiful, with a face and figure that would have attracted attention in any assembly. But even when she and Letty were standing side by side and comparison was unavoidable he could see a charm in that odd, pale, childish little face which the lovely one lacked. Each time his eye moved back to Letty with a sense of home-coming.

Then Mrs. Rowan arrived and the rumour-nurtured suspicions which had suffered a slight, but definite blow from the appearance of the Coffee House, reeled again. Nothing more intensely respectable than Mrs. Rowan could be imagined.

She was a tall woman, taller than either of her daughters, and she held herself very upright and moved with great dignity. She wore an austere gown of stiff black silk, high in the neck and long in the sleeves. Her black hair was parted smoothly and dressed in a coil of plaits low at the back of her head, and she wore upon it a little white cap with a black velvet ribbon in it. Her face was long and sallow, the eyelids and the skin under her eyes deeply pigmented. It was said that she never left her own premises — unkind people said that she dared not venture into the street — and her appearance was that of a woman who had been housebound, lacking fresh air, for a long time.

Mrs. Rowan did not help with the serving. She stood for a few minutes surveying the room and then moved to one table and began to talk to the men seated by it. Presently, during a momentary lull in the gabble of talk Humphrey heard her say, "But it's in the paper." She stretched out a long arm and lifted a paper from the centre table, turned it about, ran her eye down the page and then pointed with her finger. Her expression was grave, confident, judicious. A lively argument seemed to break out at that table, the paper was handed from man to man. Mrs. Rowan took her share in the discussion and it was easy to see that her opinions were — if not accepted — listened to. The candle-lighted faces lifted towards her when she spoke were eloquent of interest and attention. Presently she seemed to tire of the argument. She moved one hand in a gesture of admission or dismissal, and then she walked straight across to Humphrey's corner.

"It's Doctor Shadbolt, isn't it?" she asked with a slight smile and sat down upon the opposite side of the table. "I am glad to have this opportunity of speaking to you. I *almost* wrote to you. I did want to thank you for all your kindness to my niece. The silly child hadn't advised me of her intention to travel; and she had so little money that she had to spend her night at Cambridge in a hovel and forego her breakfast. I understand that you fed her and escorted her to my door. I can't thank you warmly enough."

Her deep, rather unfeminine voice was warm with feeling. Nobody but a churl of a fool could have doubted the sincerity of the speech.

"It was nothing, Mrs. Rowan."

"It was a kindness, of a sort all too rare. Have you seen Letty yet?"

"Yes. Just for a moment."

"I'm sure she was glad to see you. I expect it all seems a little strange to her. I *think* she is happy here." She paused and looked thoughtful. "Tell me, Doctor Shadbolt, did you find her communicative? With us she seems — not shy exactly — one couldn't say that. But she does look at times as though a great deal were going on in her mind which she couldn't talk about. But there, I don't suppose you've noticed that."

"Oh, but I have," Humphrey said quickly. He found himself warming to Mrs. Rowan, liking her because she seemed to be taking an intelligent interest in Letty as an individual; and because she had observed the same thing as he had done himself.

"She was delighted by her welcome," he said. "When I left her she was rather conscious of arriving without notice. I . . . I really came across tonight to see if everything was all right."

Some of the benevolent graciousness faded from Mrs. Rowan's face.

"It is very good of you to follow up kindness with interest; but I can't help wondering whether Doctor Coppard would *quite* approve."

The abrupt reminder of his 'prentice state made Humphrey angry.

"Why shouldn't he?"

"Well, I, naturally see no reason. But you do realise, don't you, that Doctor Coppard is one of the gentlemen who regard this place with very jaundiced, very prejudiced eyes. And its been my sorry experience to find that disinterested kindness is seldom accepted as such. Especially by the elderly."

Once again she had managed to express Humphrey's very thought. The old man's view of this place was jaundiced and prejudiced and he would not be capable of understanding that his apprentice had visited it out of disinterested kindness. (Would he have been right? Wouldn't those dreaded jokes about the lure of a pair of bright eyes have been substantially justified? Push that thought away.) But Mrs. Rowan understood. She was obviously an intelligent, tolerant, understanding woman.

At the back of his mind there floated a scrap of information, remembered from his school days. Hadn't the Greeks had some women intelligent, witty, accomplished and informed, though socially outcast, to whom men repaired for the pleasure of enjoying feminine company divorced from tiresome domesticity. It began with H . . . hetairai or something like that. He couldn't quite remember. Maybe Mrs. Rowan and her daughters in their comfortable nineteenth-century Coffee House served the same purpose as the hetairai of Greece. It was a nice thought, but hard on its heels came another, not so pleasant. The hetairai had plied another trade. They had been prostitutes.

He could accept the idea that, unlikely as it seemed, Mrs. Rowan had been a prostitute, and that her two daughters were prostitutes . . . but then, what about Letty? Fear began to snake through his entrails again. He was suddenly aware of the need to get away from this rather overwhelming woman and put his thoughts and impressions in order. He would have liked to have had ten minutes, just ten minutes alone with Letty. But that looked to be impossible, for the room was crowded now, and although both Cathy and Susie Rowan moved briskly when they moved at all, they were inclined to linger at some of the tables and either make jokes or flatteringly receive them. There was always laughter at any table where one of the girls stood. Letty, who was as yet familiar with no one and seemed to be in a state of fluttering shyness, was left to make the majority of the trips through the service door and he was not yet sure enough of his ground to make a bid for her attention.

And time was getting on. A glance at his watch informed him that he had already outstayed his hour.

As though she had read his mind Mrs. Rowan rose, unhurriedly, gracefully to her feet.

"Well, I mustn't sit here all evening. I'm so glad to have a chance to tender my thanks to you. I hope you will come in again."

"Indeed I shall," he said. He would continue to frequent the place until he knew its secret, if it had one; and if he found that just one thing that rumour said about it was true he would have Letty out of it as quickly as he would whip a splinter out of a festering finger.

"I expect Letty would like to say goodnight to you," said Mrs. Rowan. She beckoned, and then moved away. Letty began to thread her way through the crowded room and once again all his pulses drummed. But when she stood near him he could think of nothing to say except, "I must go now. I thought I'd like to say goodnight and that I'm glad you found everything all right." She looked at him, not speaking, but with that look which her aunt had summed up so shrewdly, and under its influence he said, quietly, rapidly, secretively, "It is all right, isn't it?"

"They're all very kind," she said. "And it's very kind of you to bother about me. I'm all right now."

"Well, goodnight then. I shall be over again."

She said goodnight and turned away.

He had reached the door when a voice hailed him, "Shadbolt! Ah, so it is you. Mercy on us, how the boy has grown. You remember me, surely?"

"Of course sir. I saw you come in. I didn't expect you to recognise me, though."

"Oh, I never forget a face. What on earth are you doing here?"

"Just taking a cup of coffee, sir."

"Obviously. I mean what are you doing in town at all?"

"I live here. I've lived here for four years. I'm apprenticed to Doctor Coppard on the Abbey Hill."

"Indeed. I didn't know that. I'm glad to hear it. I had an idea that you'd gone back into the wilds. Fancy never meeting you before. We schoolmasters lead cloistered lives. You've chosen a nice trade, Shadbolt, fattening upon the ills of mankind. I wish I'd been a doctor."

"They're never off duty, sir. As a matter of fact some ill is probably waiting to fatten me at this minute. I must be off, sir."

"Well, I'll look out for you in future. I'm here most nights when I'm not on duty at the brain shop. Goodnight, Shadbolt. Nice to see you again."

"And nice to see you again, sir, goodnight."

The trivial encounter had ruffled him a little. He had never liked Mr. Bancroft very much; the man's sardonic and grudging attitude towards the profession in which he had placed himself had been reflected in his behaviour to the boys. And allied to this personal antipathy was a young man's distaste for the company of one in whose presence he must, automatically, become a boy again, a feeling natural and universal, only to be overcome by genuine affection upon one side or the other.

But, walking swiftly across the Abbey Hill, shrouded in chilly banks of fog, Humphrey saw one advantage in the encounter. If, as seemed only too likely, Doctor Coppard learned of his visit to the Coffee House he could say, with a certain amount of truth that he had been there in the company of his old schoolmaster. That gave the thing a most respectable flavour. Also Mr. Bancroft's last words could be twisted into an arrangement for future meetings. That might be useful.

As he pushed open the heavy front door and assimilated, without conscious use of any sense, the atmosphere of the house which for four years had been his home, the place where he had known most of his true happiness, he became aware that, for the first time, he was planning deceit and dissimulation. His lively conscience, tempered upon Josiah Shadbolt's non-conformist fervour, administered a sharp stab. But reason salved the wound. It was really Doctor Coppard's fault. The man who could joke about Letty and her position could not be confided in. And those who could not be confided in must be deceived. That was Humphrey's first experience of sophistry.

★ ★ ★

The old man was dozing over his Blackwood's.

"Ah, there you are. Mrs. Naylor sent round that unfortunate little boy to say that she really was dying this time. I did look out, but it seemed so damned thick and raw. And you've been out Humphrey and haven't got your things off. I thought . . ."

"Of course, sir. I'll go right away. It's probably a false alarm, but she *is* going to die one day."

They laughed.

"I may be a fool to let you go," said Doctor Coppard, settling more comfortably into his chair. "She's got to leave her money to somebody . . . if she has any which is a matter of opinion. You may all unknowingly be qualifying for a fortune."

CHAPTER
FOUR

Mrs. Naylor, who suffered from — among other things — a severe type of asthma, was genuinely ill. And on the evening of the next day it was a simple matter to say, immediately after supper, that he would just run round and assure the old woman that she would not die in the night. Her huge, grim, indescribably dirty house was only about two hundred yards from the Coffee House. The visit was very brief for the old woman was asleep when he arrived and never wholly awakened. So he was again an early customer and again took possession of the table in the corner. Letty came towards him at once and gave him her open, childlike smile of welcome, and again all his blood moved towards her and again he found difficulty in finding things to say.

The third and fourth visits, made on successive nights, followed the same pattern. On the Friday morning he realised that by tomorrow Letty would have been at the Coffee House for a whole week and he had been in love with her for five days — unless the truth was that he had fallen in love with her on the coach — and that he had made no headway at all, either in his relationship with her or in discovering whether the place she had come to live in was what it seemed or what people said it was. And it occurred to him that he might go on in like fashion for a year.

So on Friday evening, when Letty had brought his coffee and they had exchanged their few stilted routine little questions and answers he said, "Wait a minute. There's something I want to ask you. I've been wondering. Do you ever go out? I mean, I think you should. It isn't very nice weather for walking, I know. But tomorrow I have to drive to Thurston. I wondered if you . . . I mean I wish you would come with me. It's a pretty drive and the air would do you good."

She looked pleased. No doubt about that.

"I'll ask my aunt. They tell me Saturday is a kind of market day here. They might be busy. How long would we be away?"

"Two hours. Or three. But you weren't here to help last Saturday, you know. You were on the coach and they didn't even know you were arriving. I think they might manage without you."

"That's true," said Letty, smiling. "I'll ask my aunt."

She did not return to the table; but presently Mrs. Rowan herself came towards him. Tonight she was dressed in grey, with a bow of lilac coloured ribbon in her cap. She smiled as she reached him and he noticed for the first time that when her long upper lip lifted it creased and a crescent formed across it. It was fascinating, but so unusual as to be a little disconcerting.

"You know," she began abruptly, without greeting, "you are a very reckless and thoughtless young man.

Appearances are deceptive." She sat down and folded her long slender hands upon the table. "What a mercy it is that the child asked my permission. D'you want to *ruin* your career before it is even started?"

"Are you talking about my invitation to Letty to take a drive with me?" he asked, taken aback.

"What else should I be talking about. Haven't you any imagination? Can't you see what it would mean for a young man in your position to be seen driving with my niece? The whole town would buzz with the news. You would be entirely discredited."

"Mrs. Rowan, why?"

"Ah, why?" An expression, at once mocking and wistful came into the shadowed eyes. "If I could answer that question, Doctor Shadbolt, how easy my mind would be. But I can't. But I can assure you, and that most earnestly, that for you to be seen in public with anyone from this house would cause a major scandal. Also," her voice changed to a slightly minatory note, "I don't know whether you have realised it or not, Letty's very young. She won't be seventeen until next April. She's had a hard time in the last couple of years — it would shock you, I think, to hear what that child has endured — and I agree that she looks older. But she is only a child and I think she is too young to go out alone with any young gentleman." An almost inaudible sigh came from her pale lips and she said, half to herself, "I don't know. Maybe I'm wrong. Perhaps poor Letty will suffer the fate of my own daughters. When they were young I protected them, then this inexplicable rumour about us got abroad and they lost all hope of making

42

respectable marriages. They're popular with men of course and enjoy their popularity, but that only leads to more rumour, naturally. Still, that can't be mended now. I don't worry and I don't think the girls do. We all have to make the best of life as we find it, don't we? I'm sorry to seem obdurant about the drive which I am sure was a harmless suggestion. But later on you'll realise how right I was."

She spoke with finality and moved away before Humphrey could utter a word. But when, with the bitter taste of disappointment and frustration in his mouth he was on his way out and had stopped for a moment to say goodnight to Letty, Mrs. Rowan came up and spoke over the girl's shoulder.

"Letty, I've explained why Doctor Shadbolt's suggestion was impossible; but I don't want to be harsh. If you'd like to spend some time together why not ask him upstairs?" Then she moved away; and he looked down to see Letty's neck and face all suffused with burning scarlet.

"Upstairs doesn't mean what they say or what you might think," Letty said, jerking out the words in a terrible confusion. "It's just that the living room is upstairs. And the girls have their friends to supper."

"And I'm your friend, aren't I, Letty?" he asked, fatuously and humbly because he was in the grip of such a terrible pity. "Would you like me to come — upstairs? Can I come to supper too?"

Pleasure visited her face again.

"Oh yes. That would be very nice. If you didn't mind it being rather different from this." She looked round the room with — considering her ordinarily meek and shy demeanour — an astonishing scorn. "Tomorrow?"

"All right, tomorrow. What time?"

"Oh, dreadfully late. After we close. Half past ten."

"I'll be there. Goodnight, Letty."

"Goodnight."

He went home with a good deal to think over. He had, at least, advanced a step towards his objective. If the prim and orderly Coffee Room were indeed an elaborate facade his invitation would take him behind it. If he couldn't, by tomorrow midnight, give himself an answer to his tormenting question he must be either blind or a fool. And now that he came to think about it it seemed that Mrs. Rowan's long speech contained a pointer, was indeed rather in the nature of a preparation for the invitation. And Letty's words, "The girls have their friends to supper", was in all innocence and ingenuousness, another pointer.

There remained to bother him the question of the time. Half past ten was too late, even for Mrs. Naylor to serve as an excuse.

But, soaring above all these speculations and problems was a bright banner of the thought that he would, tomorrow, really see Letty, by which he meant to be near her and be able to talk to her in leisure and — compared with the Coffee Room — privacy. The urge to explore, which carries a few peculiarly-dispositioned men to the ends of the earth, and which most men satisfy by learning the ins and outs of a woman's personality, came upon him. He wanted to learn Letty's thoughts, what she liked and disliked, what her past had been, and above all how she was affected by him.

CHAPTER
FIVE

At ten o'clock on the following evening Doctor Coppard, as was his wont, went to bed and Humphrey, as usual, followed him upstairs, after making fast all the doors and all the windows, save one. Safe in his room he washed, fingered his chin and then shaved in cold water, and put on his best suit.

The house, and the street outside seemed suddenly very quiet as though to emphasise the lateness of the hour and the enormity of the thing he was about to do. And as he took the fresh suit from the cupboard his bubble mood of excitement and exhilaration broke upon a spiked remorse. The old man, by this time asleep, not dreaming of the deception being practised upon him, had ordered and paid for these clothes. "Lord love us, boy, it's to my advantage to have you looking fine and dandy. Your mother, bless her, has other things to do with her money than pander to my vanity. Besides old Fothergill owes me ten pounds, the rogue, and he'd rather make you a suit of clothes than hand over the cash I am sure. So run along and be measured and don't let me have any nonsense." It was a handsome suit too, the long, close-waisted, full skirted coat and the trousers of a pale cinnamon colour, the waistcoat a bright canary yellow, with brass buttons. Doctor Coppard had certainly never imagined it gracing Mrs. Rowan's supper table.

But Doctor Coppard had laughed about Letty. So he must be deceived for a time. Not for ever, of course. Humphrey would explain and apologise one day. When? Well, that depended. Not later, certainly, than next Midsummer, when he would have taken his examination and fulfilled his articles and would step forth as a fully qualified medical man. Then he would tell his master everything; and say that he intended to marry Letty. There would be objections and arguments at first, but they would be quelled when the old man saw that he was determined and meant to marry the girl he loved even if it meant leaving the town and taking a post elsewhere.

But that, he thought, arranging his neck cloth with meticulous care, was, of course, a far cry ahead. First he must discover whether the Coffee House were a fitting place for Letty to remain in between now and Midsummer. And he must find out whether she loved him; or — and he remembered her extreme youth — whether she had a feeling towards him which might grow into love. He was himself almost twenty-one; Letty was only sixteen; but women were supposed to come to maturity sooner than men, and Mrs. Rowan herself had said that Letty was older than her years. Anyway he would have patience and hope.

He leaned forward and studied, in the dim, candle-lighted mirror, his own reflection, with anxiety which he had never felt before, and which did little to enhance his appearance. Seen at such close quarters his face was repulsive, the nose was too long, the black brows too heavy, the cheeks too lean and hollow, and the mouth too full, still deplorably childlike. Yet, when he stepped back so that the mirror could reflect also the long, elegant lines of the coat, the broad spare shoulders, the bright waistcoat and the dazzling white neckcloth, the effect was very different. And Letty, at least would see the whole of him, not just a face at close quarters. Not . . . that was . . . until . . . he kissed her The even flow of his blood was disturbed again.

He tiptoed down the stairs, into the back hall, climbed nimbly — careful of his trousers — out of the window which he had left open, dropped into the garden and made his way out of the back gate.

CHAPTER
SIX

He knew the approach to the Coffee House from the rear. There was a small walled garden jutting out into the churchyard; and, seeing the front of the house in darkness, and remembering old Duffle's words about when the street door was shut, he made his way to the back. There was a little paved space and then the back door, but that was closed too. He felt about and found a bell. The door was opened, immediately, by Letty.

"We were afraid you wouldn't find it," she said. "My aunt said I should have told you. She doesn't like people going to the front after closing time."

The door opened upon a little white-washed lobby lighted by a hanging lantern which gave hardly any illumination. In the dimness Letty's small face looked radiant. Immediately behind the lobby was a huge kitchen, running the width of the house and smelling of freshly ground coffee and onions. Letty led the way across it and up a flight of old, uneven, curving stairs with heavy posts and hand rail, through a dim passage and into a room which blazed with light and colour. The warmth of it met him at the door, and he stood for a moment staring around the apartment with something akin to recognition, knowing that it was this that he had expected to see when he entered the Coffee Room. This big, overheated, overlighted, garishly coloured room with its air of sluttish comfort conformed to the town's opinion of the house, while the Coffee Room protested against it. He had an idea that tonight he would penetrate the secret.

Mrs. Rowan was standing alone by the great log fire, drinking a cup of tea.

"Oh, come in, Doctor Shadbolt. I'm so glad you could come. I suppose it's no good offering you a cup of tea. I always have one before supper. I find it so refreshing. No. Well let Letty give you a drink. She has mastered the difference between port wine and brandy now, haven't you, child? What would you like?"

He chose the wine, because by name at least it was familiar, and because Doctor Coppard consumed quantities of it, apparently without ill-effect, though he held spirit-drinking to be detrimental to health. Letty went to a table at the side of the room and there was a clink of glass and then she proffered him, with a pleased and proud look, a tumbler holding almost half a pint, full to the brim. Mrs. Rowan laughed indulgently.

"Look, child, these are for wine. Will you remember that? Not that it matters much. I daresay Doctor Shadbolt will forgive you. Now pour some for yourself, and you can entertain one another while I tidy myself and hurry the girls. Oh, and Letty, just see that the table is right. Plant will be coming for certain, and Chris and Mr. Everett; but Stevie may arrive too. So see to the places, there's a dear."

50

She walked, a little more briskly than usual, out of the room. Letty came back from the side table with about a tablespoonful of port wine in a glass.

"I've learned to be careful with this," she said in a confidential intimate voice. "I don't know how people drink glasses of it and stay friends. I found out that after a bit I began saying the first thing that came into my head. And that wouldn't do." She smiled, and it seemed for a moment as though they shared a secret.

"I don't want you to drink too much, but I would like to hear you saying the first thing that came into your head."

"So did they!" her voice was rueful. "They all laughed their heads off. Then I got angry. Then I cried. Oh dear, I did make a raree-show of myself."

"When was this?"

"The night I got here. Last Saturday. My aunt said I looked starved and gave me such a supper; and I told her I wasn't starved because you'd been so good to me. And she said port wine would put some colour in my face. And then it happened. Would you believe that before I knew where I was I was telling her why I'd put off coming here for two years."

"And why was it?"

For a moment she looked secretive and the old suggestion of having much to say but lacking the ability to say it showed in her eyes again. Then, in a less confidential voice she said:

"Oh well, *you* know. What they say about her and Cathy and Susie. You see, my father had the same idea. He just didn't understand."

51

"Was your father Mrs. Rowan's brother?"

"Oh no. Mrs. Rowan is my aunt because my father's brother married her. So she really isn't related to me by blood at all. That makes her kindness to me the more surprising, don't you think?"

"And she is kind to you?"

"Oh yes. Even that night I was telling you about, when I was so rude to her, she didn't bear any grudge. She told Cathy to take me to bed — and do you know I can't remember anything about that? — and then, next day, she explained everything."

"And what did she tell you?" At the back of his mind there was a thought that this sounded more like a cross-examination, or a consulting room conversation than the first private talk between two people, one of whom, at least, was deeply in love. But this was his chance and he must seize it.

"Well," said Letty, a little reluctantly, "she said that what my father had said was what the people here said too. She said all girls who had to work for their livings got a bad name because everybody knew they had to get money so they chose to assume" (Mrs. Rowan's phrase fell oddly from Letty's lips) "that they'd do anything for money. So Cathy and Susie hadn't made respectable marriages, but they couldn't live like nuns. I could understand that, in a way. Can't you?"

"Oh yes." At least Mrs. Rowan's story had the virtue of consistency. This was almost an exact repetition of what she had said to him. It was not without plausibility. But it had a flaw in it. Where had the tainted rumour started?

"A great many girls who work for their living *do* get married." he said gravely. "And quite respectably, too."

"Oh yes, I know. Two that worked alongside me did. But one married a cobbler and the other a coachman. That wouldn't quite do for Susie or Cathy, would it?"

He would have liked to say that any marriage, however humble, was to be preferred to the invidious position in which her cousins found themselves; but Letty was regarding him so seriously and so evidently believed what she had been told that he was forced to remain silent.

"You see," said Letty earnestly, "they can read and write and understand things in the papers. They make me look very ignorant. And they're used to nice things." She glanced round the room with admiring appreciation. "And they have nice clothes. Those two who worked with me were poor, roughish sort of girls. The truth is Cathy and Susie don't fit in anywhere, so they have to make the best of things."

It was the longest speech she had ever made in his hearing. And its patent unoriginality sounded a warning signal. With the subtlest cunning they were beginning to work upon her already, turning her thoughts away from the idea of marriage, undermining what principles she might possess by emphasising the advantages of their own way of life. And she was so young, so malleable. It took but the slightest effort of the imagination to see how attractive and superior the Rowan girls must seem to one accustomed to "poor, roughish" workmates, how comfortable and free and easy life in the Coffee House must be to one who had tried — and failed — to keep herself from destitution by plying her needle.

The more vulgar and obvious of his fears fell away leaving behind them doubts and anxieties of a more subtle and complicated kind. At the moment it wasn't so much the virginity of Letty's body which was in danger — it was the purity of her mind. Once she had grown accustomed to, and come to rely upon, the material things which the Coffee House offered it would be so easy for the Rowans to say, "Now, in order to live like this you must . . ."

He pulled himself up sharply. He had, as yet, no reason for thinking such things. Anyone who could realise how much environment coloured attitude of mind ought to be sensible enough to see that his own attitude towards the Rowans was biased by his own environment. He mustn't blindly accept the town's opinion; he must judge for himself.

"I nearly forgot," said Letty. "I've got to look over the table."

"I'll help you," he said, emptying his glass and getting to his feet. "I *can* count. But Mrs. Rowan mentioned so many names, so quickly, I'm a little confused."

There was a round gaming table at the far end of the room, half under the shadow of a kind of gallery which spanned it. The table was covered with a cloth of fine linen inset with lace, rather grubby in places; there was a good deal of silver haphazardly arranged and an assortment of dishes and glasses.

Letty moved a few things ineffectually, almost purposelessly. Then she sighed.

"I don't know how many there'll really be. And everybody'll want to sit by Cathy or Susie . . ."

"Not me. I want to sit by you, if I may."

She smiled and looked gratified.

"Yes. Tonight I shan't be out of it, shall I? Let us have these two places and the others can sort themselves out."

She had offered him a clue, which, noticed and remembered, might have helped him to understand a good deal of her subsequent behaviour. But he was dazzled by her smile and by the suggestion that his company was as desirable to her as hers was to him, so he missed the significance of the sentence. The prospect of sitting by Letty, of continuing their private conversation under cover of the general talk, induced in him a mild form of intoxication. And the half-tumbler of port wine in his unaccustomed stomach was not without its effect.

If, during the next hour or two he remembered Letty saying "tonight I shan't be out of it", he did so with sympathetic understanding. For until another glass of wine, taken with his supper and a third afterwards for sociability's sake, had dulled the edges of his self-consciousness, he was acutely aware of being "out of it" himself. In all there were five guests; two, Mr. Hatton, whom Mrs. Rowan called "Chris", and Mr. Everett, were gentlemen, there was no doubt about that. Two others, Stevie and Midge, were working class men though better dressed and in possession of more money than any honest working men — Humphrey thought — had any right to be. The fifth man, the last to arrive, and distinguished by his odd name — Plant Driscoll — by his odd, monkeyish face, and his odd trick of over-emphasising certain words in every sentence, was less easily placed. He was as well-dressed and confident of manner as Hatton and Everett, but there did not hang about him the indefinable yet unmistakable suggestion of great houses and ancestral acres in the background which was inseparable from the others, silly as Chris Hatton might seem, gross as Mr. Everett undoubtedly was. But it was equally plain that Driscoll was not, like Stevie and Midge, a roughish fellow out in his best clothes and on his best behaviour. Perhaps on account of this "classlessness" Humphrey felt drawn towards the man and would have talked to him after supper while the girls were hastily clearing the table and the men stood about aimlessly; but there was in Driscoll's face an expression of curiosity and a faint amusement which Humphrey found disconcerting; the conversation died of its own inanity and after a minute or two Driscoll turned and laid his arm over Stevie's shoulder and the pair drew away from the others and began to speak in lowered tones with an occasional burst of laughter.

Then everybody except Letty moved back to the table, and Mrs. Rowan, sorting a pack of cards with swift, accurate hands, called:

"Will you play, Doctor Shadbolt?" and Humphrey, conscious of his empty pocket as well as his ignorance of any game except Nobbin, shook his head, and feeling conspicuous and ill-at-ease, dropped down into a chair by the fire.

Presently Letty joined him.

"Aunt Thirza says I'm to give you a drink. She didn't think you were enjoying yourself very much."

"I just don't play cards," he said a trifle grumpily — because he felt awkward, and because Letty hadn't come across as soon as she saw him sitting alone but had waited to be sent. "I've never had time to learn."

"There's nothing to *learn*," Letty said. "I picked it up the first time I tried. But I always have bad luck and lose my money. And then they try to lend me some and laugh at me, and make me feel like a baby." She turned to the side table and poured him a glass of wine, correctly this time.

"I saw you talking to Plant," she said, taking a chair near Humphrey's. "He's nice, don't you think?"

"I really couldn't judge. He's all right, I suppose." He knew that he sounded grudging.

"He's Cathy's absolutely favourite friend."

"Yes, I thought they seemed on very good terms."

He didn't want to talk about Cathy and her friends, but he lacked the skill to turn the conversation, so he sat dumbly, drinking his wine and staring at Letty with an adoring, but rather stupid expression. The evening was passing — was, in fact almost over — and it had been a disappointing affair.

"Look," said Letty at last. "I'll get a pack and we'll play here, just by ourselves. Then it won't matter if you make mistakes or if I have bad luck."

She proceeded to initiate him into a game so simple, so easily understood that within ten minutes he was deliberately making mistakes in order to have the pleasure of hearing her admonish him and explain all over again. Seated thus, with only the tiny table between them, and with her whole attention focused upon their common occupation, he felt quite happy and lost sense of the passage of time. It was with a start of surprise that presently he looked up to find Mrs. Rowan at his elbow, offering him another glass of wine, and glancing at the table, the cards, Letty and himself with a wide, inclusive smile of approval. Looking past her he saw that the big table was now occupied only by Mr. Hatton and Mr. Everett, deep in some game.

"I'm glad to see Letty playing the part of instructor," said Mrs. Rowan, gently teasing. "She's had so much to learn in the past few days it must be pleasant for her to turn the tables."

"Why," exclaimed Letty in surprise, looking across the room, "has everybody else gone? Has Plant gone?"

"They're around, somewhere," said Mrs. Rowan, in a changed voice. "But it's time everyone went now. At least . . ." she glanced at the pair at the table and left the sentence unfinished, cut short by a yawn. "I'm tired. Letty, your legs are younger than mine . . . run up and see whether those towels went up into the tapestry room for Chris. And shut Mr. Everett's window as you come down. He likes it closed but he never can manage it properly. Then give Doctor Shadbolt a night-cap and come to bed. I'm going up now. Goodnight," she turned to Humphrey with a smile, "I'm afraid it's been a trifle dull for you, but Letty will learn to entertain her friends presently; it's better for me to let her stand on her own feet, don't you think. I hope we shall see you often."

He could feel that the smile upon his face had a certain fixity, and he straightened his face abruptly. He stood up, and his feet seemed a long way away and his knees less firm than usual. He watched Mrs. Rowan as she walked to the stair door and at one point the outline of her figure grew vague, and wavered, and spread about until there were two of her. He blinked his eyes fiercely, the illusion passed. In the silence he could hear, from somewhere in the house, a peal of high, mocking laughter and following it a male voice, expostulating. Then Letty came back and he could see that she looked very tired and very fragile. He wondered that he had not noticed it before, and blamed himself for selfishness. She went to the side table and had lifted a glass when he stopped her.

"Please, if that is for me, don't. I've had quite enough to drink; and I must go home now. I'm afraid I've been keeping you up."

"She said you were to have a night-cap . . ."

"I've had it, she gave it to me herself." It was odd, he thought, he'd felt perfectly all right while he was sitting with Letty and concentrating on the game. Perhaps that last glass of wine was to blame. Or standing up. Or looking at distant things. Everything more than a few paces away seemed blurred and unsteady. He must be looking peculiar too, for Letty was regarding him anxiously.

"You haven't very far to go, have you?"

"No. I told you where I lived. Don't you remember?"

She nodded and smiled and began to lead the way towards the door. They had to pass close by the table and one of the men — Everett — reached out and caught her wrist in his hand.

"Losing your cavalier?" he asked, jokingly, and then added something in a whisper.

Letty jerked herself free, her face reddening.

On the stairs Humphrey asked, "What did he say?"

"I didn't really hear. Something nasty I expect. He's always teasing me."

"Teasing?"

"Yes; making pretend that I'm about ten years old. They all do it. I hate it. I wish I was six foot tall and as big round as Susie and twenty-five years old."

"Letty you are going straight up to bed, at once, aren't you?"

"Of course I am. I'm last as it is."

"Is that my fault? Have I stayed too long? I'm so sorry. I just waited . . . I thought I'd see somebody else going. I didn't like to be the first to leave . . . and I was interested in the game."

She did not answer. They reached the lobby and she stood on tiptoe and lifted down the lantern from its peg. Then she opened the door. Once it was open and he had passed her and was standing on the other side of the threshold some kind of constraint fell from her manner. She said, quite warmly, "Thank you so much for coming. It was nice for me, having you there. Goodnight."

He guessed that she had waited until he was outside and she was in a position to slam the door upon him before showing even that amount of friendliness. Such caution was appalling in its implication. He remembered suddenly that she had to go back, up all those stairs, past the door of the room where those two men still were. Suppose . . .

He would have turned back, made his suspicion and his care for her very plain and offered to see her to the door of her room, but he knew, with deadly certainty that within the next minute he was going to be sick.

So he said goodnight hastily, and blundered dizzily out of the little yard and out into the churchyard among the graves. There, leaning upon a convenient tombstone he vomited up his supper and all the port wine and a good deal of his self-respect. He'd failed Letty dreadfully, he felt.

But at least he knew now that it was not a fit place for her to stay in, and he would take immediate steps to get her out.

CHAPTER
SEVEN

He had planned the steps as he lay there, in an abandonment of self-disgust, under the frosty stars. But he underestimated the amount of courage it would take to look across the breakfast table and shatter the atmosphere of goodwill by saying, "Sir, I have something to tell you that may make you very angry. But I need your help." The old man smiled and went on loading his fork, imperturbably.

"Been trying out one of your new-fangled methods, I suppose and found it didn't work. Never mind, Humphrey. Everything has to be tried — once. We'll talk about it after breakfast."

"It . . . isn't anything to do with the practice, sir. I'd leave it if it were. I feel I've got to snatch a moment. You remember I told you that I met a girl on the coach, a girl who was going to Mrs. Rowan's . . ."

Doctor Coppard halted his fork half way to his mouth and looked, for a moment, startled, attentive, apprehensive. Then he said:

"Yes, I remember. What about her?" and carried the fork to his mouth, deliberately, as though announcing that nothing should be allowed to come between him and his food. But before Humphrey had finished his story the fork was moving more and more slowly, and sometimes he loaded it blindly without taking his eyes from his apprentice's face. And his eyes, small and bright, between puffed lids and fat cheeks, grew hard and wary.

"Well," he said, quite shrilly, when Humphrey had done. "You have astonished me. So you've really been into the old bitch's den. I'll be damned. You, of all people. I suppose, my boy, I ought to go bald-headed for you for sneaking out at night. That's what you're expecting, isn't it? That's what makes you so white round the gills. But we'll cross that off. You've told me, made a clean breast of it and we'll say no more. What interests me is that you've really seen behind the scenes. That was the trouble at the inquiry. Nobody came forward to say that there were any proper goings-on. It seems to me that this visit of yours might lead to something. We may catch her yet. Tell me . . . which wench did you have, and how much did you pay her?"

"I, sir?" said Humphrey in a blaze of embarrassment. "None, of course. I didn't go there for . . . that purpose. I told you. I went to see if I could find out whether it were a fit place for Letty to live in, and I told you, sir, it isn't and we've got to get her out today."

"I beg your pardon," said the old man, a little ironically. "I'm old and ignorant, you know. I didn't realise that handsome young men could spend evenings in brothels and emerge unexperienced."

"But I told you, sir, I haven't any actual proof that the place *is* a brothel. There were men there, at supper

63

and afterwards, and the . . . the general atmosphere, sir, everything about the place . . . but they didn't . . . I mean I didn't see . . . Some of them stayed the night, Mrs. Rowan made no secret of that. But even that seemed reasonable enough. Mr. Hatton had come all the way from across the Essex border, Mr. Everett was from Newmarket; they obviously came to play cards, I doubt whether Mr. Hatton has another thought in his head. But there were the others. And you see, sir, they are deliberately keeping Letty in the dark. She's so innocent, and young. They can explain anything to her."

"Now look here, my boy," said Doctor Coppard, passing his plate for re-filling. "You've got to be a little clearer in your mind. Either the place is, or *isn't* a whore-house. If it is we can get it closed. It stands on Church property, after all. And if it's closed this little girl will have to find another job. If it isn't . . . well, what are you bothering about? You've been in it, you're an observant chap, you went to investigate, surely you must *know*. I mean, if Mrs. Rowan just had a few friends in to play cards, and if they got drunk and romped with the girls a bit, and if two of them were her guests for the night because their homes were a long way away; we're going to look silly if we start anything."

"So long as Letty gets out I don't want to start anything. What the others do is their affair. But I could see, just from last night, sir, that the atmosphere is evil. Gradually — in her case very gradually, because they're so clever — they'll lead her to think nothing of drinking and . . . romping . . . and all the rest of it. If that should

64

happen, sir, and without my making every effort to prevent it I should never . . . never forgive myself." He ceased the pretence that he was making a breakfast and pushed his plate away, put his big, boyish-looking hands on the table and leaned forward. "Sir, you know how I am placed, I've no money, no influence, no home of my own where I could offer her shelter. I beg you, do something, suggest something. I don't want her to stay there any longer."

Doctor Coppard began to look uncomfortable, and observing this, Humphrey took heart a little. He knew that look. It was a sign that the old man's sterling good-nature was striving with his judgment; and in the past Humphrey could remember many victories to sentiment, hardly one to sense. But the silence lengthened, and gradually the look of discomfort gave way to one of mulish obstinacy.

"I can't have her here," he said at last, flatly. "So if that's what you're hinting at, put it out of your mind, my boy. It'd upset Mrs. Gamble and cause a scandal. Besides — no, frankly impossible. And I'm not sure," he added, dragging out the words a little, "that we have really any cause for interference. You're more than half in love with the girl — no need to tell me that — and I do appreciate how you feel about the position. But even you didn't come out with the proof that you went in for, did you? And in view of that fact I'm more than half inclined to think that it's just a drinking, gambling den and maybe those wenches have fancy men of their own. The girl may be as safe there as anywhere. After all, you seem to be in her confidence. Did she say anything to suggest that she wasn't happy, or that her virtue had been attempted?"

"No sir. The point is that she is very happy there. They're kind to her, and I gather that kindness itself is a novelty to her. She doesn't see that their damned kindness is a leading string. But I can see that; and that throws the responsibility upon me. I know it's asking a lot, sir, but couldn't you have her here until we could think of something else?"

"No," said Doctor Coppard flatly. "I could not."

"Then I must think of something else." He spoke dismally; aware that he had no other idea. The old man's face softened, weakened, and finally became peevish.

"This is a devilish business, Humphrey. Why the hell did you have to take up with the little faggot and let her get you by the nose. Just when you need all your wits and your mind on your job! God blast Mrs. Rowan and all her breed. All right, all right. Exempt her niece-by-marriage!"

He looked at his apprentice, and as he did so, became aware of a challenge. For four years he had been — no, it wasn't blasphemous to think it, it was so nearly true — God to this boy. There hadn't been a question to which he hadn't been able to concoct some kind of answer, there hadn't been a problem he hadn't been able to solve or smooth away. The relationship between them had been phenomenally pleasant. It mustn't be shattered now on the reef of some wretched little bundle of female flesh.

"I suppose you're just panting for Midsummer and intend to marry this Letty as soon as you come out of the examination room."

"I couldn't answer that question, sir. She's very young. I haven't any reason to think that she is in love with me. I should think she is too young to have any thoughts of the kind. That is what makes the whole thing so horrible."

"Hmm. Juliet was . . . what was it . . . fourteen? Anyway, I take it that you are in love with her."

"I don't know, sir. I've never been in love before. The whole thing's new to me; and all mixed up with wanting to get her out of that place. But I think I am."

"That's enough. Now look here, Humphrey. If I help you, if I find a place for her to go — a nice suitable place — will you make me a promise? Promise me that you'll do nothing for a year. That's all I ask. See her, talk to her, kiss her if you must, but don't think about marriage for a year. More young men are ruined by marrying the first girl they take a fancy to than by any other single cause under the sun. You're a clever boy. You're going to make a respectable place in the world for yourself. I look forward to seeing you in my shoes before I die. But I don't want you to spend your life with a clog round your neck simply because at a critical moment a girl stirred your pity. Promise me to be sensible for a year and I'll get her out . . . if only to set your mind at rest."

"I can promise you that, sir. If Letty could be safe and happy . . ."

"Then she shall be. I'll arrange everything."

That brought back the old, admiring, almost worshipping look upon which Doctor Coppard had come to rely, and never known how much he valued it until it was momentarily withdrawn.

"I shall be grateful to you, all my life."

"I expect you will. I quite expect you will."

They sat down, as usual, to dinner at three o'clock. And at once, even as he carved the leg of mutton, the old man said:

"Well, that's all fixed. I went to see Miss Julie Pendle and she'll take your little friend whenever she likes to go."

A great wave of relief broke in Humphrey's brain and went flooding through every tense nerve and muscle. Following upon it was a feeling of wonder as to how the old man had managed it. Even if he had thought of it himself he would never have considered it possible.

Miss Julie Pendle was one of the town's eccentrics. She had run, for more than thirty years, a struggling, would-be-exclusive dressmaking establishment. The wives of the lesser gentry and of the most prosperous farmers and tradespeople had composed her clientele and she had paid her way, managed her two or three apprentices and appeared doomed to a life of respectable obscurity. But it chanced that the Duchess of Belfrage, one of the reigning beauties of the day, credited with having eclipsed Lady Jersey in the Prince Regent's affections, came to stay at Culford. And while she was there an old, exiled admirer sent her, from India, a length of embroidered silk, the like of which had never been seen in England before. The pampered lady conceived the fancy to have it made into a dress to be worn at a ball on the next evening and out of the confusion into which the suggestion threw the whole household Miss Pendle's name presently emerged, a dim star upon a turbulent sea. Miss Pendle and her four apprentices travelled to Culford in a chaise and for eighteen hours on end only laid down their needles in order to lift cups of tea to their panting lips. The gown was finished in time and was the sensation of the season. Her Grace, well-pleased, and with a desire to appear "original" told all admirers that it had been made by little, unknown Miss Pendle of Bury St. Edmunds. Miss Pendle awoke to find herself famous — and, even better — in great demand. Then the little humble dress-maker who had wept from nervousness all the way from Bury to Culford, and whose hands had so trembled during those fittings that they could hardly hold the pins, suddenly revealed a vast and cynical sense of strategy. To the first great lady who came posting into the shabby establishment demanding a gown as like the Duchess of Belfrage's as possible, Miss Pendle replied that she could not accept the order, the result would not do her justice, her ladyship must know that her Grace's figure was largely responsible for the gown's success. Her ladyship, who was short and portly retired in a towering rage, but could not refrain from telling an intimate friend or two how she had been insulted. Competition for Miss Pendle's services grew keener. She refused three orders and then accepted one and the lady upon whom she bestowed this favour received it as an accolade, boasted about it. The thing became ludicrous. Ladies from six counties travelled to the little country town with lengths of lovely material among their luggage to test — as it were — their claim to beauty against Miss Pendle's arbitrary touchstone. Miss Pendle never wavered, and finally touched a dazzling zenith, when, at a Ball at Devonshire House seven of the most widely acclaimed beauties of the day were clad in confections designed and stitched in a little workroom seventy miles away.

The fashion lasted for about eighteen months and then died, as fashions do. The great ladies moved on. But Miss Pendle had money put by in Thorley's bank and a reputation which, in the preservative atmosphere of a country town, would last her life-time and longer; and she had her old clientele, for never, even during the wildest rush of business had she refused to work for a former customer; and she had for apprentices the pick of all the Suffolk girls who hoped to make a living by dressmaking. To have been trained by Miss Pendle was a mark of a standard widely recognised. In the old days she had taken girls without premiums and even paid them a few shillings a week during their training; now she asked twenty pounds for six months' tuition and thirty for a year.

Surely, Humphrey thought, astounded, the old man hadn't plumped down twenty pounds on behalf of a girl he'd never even seen.

"That is wonderful news, sir. How on earth did you manage it?"

"Oh, I talked to her," said Doctor Coppard, looking flattered and pleased. "Julie and I are old friends. She broke a needle in her finger when she was just a slip of a girl . . . one of the first little jobs I ever tackled. Both sweating like pigs we were by the time I had it safe. She'll take the girl and do her duty by her. But there's a condition . . . She doesn't want any running backwards and forwards between her place and Mrs. Rowan's. That's understandable enough."

"I suppose so. Did she say when?"

"Just when you like. Tonight. Tomorrow. You'd better go across to the Coffee Room and talk to her about it this evening. I shouldn't — if I were you — make a song and dance about it. Madam won't take kindly to the idea. But you can tell the girl that if she likes to walk out at a convenient moment I'll send Davie across for her gear."

"You don't imagine, sir, that Mrs. Rowan would attempt to keep her there against her will?"

"She would if what you suspect is true," said the old man, looking wise. "She might in any case. And in any case she won't take your interference — or mine, if she hears of it — very kindly. Thank God I don't drink her coffee!" He laughed, as though the idea of Mrs. Rowan doctoring his coffee was the greatest joke on earth. But though the mirth was a little discordant Humphrey could see that the old man had done his best, had acted swiftly and sensibly, and that the offer of Davie's assistance in the removal was prompted by keen perception.

"I can't thank you sufficiently, sir. And you've hit on just the right thing. Letty used to do sewing in London, I believe."

"And she'll be safe with Julie." That was very true. Miss Pendle's young ladies could have gone straight to a cloister without feeling any loss of freedom.

"I'll tell her tonight." A feeling of responsibility and foreboding which had weighed upon him for a week lifted. "You've made me very happy. And very grateful."

"I trust those feelings will last for a year, Humphrey. You'll remember I also made a condition."

Privately he thought that, for an old man, not much practised in craft, he'd done very well. The little baggage would be far more inaccessible in Julie's house than she would be in the Coffee House. Two or three visits to the prim sitting room where Julie's girls were allowed to receive their guests would be as much as Humphrey would be able to attain in twelve months. Miss Pendle did not allow "followers" or "walking out". And the whole onus of the separation was squarely laid upon Miss Pendle's shoulders. That was the beauty of the scheme. No need for Doctor Coppard to interfere. No blame to Doctor Coppard, who had been helpful and understanding at a critical moment. And twelve months was a long time. Half Humphrey's interest in the girl was an adolescent knight-errantry. Once the reason for that was removed, and the subject of it out of easy reach the thing'd die a natural death. By next year at this time Humphrey would have forgotten all about the wench. Ah yes, you couldn't beat an old man when it came to a little scheming.

72

CHAPTER
EIGHT

"But whatever made you think of doing that? Whatever made you think I wasn't ever so happy here?" Letty asked, when, with many a stumble, hesitation, apology and apparent contradiction, Humphrey had at last reached the end of the speech which had begun, "Letty, stay and talk to me for a moment. There's something I want to tell you."

He had been far more nervous than — remembering the Latin speech which as head boy it had been his duty to deliver on Founder's Day to the assembled Governors and notabilities of the county — he could have believed possible. Relief of mind and hope for the future had carried him into the Coffee Room and made him make the bold bid for Letty's attention. But as soon as he started he realised the difficulties. Without maligning the aunt and the cousins who had received Letty kindly and treated her well and deceived her cleverly, it was impossible to make her understand the danger from which he proposed to rescue her. Upon the face of it, hampered as he was by the impossibility of plain speaking, it did appear as though he were offering her an alternative employment, and that alternative somewhat duller, and, in a way, socially inferior, to that in which she was at the moment engaged. Almost any girl would prefer the cheerful, club-like atmosphere of the Coffee House to that of Miss Pendle's establishment, and, short of the brutal truth there seemed no reason for the suggestion of change. Humphrey began to feel foolish, and the feeling grew as he blundered on. The plaintive wonder in Letty's voice as she replied to him came as no surprise.

"I didn't think that you weren't *happy*, exactly. It was just that I thought Miss Pendle's would be more *suitable*, I thought . . . you see, you're good with your needle . . . and it was a lucky chance that she had a vacancy, usually she is besieged by young ladies . . . Well, anyway, I thought I would mention it."

"I see. That was very kind." The long lashes met and then parted upon a shining look of gratitude which went out like a blown candle, leaving that dumb look of mourning which was the essential Letty. "You couldn't know how I hate sewing. In the last couple of years I've had enough sewing to last me the rest of my life. It looks easy enough, doesn't it? But it's cruel work. Honestly. I've sewed and sewed till I was nearly blind and ached in every bone of my body. Even your toes'll ache if you sit at it long enough. It was kind of you to think of me, but I wouldn't go back to sewing again for anything. This is much nicer."

"It isn't *this*, so much," he said faltering, looking round, as she had done, upon the crowded, cheerful room. "It's . . . afterwards. You weren't completely happy, not all the time, last night, were you?"

74

Something shrouded and defensive crept into her face.

"Well, I told you. I don't like it rowdy. But it's my aunt's house, isn't it; and while I live in it I can't tell her I'd like it quiet, can I? I don't have to stay up when they begin to lark about. Last night, I . . . well, I'd asked you round, I kind of felt you were my guest, so I stayed up. But generally I go to bed. And anyway, it'd be silly to give all this up that I like and go and sew which I hate just because Cathy's friends and Susan's kick up a clatter."

"And get drunk. And try to make you drink . . ."

"I didn't, did I?" she said quickly. "I told you. I've had my lesson about that." A little look of mockery, not without any accompanying affection and an odd suggestion of intimacy, came into her voice. "You shouldn't talk about getting drunk . . ."

"I know," he said humbly. And somehow the whole shining scheme of rescue faded and shrivelled into nonsense. He hadn't a foothold at all. The girl didn't understand; she didn't want to be rescued; he'd no proof that anything worse than drunkenness went on in the damned house; and to crown all he'd been drunk himself. Despair brought with it a certain lucidity.

"I know I was drunk, and I know you think I'm a busybody, but it's only because I'm interested in you, Letty. And frankly I don't think this is the place for you. You're not like Cathy and Susan, you're different. It's all very well to say that if I hadn't been there last night you'd have gone to bed and that on other nights you do go to bed. When you've been here a little longer and they get used to you they'll laugh at you for that — and you don't like being laughed at. So then you'll stay up and you won't like that either. And I shan't like it. I wish you'd just think about Miss Pendle's offer. It'd be the best thing — in the long run."

"I don't want to sew any more. I'm quite happy here. And I can look after myself." The three short sentences rattled out in a manner which in any other person he would have found extremely offensive. Spoken by Letty they filled him with dread lest he had offended her. And if that happened not only would his life be darkened, but she would be cut off from the only true friend she had in the world.

He began a hasty speech of explanation and apology; but just then Cathy beckoned Letty away and he sat for almost an hour waiting an opportunity for further talk. When it came and he blurted out the sentences which had been milling and milling around in his mind Letty received them kindly.

"That's all right. I know you meant it kindly. I just couldn't do it. But thank you all the same."

Letty had made herself an enemy. Like many kind-hearted people old Doctor Coppard expected his kindness to be accepted with unquestioning gratitude. When Humphrey reported the result of the interview and miserably tried to explain that Letty did not understand the position and preferred to stay where she was, the old man was affronted. He had made an effort on the behalf of an unknown little draggle-tail and she had dared to render it abortive. He was incapable of dismissing the matter with a shrug, of saying, "Well, my boy, we've done our best. Now she must take her chance." But at the same time he was too clever to expose his own wounded vanity in a fit of healthy fury. He'd wanted the girl out of the way, and that feeling of responsibility off Humphrey's mind; and at the same time he'd intended a kindness. The girl had thwarted him. But it was possible that her refusal could be used to good purpose. If he could just wait long enough to speak coolly, judiciously.

"I was afraid of that, my boy," he said, when he was quite sure of his voice. "All along. I didn't want to disappoint you, and I did what I could, naturally, to help. But I expected exactly that answer. She's tainted already. And a taste for that kind of life is as incurable as a taste for drink. I'm afraid if you'd persuaded her to go to Miss Pendle's she'd have gone back within a week."

Humphrey realised the import of the speech, but the word "persuaded" struck through the realisation like a blow.

"I'm afraid I didn't even try to persuade her, sir. I should have. I see that now. But it was all extraordinarily difficult. I couldn't even say what I suspected. I messed the whole thing up. But you're wrong about the taint, sir. It isn't that. I swear it isn't that. She doesn't even know. She's like a child. She calls the place rowdy and says she can always go to bed."

"She says that to you, Humphrey, because she thinks you don't know. She probably thinks *you* are like a child. Forgive me for saying this, but your very credulity shows how very innocent and inexperienced you are. It's a horrible fact, but it is a fact . . . there're girls of twelve who'll sell themselves for sixpence. She's probably one of them . . . knows all about the place and is keeping the secret. Is it reasonable to suppose that otherwise she would prefer to stay there?"

"It sounded reasonable enough when she said it," Humphrey said, struggling not to be angry. "And the rest just isn't true. I can't tell you how I can be certain, but I am certain. If she really understood what the place was she wouldn't stay in it a minute."

"Then why didn't you tell her?"

"Because I don't know. And because if I did know it'd be such a dreadful thing to say. Don't you realise, sir, that they've been kind to her and you've only to look at her to see that nobody's ever been kind to her before. She looks on me as a friend because I gave her a handful of food — and look what they've done — given her clothes and a home and a kind of . . . well they laugh at her and consider her, make a kind of pet of her. And then I go along and offer her a place in a strange establishment, doing something she hates. No wonder she refused."

"Bless you, Humphrey. There should be an addition to the Beatitudes, Blessed are they that believe the best, for they shall know the worst. I've warned you."

"I don't want to be offensive, sir, or to quarrel with you over a girl of whose very existence I've only been aware for a week . . . but I would ask you to remember that I *have* seen her and talked to her and you haven't. If she were a patient and we were talking of symptoms you would at least admit that gave me a certain advantage, wouldn't you?"

"Not if it were a disease which you had never seen before and with which I was familiar, Humphrey. And I'm afraid that in this case it *is* a disease — sheer badness. And one thing that makes me think so is this. I don't think an entirely inexperienced, innocent young woman would have got her hooks into you so quickly. I perceive the skilled hand. But there, I don't want to quarrel with you. I refuse to quarrel with you. You asked me to help to get an innocent young girl out of a bad house; I find her a place. She refuses it. Draw your own conclusions. So far as I'm concerned I'm happier than if you'd lost your head over, say, little Anna Duffle. You might have had to marry her. You'll get this one for half a guinea presently, or I'm a Dutchman."

He had worked off his rage. He could look at his apprentice with his usual benignity, and attribute the tenseness of the boy's attitude, the close pressed lips and the silence to the fact that one, at least, of his several bolts had gone home.

When those of whom one is fond behave in an unexpected and disappointing manner excuses must be found for them. So Humphrey, bitterly outraged by his master's manner, took refuge in the thought that the old man did not understand. He was blind and bitter, as all old people were. It had been a mistake to confide in him at all; for now there would always remain between them a subject about which it was not safe to speak; even to maintain silence upon it would be significant — an admission of danger. The old, complete harmony could never be regained. But he must remember that Doctor Coppard had, in the beginning, meant to be kind, and that his failure was failure of understanding, not of good will; and he must above all things remember the many, the uncountable favours which the old man had shown him in the past.

So he dismissed Doctor Coppard from his mind and began again to worry about Letty.

CHAPTER
NINE

More and more during the next few days he found his mind reverting to the little farm where he had been born, but which had not really been his home since he had left it, a boy of twelve, to attend the Grammar School. There was the farm, and there was the little shop which was his mother's particular province. Surely another pair of hands would be welcome there. And Letty wouldn't be lonely, with his mother and sisters for company; and helping in the shop would bring her into contact with people; it wouldn't be such a dull alternative as entering Miss Pendle's workroom.

His mother would need a good deal of persuasion. In fact, when the idea first occurred to him he had dismissed it, judging Hagar's opposition to any such scheme unsurmountable. But as the days went on, as each night brought the thought that Letty was still in that house, his secret fear of his mother dwindled; the idea of Letty safe and busy at Slipshoe Farm became brighter and more attractive until finally he took refuge in a kind of desperate optimism and felt that he had only to see his mother, talk to her, reason with her and all would be well. He

determined that when he went home at Christmas —
now only three weeks distant — he would lay the
proposition before her. Meanwhile he would continue
to frequent the Coffee House and keep his eye on
Letty. Most likely her attitude would change
presently; the Rowans would grow used to her
presence, cease to pamper her, stop trying to deceive
her. By the time he came back from Slipshoe with
his mother's invitation Letty might be very glad to
receive it.

Once he had decided upon this plan his mind grew
easier. There were moments, when he was walking or
driving alone, or when he lay in his bed between
sleeping and waking, when his imagination presented
him with a terrifying picture of himself first broaching
the subject to Hagar. Undeluded then, he knew that
it would be a very difficult moment, and wished with
all his heart that he could see some way to avoid it.
But such moments passed; and after all it would be
a despicable fellow who could not face a little
embarrassment and unpleasantness for the sake of the
girl he loved. And he had only to go across to the
Coffee House, to watch Letty walk towards him, so
young, so defenceless, so very dear, in order to feel
himself equal to anything; and he had only to think
about the hours when the Coffee House was closed to
wish that he could go to Slipshoe before Christmas, or
that the time between now and that interview could be
hastened away.

★ ★ ★

Something happened first. A thing apparently irrelevant and insignificant, but which was to have importance.

He was in the Coffee House. Most evenings found him there now. Sometimes, when the whole long session had gained him only a few brief words with Letty and the painful joy of watching her as she moved about the room, he would swear to miss an evening. But although he could walk to the very door and then turn and go quickly in another direction he always came back, and always entered at last. It was a criminal waste of time which should have been devoted to study; and it was a waste of money, a long evening often cost a shilling which he could very ill afford; it got him nowhere; it solved nothing; but he was simply unable to remain, of his own will, away from the place where Letty was. Once or twice he had been involuntarily absent, chained to duty; and each time he had hoped that Letty would notice and give some sign. But her greeting never varied. She always looked pleased to see him, always stood by smiling while he ground out his little mundane remarks, always replied in kind and then with a final smile moved away. But now her going did not always leave him in conspicuous isolation, Mr. Bancroft, on his off-duty evenings, was anxious to share a table and chat, and there were other men who seemed disposed to friendliness. The fact that most of them drank brandy with, or instead of, coffee, and took turns in paying for the rounds of drinks made their company less pleasant than it might otherwise have been. However, it was easier to sit and watch Letty from an occupied table than from one by himself, and if the men with whom he sat thought him mean and stingy that couldn't be helped.

On this particular evening he was sharing a table with Mr. Bancroft and another Grammar School master, and this man, plainly very junior, had just looked at his watch and said that he must be moving. He had to be in at the half hour, and couldn't hurry uphill. He began to be confidential about his symptoms — as, Humphrey had discovered, many people tended to do when they found themselves in a doctor's company, rather as though they hoped for some casual word of advice which they could use without paying for. But the poor man received scant attention from Humphrey who had just seen Cathy Rowan, her face very white where it wasn't painted, hurry into the room and unostentatiously draw Mrs. Rowan aside and whisper. Mrs. Rowan immediately hurried out. Letty was not, at that moment, in the Coffee Room, and Humphrey's imagination, excessively vulnerable where she was concerned, immediately presented him with the proposition that there had been an accident and that Letty was involved in it. She had cut her hand with the bread knife; she had turned a boiling kettle over upon herself. Mrs. Rowan did not come back, but Cathy, still very white-faced, did presently, and then after a short, agonising interval, Letty herself, paler even than Cathy and looking quite distraught. Once, as she passed Susie, she leaned for a moment against the plump girl's shoulder and whispered, and Susie immediately hurried away, only to return after a moment with her face white in its turn. Something very upsetting must have happened in the Rowans' kitchen; but since Letty was safe the sharpest edge of Humphrey's interest was blunted and he could return his attention to the little schoolmaster who was concluding his account of his physical state by saying, ". . . could wring it out. So you see I absolutely must not hurry uphill."

"Very awkward for you," said Humphrey unhelpfully. To do him justice he had still enough amateur enthusiasm in him to have let fall a helpful hint or a suggestion had he been in a position to do so. He was young enough to enjoy giving advice; but he had not heard a word of the long, self-pitying discourse.

"Well, goodnight," said the little man in a deflated voice.

"I'll come with you, I think," said Mr. Bancroft, sacrificing the extra hour to which his seniority entitled him for the sake of company on the way home. "'Night, Humphrey."

Humphrey sat firm. Somebody would have to remove the cups and the glasses from the table and it might well be Letty. He liked her voice to be the one to bid him a final Goodnight. But when he looked round she had vanished again. And then Cathy disappeared too. Susie, left alone in the Coffee Room began to make premature — and unusual — preparations for closing. Humphrey saw her deliberately move a log on the hearth, not to make it blaze the brighter, but to the side of the embers where it smouldered to extinction. Then she blew out the candles on the unoccupied tables.

Finally she began to tidy the papers and periodicals on the centre table, and even took one away from under old Duffle's elbow. "Finished with this?" she asked in a curt way, utterly alien to her usual manner.

In the oddest way she had succeeded in destroying the atmosphere of the place. The dying fire, the stink of the blown candles, the tidiness of the centre table and something that emanated from Susie herself made the hour seem suddenly late. Men who, engrossed in their company or their thoughts had not noticed, as Humphrey had done, each detail of Susie's movements, became aware that they were not so warm and comfortable as they had thought; one by one they began to leave until at last there was only old Duffle, who, after a glance at his watch, pulled his chair nearer the dying fire and sent Susie for more coffee, and Humphrey himself, still hoping, though rather despairingly, that Letty would come back and say goodnight.

Finally he gave up, and rose and went into the dimly lighted passage and took his hat and coat from the peg. He slung the coat over his arm, not worth putting it on just to cross the hill, and was lifting his hat when his elbow was seized and Letty's voice said:

"Humphrey." He was startled, both by her presence and the fact that she had used his Christian name. She had always called him Doctor Shadbolt and he had never dared suggest the more intimate usage. The moment when one first hears one's own name upon the lips of the person one loves has a peculiar excitement. (One forgets, of course; the wonder stales; glory vanishes; but it was there, once.) He turned and said in a breathy, tense whisper, "Letty." And he thought that she had waited for him, laid in wait for him, called him Humphrey because . . . because something of his own glorious, agonising state had brimmed over and informed her.

She said quickly, secretively, "Will you come into the kitchen and help Aunt Thirza. Plant's there, and I'm sure he's bleeding to death, but they won't get a doctor. Plant didn't want anybody to know he'd been hurt. But when they see you they'll be glad really, and know I was right."

So that explained all their white faces and curious behaviour. Somebody bleeding to death in the kitchen was enough to upset any household, especially a household of women. And of course the likelihood was that it wasn't a serious case at all, a slight cut or something making a lot of mess, and the man making light of it, knowing that a doctor's attention was quite unnecessary.

Nevertheless he was pleased that Letty had asked his aid. For the first time he stood within the precincts of the Coffee House by right of his profession, needed, not tolerated, important, not to be ignored.

"Of course," he said, "I'll be glad to do what I can. It probably isn't 'as bad as you imagine."

"Aunt Thirza can't stop it," said Letty simply, as though anything which defeated Mrs. Rowan's omnipotence was very serious — and very rare. "We'll go this way, it's nearer." She turned and plunged into the darkness which, beyond the radiance of the little lamp, filled the passage. He heard a door handle turn. Then Letty said,

"There're two steps down. Be careful." Her hand sought and found his and at the touch every nerve in his body leaped in response. But though her clasp was tense and nervous it was completely impersonal and as soon as she had opened a second door and a ray of light pierced the darkness she tried to withdraw it. His own fingers, almost against his volition, clung for a second, dumb, communicative, pleading, and they did actually step into the kitchen hand in hand.

But nobody noticed. All the Rowan women, with sick white faces were busy about Plant who lay slumped in a chair, his face the colour of boiled milk, his eyes open but fixed in a dreamy, far away stare which reminded Humphrey of the theory that of all ways of dying that by haemorrhage was easiest and least painful. His sleeve was pushed back to the elbow and about his wrist and hand was draped a towel, its thick white folds reddened and heavy with blood, and behind him on the table lay a heap of others which had been used and discarded. People always seemed to think that a fresh cloth would be effective.

Mrs. Rowan turned her head. Her first expression of dismayed defensiveness slowly gave way to relief.

"Mr. Driscoll's cut himself," she said, somewhat unnecessarily. "Stand back, Cathy, and let Doctor Shadbolt look."

Humphrey raised Plant's arm until it was level with the back of the chair, and then removed the towel. No wonder all the women looked so sick, he thought. At first sight it appeared as though a determined effort had been made to sever the hand at the wrist. A nasty sight, even for one accustomed to such. But as a job it seemed simple and straightforward. With the pressure of his finger he staunched the spouting artery, and said over his shoulder: "Get me a piece of string or tape, something I can tie. And a wooden spoon or a skewer."

The hand which delivered the article was Letty's and what she held out was the blue ribbon from her hair. She must have tugged it out with some violence, for a strand of long brown hair, almost a complete curl still clung to it. Cathy found a spoon. In three seconds the hasty tourniquet was in place.

"Now," he said, "stand away, all of you. I shall want a cup of black coffee with a teaspoonful of brandy in it; and your workbox, Cathy. Mrs. Rowan, you may hold the cup for him, if you like. The rest keep well away."

There was something pleasant in being, if only for a few moments, in a position of such supreme authority. And it was particularly gratifying to display one's skill before Mrs. Rowan who had always treated him with a degree of condescension, before Cathy and Susie who on that gay rowdy Saturday evening had had no glance to spare for him and above all before Letty — though for quite different reasons. No trace of this youthful conceit showed in his manner. He worked as though he and Plant were alone in the world. When the wound had been stitched and bandaged and the hand laid to rest in a sling contrived from a scarf, he relaxed however, and blew out his breath and turned to Letty and said, "Well, that was touch and go. You were quite right. You've saved his life without a doubt."

His words seemed to break the spell which lay upon the room. Everybody drew deep breaths and made little purposeless movements. Even Plant Driscoll disembedded his top teeth from his lower lip and stretched his monkeyish mouth into a caricature of a smile and said, "I'm obliged to you . . . no idea you were such a good surgeon."

"We are *all* most deeply grateful," said Mrs. Rowan with an air of finality.

He found himself the centre of a flattering female circle. Cathy fetched a bowl of hot water for his hands, Susie rummaged out yet another fresh towel; Mrs. Rowan poured a glass of brandy.

"I'm sure you need a drink, Doctor Shadbolt. I know I do."

"And what about me?" Plant asked in a faint, wryly humorous voice.

"You have the same again," Humphrey said with authority, and, sipping his own brandy, watched with approval as Letty poured another cup of the strong black coffee, measured into it a meticulous teaspoonful of brandy and held it for Plant to drink. Then he became aware that by watching his patient he was causing an atmosphere of uneasiness which — owing to Letty's hint — it was not difficult to guess the reason. They feared that now, with the operation completed, he would ask an awkward question. As he easily might have done, but for the warning. A little amused, enjoying the sense of power, he watched until Plant had emptied the cup. Then he said:

"And now . . ." and paused just long enough to feel the tension, "you should go to bed as soon as possible."

Mrs. Rowan, Cathy and Plant all began to speak together. Mrs. Rowan said, "There's a bed all ready for him — this is his second home as you might say." Plant said, "Right willingly I *do* assure you." Cathy said, "I've got a hot brick in the oven. Just a minute, Plant, and I'll help you."

She stooped and took a piece of flannel from the hearth and then opened the oven door and drew out the hot brick and wrapped it, firmly and competently in the flannel. As she did so Letty moved towards Plant's chair and said, "You can lean on me, Plant, as hard as you like."

To Humphrey, a little dizzy from triumph and a gulp or two of brandy the words sounded immeasurably pathetic and brave. She was so small, so fragile — and she had more sense than the lot of them put together. They didn't appreciate her properly. Even when he had praised her a moment ago no one had noticed it. He said, rather loudly:

"That's right, Letty, finish off your good work. But for you he wouldn't have gone to bed again."

It was, perhaps, he reflected as soon as the words were spoken, a back-handed form of self-praise, a little vulgar, not *quite* the thing to have said. ("Always conceal from a patient the gravity of his condition.") Was that why Cathy, rising from her knees and tucking the wrapped brick under her arm shot him that glance of unmistakable pity and contempt? As though he were a little boy, clever with his fingers and blown with pride and blind to the fact that in every other way he was hopelessly stupid. Well, after all, there were times when it was good to be clever with one's fingers.

Nevertheless the glance crushed him; and to put himself right with Cathy he moved forward and said, "I'll help."

"No, you've done quite enough," said Cathy crisply. "Letty and I can manage, can't we, Letty?"

Susie, with an air of conveying that when a man who was bleeding had ceased to bleed to death in the kitchen all was well again, said, "Well, I suppose even old Duffle has gone now. I'll lock up," went away into the front of the house and when Letty, Cathy and Plant had made their slow way to the stair door Humphrey was left with Mrs. Rowan.

She had seated herself on the shabby settle by the hearth and was leaning back, not even drinking from the glass she held, as though she had finished with some matter which had completely exhausted her. He saw that she looked tired and old. Automatically he softened towards her, laying suspicion aside, remembering that she had done her ineffective best to deal with a nasty situation.

"You're very tired, Mrs. Rowan," he said.

Experience had taught him that women were peculiarly susceptible to that kind of remark; the weariest woman, worn out by nursing, would brighten and actually take new strength from the thought that someone had noticed her exhaustion with sympathy.

And though he had spoken the words sincerely, as soon as they were spoken he expected the normal response. It might even be that, weary, touched, she would forget to be defensive. But Mrs. Rowan only sighed, a little impatiently.

"Yes, I *am* tired. I'm tired of being depended upon and not confided in. Tonight, for example, calls for some explanation, surely. I have none. Plant just arrived, like that. There are some men around here who would, I verily believe, run to me if their heads were cut off and expect me to fix them on again. One grows weary." She lifted her glass and drank deeply.

"I appreciate your lack of curiosity," she said in a lighter tone. "As for my own, that will go unsatisfied, as usual. Plant never tells me anything, and I never ask him any questions." A slight dash of venom came into her voice. "Plant had his usual luck. He got here, and Letty was inspired and you were on the spot. You must send him your bill, Doctor Shadbolt."

"Oh, I'm not worrying about *that*," Humphrey assured her. Indeed how could he charge for a job which he had so much enjoyed doing; for an experience which had brought him such complete satisfaction.

Mrs. Rowan's interest detached itself again. If he hadn't been waiting to say goodnight to Letty he would have gone home, so plainly was he dismissed. But he stood until Letty came back into the kitchen and then bade Mrs. Rowan goodnight and slowly moved to the door, looking towards Letty like a dog seeking a favour.

"I'll see you out," she said.

"And lock up," said her aunt.

"Susie said not to."

"Very well. I'm going up myself now."

Once again they stood together in the little lobby by the back door. The moon was high and full and the whole world was a-wash in its white, rather eerie light. When Letty opened the back door the faint radiance touched her eyes and mouth and lighted the pallor of her face until it seemed to float above the shadows like a white flower upon a dim pool. The sight of it and the sense of her nearness and of their being alone together in the night, combined with the brandy and the memory of his recent personal triumph to lift him into a state of heady excitement. He even lost for a moment his feeling of responsibility for her. And when Letty put her hand on his arm, in an unaccustomed, friendly gesture and said:

"Thank you for doing it. You are clever. It must be wonderful to be so clever and able to save people's lives! And then you said that nice thing about me ..." a great wave of recklessness thundered through him and he stooped his head and kissed her.

Her mouth was cool and unresponsive, she leaned back a little, withdrawing from him. It was like kissing a flower. But he had never kissed a girl before, even in fun and he was as shattered and excited by the brief contact of lips and by his own daring as a more experienced man would have been by the closest and warmest of embraces. Now she would know, begin to share his feelings.

"Oh, Letty," he said in a strangled voice, "I do love you so much. I loved you the moment I saw you, on the coach. I'll never love anybody else as long as I live."

Time and all its menace, the changing, hardening, threatening years stood off before the innocent shining challenge. Never again would it be the first time; to no other lips could the first kiss be given. Already, unconsciously, the process of experience had begun, grooving the mind for comparison, memories, disillusionments. But as he lifted his head he believed that this love would last for ever, and that it would beget love.

Letty stood silent and rigid. She had let her hand fall away from his arm and everything, the lines of her body, the expression of her face, the look in her eyes indicated a wary defensiveness, pitiable because it was so automatic, and so uncalled-for. He looked at her for a moment, waiting, and then the old, inherited knowledge that men call instinct warned him — not thus — not thus . . .

"You're not angry are you, Letty?"

"No. But you wouldn't do that in front of people, would you? They might think I was like . . . Cathy and Susie."

"Of course they wouldn't. Nobody could. And of course I wouldn't. I wouldn't do a thing in the world to displease you. It was just that you looked so sweet, and I've wanted to kiss you for a long time. Because I do love you. Letty, you do . . . you do . . . like me a little?"

"Oh, I do," she said, promptly, reassuringly. "I do *like* you. I think you're the nicest, kindest person I ever met. But you see . . . I . . ."

"Well?"

"Well, there is a kind of gap between liking a person and kissing and cuddling. It takes a bit of getting over."

A pang of remorse pierced him. She was so very young. Hadn't he himself said to Doctor Coppard that she was too young to have any thoughts of the kind. And the old man had said something about Juliet being fourteen. But Juliet wasn't a real person, just somebody in a story. Letty was real; and what she had just said, though perhaps a trifle disheartening, was also real, and true. He saw that he would have to exercise self-control and patience, and that thought made him feel suddenly very old and male.

"I know. I shouldn't have kissed you or said what I did. I'm a clumsy blundering fool. But now you do know how I feel. And I want you to know that I can wait, for years if you like, Letty. I won't kiss you again or mention the subject until you want me to."

She looked at him solemnly. "Thank you. You are so nice; and I do like you, but I . . ." She broke off as the gate in the wall opened and heavy steps sounded on the cobbles of the yard. Humphrey stepped out of the lobby and the newcomer saw Letty first and cried in a boisterous, facetious way, "Hullo, my pretty, looking out for me?" Then, seeing Humphrey, he added, "I beg your pardon."

"Susie's expecting you," said Letty in a small cold voice.

"Nice to think somebody is," said the man as he passed into the house.

"Who's that?"

"Susie's friend. They call him Taffy, I think. He's horrible. I shall go to bed now. Goodnight — Humphrey." She paused before his name and spoke it with a kind of nervous punctiliousness as though having once used it when asking a favour she could not now revert to formality, especially after what had passed between them. But the lack of spontaneity could not prevent it enchanting him again.

The arrival of Taffy, however, had broken the bounds of the little self-contained world of his personal relationship with Letty and as he walked back across the Abbey Hill the old nagging thoughts began to tread their familiar way through his mind. He had to put aside the thought that Letty had used his name, and that he had kissed her and that they had said intimate things about their feelings for one another, and consider instead that she lived in a house frequented by men who would sooner bleed to death than face an apparently harmless question, by men who addressed her familiarly and called her "my pretty". He even endured some moments of self-reproach because he had allowed himself to be side-tracked, as it were, into a display of selfish sentiment. His motive might be more honest but his behaviour was no better than that of the others. If any other man had kissed an unwilling, shrinking Letty . . . What he had to bear in mind was that whether Letty loved him or not was, at the moment, a thing of less importance than that she should be safely out of that house. To comfort himself he remembered her cool unresponsiveness. Thank God she was, as yet, completely untouched. Such innocence couldn't be feigned, whatever Doctor Coppard might say. And there were only ten days more to Christmas and his visit to Slipshoe.

Since he had confessed to visiting the Coffee House he had been free to leave and to enter Doctor Coppard's front door. Apart from that change the fact that he had become one of Mrs. Rowan's customers seemed to have dropped into oblivion. The old man, with more sensitiveness than one might have credited him with, had sensed that Humphrey's evening absences, Mrs. Rowan, Letty and Miss Pendle were subjects never mentioned between them. The silence had an ominous significance which both, at odd moments, realised as a symptom of a changed and deteriorated relationship.

Tonight the old man was just on his way to bed. He paused at the stairhead and leaned over the banister and called to Humphrey.

"That you, Humphrey? Pity you weren't back a bit sooner. You could have saved me putting on my boots. A fruitless errand too. I do wish people would understand that the one sort of body that can wait till morning is a dead one." His voice was grumbling but cheerful and gossipy.

"Who died, sir?" For whom had the old man been forced to don his boots again, what known, faithful patient had died while Humphrey spent his skill upon mysterious, knife-slashed men?

"Oh, nobody of ours. Just a man. They found him, all cut about and tangled in the weeds under the bridge on

Fornham Road. Hadn't been there long, either, or dead long. In fact he wasn't quite cold when I got there. But he was dead as mutton and they could have seen that with half an eye."

"Foul play, sir, d'you think?"

"I'd say so, undoubtedly. He was dead before he went in the water, that I do know. And carved up very fancy. Hands all cut about as though he'd resisted pretty strongly. I reckon somebody pushed him in the river hoping the current'd carry him away. Pity it didn't; then some other poor slave of a doctor would have had the pleasure of turning out and pronouncing him dead."

His voice was cheerful and callous. It was one of the genial old man's peculiarities, this heartless attitude towards corpses. Humphrey had noticed it before. Once even a valued patient had breathed his last Doctor Coppard behaved and spoke as though there had been no connection between the living person over whom he had worked and worried and the lump of carrion left lying on the bed. It had shocked Humphrey at first, but with the years he had seen that it was a form of defence reared between the old man's good heart and the sad realities of his trade. And perhaps a form of revenge too. Living bodies, so vulnerable and complicated made so many demands upon him that he derived satisfaction in speaking and acting callously about those which were beyond the help of skill and kindness.

Tonight Humphrey hardly noticed the attitude. His mind was busy with the man who had also been slashed with a knife and hadn't wanted anyone to ask how the wound had been inflicted. If a third man had set upon two, killing one and wounding the other, one would have expected the survivor to be raising a hue-and-cry. Was it that two men, each with a knife, had set upon one another? Or had one attacked, and had the victim snatched at the knife — "hands all cut about" — and inflicted one serious wound before it was snatched back and used finally?

"I wonder . . ." he said aloud, falling back into the habit of the bygone time when he and Doctor Coppard could gossip and speculate together upon any subject under the sun.

"What d'you wonder?" asked the old man.

But Humphrey had remembered. He was the only one outside the Rowan family who knew that Plant Driscoll had been injured. If he spoke now Doctor Coppard's public-spirited energy would be in action first thing in the morning, and the Rowans would know whom to blame for anything that might develop. And that would make it more difficult for him to keep in touch with Letty.

"Who killed him of course," he replied, the banal words denying the promise of interest in "I wonder . . ."

"Oh," said Doctor Coppard in a disappointed voice, "well, we all wonder that. There may be news in the morning. Goodnight, Humphrey."

"Goodnight, sir," said Humphrey, and went into his own room and closed the door and faced the startling fact that he had just connived at murder. It stunned

100

him for a moment until automatic self-justification began its soothing process. After all he couldn't be *sure* that there was any connection between Driscoll's wound and the corpse in the water. One shouldn't jump to conclusions or take too much notice of what might easily be a coincidence. But in his heart he knew that his reason for keeping silent upon the subject was in itself an argument against such plausible and comfortable reasonings. He had entertained a dark and not entirely unfounded suspicion and he had kept silent, not from a sense of justice, or from caution, but from fear. He wouldn't have done that in the old days.

On the other hand the man was dead, and not even the apprehension of his murderer could bring him back to life. Was it right to risk his access to Letty and the chance of getting her away from the Coffee House for the sake of a corpse?

Rather miserably he undressed and got into bed, pursuing the argument with himself: then, seeking relief from it he retraced the events of the evening, remembering with undivided pleasure the skill of his own fingers, and with pleasure that was sharper, though less certain, the moment when he had kissed Letty. Finally he came round again to the prospect of Christmas — now very near, and the likelihood of his mother's capitulation. Upon that thought he fell asleep.

CHAPTER
TEN

Next morning the scarecrow little urchin who did Mrs. Naylor's errands arrived with a message to say that the old lady was dying. It was a cold raw morning and the greyness of the sky seemed to have seeped down into the streets and into the spirits of the people who went, shivering and huddled, over the damp-greased cobble stones. At each exposed corner a savage wind waited to pierce through clothes and flesh and bone to one's very vitals. A fitting morning to die upon, Humphrey thought as he made his way to Mrs. Naylor's house. But she was no nearer death than usual and when he had reassured her she surprised him by asking, "When's Christmas?"

"In nine days' time," he said, wondering why she, who never knew the time of day, or day of the week, should show interest in the season.

"I shan't live to see it," she said mournfully.

"Oh yes you will. And many another. If only you'd keep care of yourself, Mrs. Naylor." He looked round the cluttered, dirty room, the rusty, unused grate, the window sealed with cobwebs, and back again at the skinny old figure seated in the middle of a bed piled high with dingy blankets, old rugs, coats, capes and under-clothes. "I do wish you'd have a fire and get the room warm and then open the window a crack. You'd breathe much more easily and be able to sit comfortably in a chair."

"I can't afford a fire."

"Nonsense. Don't you remember last spring when you said you couldn't afford milk, I went to the Bank for you and young Mr. Thorley himself came round to explain that you could afford anything you needed." He spoke briskly, but patiently. The old woman was pitiable; almost, if not quite, as pitiable as other old women he knew who lived in misery because of their poverty. Mrs. Naylor had an abundance of money, but some twist in her brain prevented her from believing it, or using it. And in a way she was worse off than the very poor, for at least their neighbours were kind. Mrs. Naylor's believed implicitly in the riches which she would not admit she possessed, so it cost her a penny every time she sent anyone on an errand.

"You don't know anything about my money," she said. "I've had heavy losses."

She had once had a little bad luck with an investment, and that had given rise to an obsession which was one facet of her madness. Humphrey knew the futility of argument; and he had other calls to pay. There wasn't time to go into her mythical financial troubles.

"Look. May I see if you have any coal? And light the fire. Just for today."

"Sufficient unto the day is the evil thereof."

"Just so. I'll see what I can find."

Humphrey found what he had expected. At the back of the terrible house which was literally falling down for lack of repair, was a coalhouse stacked with coal and a woodshed full of logs.

When he had got a fire roaring in the rusty old grate Mrs. Naylor began to weep.

"You're a good boy. A good boy. I want to give you a Christmas present. But I shall be dead long before then."

"The best present you could give me would be permission to send Mrs. Flack in to look after you. She'd do it gladly for two shillings a week."

"I don't want any females messing about with my things. Besides, I can't afford to pay for help. But you're a good boy. I want to give you a present."

The mention of a present, like her pleas of poverty, was a recurrent factor in Mrs. Naylor's conversation. It meant nothing. Nothing she ever said meant anything. But on this morning she stuck to her point and finally scrambled out of bed and shuffled over to a chest of drawers which, laden with rubbish, stood at the end of the room.

"Really, Mrs. Naylor, this is going too far. Get back into bed until the room is warm. Then you can get up and move about as you wish."

"I can do what I wish now. And I'm going to give you a present because you're a good boy and it's near Christmas."

"But I don't want you to give me anything. I do nothing except what I'm paid for. Please, Mrs. Naylor, let me help you back to bed."

"You turn your back while I get out my keys. There. Now you can come and help me to find it."

"What are you looking for?"

"I forget."

She started to rummage madly in the drawer which appeared to be full of old paper, bits of string, odd lids and corks, some bright pieces of material cut up as though for patchwork, a length or two of good lace, some broken ivory-handled knives — a representative collection from the mad miser's hoard. But finally from the very bottom of the rubbish she produced a good gold watch. She hailed its appearance with a shriek of joy and began at once to wind it so fiercely that Humphrey feared for its mainspring.

"It goes," she cried. "Listen, it's ticking. I knew it would. There, that's for you."

"But, Mrs. Naylor," he said patiently, "this is a good watch. It's valuable. You mustn't give it away. And I mustn't take it. Look, put it on this table by your bed, and keep it wound and then you'd always know the time." One of her idiosyncrasies was that she never knew what time of the day or night it was. "Shall I set it for you?"

He drew out the plain silver watch which Doctor Coppard had given him at the very beginning of his apprenticeship.

"That's not a good watch," said Mrs. Naylor. "That's a very poor sort of watch. You have this one."

"No. Really, Mrs. Naylor. It's very kind of you and I do appreciate it. But I mustn't take it. This one does quite well for me. Look, it's just a quarter past twelve.

I'll set it for you. Then you can see when it's one o'clock and the room will be warm and you can get up and get yourself something to eat."

"I won't go back to bed and I won't eat anything if you don't take my present. And I won't have your fire, either," she said shrilly. She shuffled across the room, seized the poker and began to attack the fire savagely, throwing the live coals about the hearth and even on to the carpet.

"Oh, all right. I'll take it. Don't do that. You'll set the room afire. I'll take it. And thank you very much."

"That's a good boy. And you won't tell anybody I gave it to you, will you? If they thought I'd got anything to give away they'd all be round me like hornets." She slipped the watch into his pocket, patted his shoulder and repeated that he was a good boy, and then scrambled back into the bed.

"Slam the door. Mind you slam the door."

He had taken the watch in order to prevent the crazy old creature falling into a frenzy, but he had no intention of keeping it. It was true that Doctor Coppard frequently received presents of game, farm produce and fruit in season, but that was a very different thing from accepting, at the hands of a mad woman, a valuable trinket. So for an hour or two Humphrey planned that next time he visited Mrs. Naylor he would try to talk her into a more reasonable state of mind and give her back the watch, or, if that proved to be impossible, leave it somewhere where she would eventually find it. But at some time during the course of that day his attitude changed from the professional to the practical. Exactly when the change took place he did not know; almost perceptibly the view grew upon him that after all Mrs. Naylor was right in feeling gratitude towards him, and that the gift of the watch was very timely since it *could*, if he permitted it to do so, solve the very pressing problem of pocket money.

The problem was one which had hitherto caused him little actual worry. It had always been with him and he had grown accustomed to it. On that far-off day when he had first left Slipshoe Farm for the Grammar School his mother had given him, surreptitiously, two florins, saved for the purpose with God knew what self-denial and scheming. He had felt unimaginably wealthy until he had been at school for about twenty-four hours and had discovered that for odd dues and subscriptions he needed at least eight shillings and sixpence. And since that moment his pocket had always been empty. He had felt the pinch less during his apprenticeship than in his schooldays, for there were no traditional expenses to be met. Doctor Coppard provided board and lodging as well as tuition, and had generously looked to his wardrobe. On his birthday and at Christmas his mother gave him a sovereign, a gift which seemed embarrassingly generous, and hitherto he had fitted his expenditure to his income. He had even paid his own coach fare on his journeys to Cambridge though that had meant shaving with a lather made from kitchen soap instead of the lavender-scented, emollient preparation which Mr. Duffle sold for the purpose and which, prior to Doctor Coppard's kind arrangement, he had, somewhat luxuriously, used. And it had never occurred to him to complain of his penury, or to think that he was hard done by.

But lately there had been a sharp rise in his expenditure. Every visit to the Coffee Room had cost him a shilling and already his finances were in jeopardy. Also, during the last few days, when people were beginning to speak of the imminence of Christmas he had thought that it would be pleasant if he could give Letty a present. But whenever that thought had occurred to him he had pushed it away with the vague idea that when he came back from Slipshoe after Christmas he would have his mother's gift in his pocket. He would buy Letty a present then. After that he would be in a horrible muddle; he'd certainly have to ask Doctor Coppard for his coach fare next time; but the future must look after itself. He had, in fact, the somewhat insouciant attitude towards money which is the prerogative — and the compensation — of complete and hopeless poverty.

But on this December day, as he slipped his hand into his pocket and fingered the watch which the mad woman had placed there, a warm and lovely feeling swelled through his hitherto atrophied financial sense. If he took the watch to Pawny Sabberton he might get as much as a sovereign, or twenty-five shillings. Be able to buy Letty a necklet or a pair of ear-bobs. Have a few shillings left for coffee.

The real Humphrey thrust the thought away several times. It was disgraceful to imagine a doctor, a respectable man, going into Sabberton's dreadful little shop in order to dispose of a watch given him by a patient — and she not wholly right in the mind. But even hot-faced, sweating self-contempt could not wholly banish the thought. He began to reckon over all that he had done for Mrs. Naylor, things outside the scope of his professional duty, several times, called to what she chose to think her death-bed, he had discovered that she had eaten nothing for twenty-four hours. He'd always made her a meal of some sort. He'd gone to the bank for her. He'd set a trap for one particularly bold rat. He'd pasted back a piece of wallpaper that trailed across her bed. And there were many things he had forgotten. After all, she had lucid moments, and probably it was in one of them that she had conceived the notion of rewarding him for his kindness. Shouldn't he take the gift and be grateful and make the best use of it? The struggle lasted for four days, with idealism putting up less and less resistance, and then, five days before Christmas, he walked, set-faced, stiff-legged from embarrassment, into Sabberton's and pawned the watch for twenty-four shillings.

The moment he had the money in his pocket he became so excited and happy that a detached part of his mind, a part which had taken no part in the struggle, commented acidly that all his scruples had had their roots in a distaste for a visit to the squalid little shop. But the comment, like the scruples, vanished in the joy of going shopping for Letty.

He chose a necklet, seven plaques of blue enamel painted with little flowers, slung on a silver chain. It was the prettiest thing he found in his search, and immediately he saw it it seemed so appropriate, so entirely Letty's ornament that it seemed to belong to her already. It was priced at twenty-four shillings, but he could have cried with relief to know that it was just within his power to purchase it. It would have hurt him unbearably to be obliged to leave it there — looking so like Letty.

Early next morning, while he was shaving, Mrs. Naylor's messenger arrived to say that the old woman had rapped on her window and sent him to fetch Doctor Shadbolt. Humphrey, dabbing at his face, snatching up his jacket, rushing away from the appetising breakfast odours and into the frosty morning air, certainly thought of the watch, for the thing was inextricably linked with its donor in his mind, but his thoughts were complacent. Think of the number of calls like this which he had answered in the past two years — hadn't he earned that twenty-four shillings, hard and fairly?

But Mrs. Naylor's unbalanced mind had turned another cog and she greeted him with the words, "You'll have to bring it back you know. You'll have to bring it back."

"D'you mean the watch?"

"Yes. The watch. The watch. The watch." Her voice rose in a crescendo of passionate wailing. "It was his. My husband's. He will have it back. The things he's said to me. You wouldn't believe. Look. I've found up all his things but he won't be satisfied. He must have the watch."

Humphrey followed the direction of her wildly waving hand and saw that, for the first time, the cluttered room appeared to be set out in some sort of order and with some suggestion of unity. Suits of clothes, all of a fashion of fifty years ago, topcoats, hats, cravats and mufflers were laid out upon the chairs, the bed, the floor. Eight pairs of boots marched in an orderly line across the hearth before a grate full of dead ashes. Nearby lay a hunting flask, a riding crop, two silver-topped canes. On the seat of one chair was a case of razors. On another, a set of brushes. A collection of wigs lay huddled, like a deformed, excessively hairy animal on the foot of the bed.

"Everything he ever had," said Mrs. Naylor dismally, "but he won't rest. He will have the watch." Her thin, discoloured face with its mad eyes took on a sly, defensive look. "I told him. I explained. I told him you'd taken it when I wasn't looking. I wasn't to blame."

"But you gave it to me, Mrs. Naylor. I didn't want you to. Don't you remember. You said if I didn't take it you'd throw the fire all about the room. So I did take it. And now you've put me in a very awkward position. You see, I haven't got it here."

She broke into a shrill screaming. The window through which she had earlier hailed her little messenger was still open, and suddenly, before Humphrey could move she had her head out of it and she was shrieking into the street, "I've been robbed. I've been robbed."

"Mrs. Naylor," said Humphrey, darting after her and trying, with his hand on her shoulder to draw her back into the room, "you'll rouse the street. You haven't been robbed. You gave me the watch. But I'll bring it back. I'll go for it now."

But the damage had been done. A crowd of people was gathering by the window and a tidily dressed, responsible-looking man was thrusting his way through it. When he reached the window he looked up to where Humphrey was still trying to hold Mrs. Naylor back and asked pompously, "What's this, Mrs. Naylor. Did you say *robbed*? I always said you would be, living there alone. When'd it happen?"

"Yesterday. Yesterday. My husband's watch. He abuses me so. Says I've taken care of my things and let his go. What shall I do?"

"Well, you couldn't do better than tell me. I'm the constable. I'll come up." He stepped back, sprang at the window, hooked his hands inside the sill and pulled himself up.

"Why," he said, seeing Humphrey plainly for the first time. "Good morning, sir. I didn't see you. What is this? The truth or just one of her mad fits?"

"It's both," said Humphrey, feeling sick, but thinking that the best way was to forestall — with the truth — anything the crazy woman might say. "A few days ago she would give me a gold watch. I didn't want to take it, but she started to throw the fire about, so I took it to pacify her. Now she says her husband wants it back. And naturally I haven't got it on me. Poor soul, she won't even listen while one tries to explain."

112

"Oh. I thought maybe she had been robbed. It'd be likely enough. They say there's a thousand pounds hidden about the place. One night someone'll crack it. Her too I shouldn't wonder." He gave a bark of unsympathetic laughter. "Well, if that's the way it is there's no call for me to do anything." But the habit of interference was strong upon him and he turned to Mrs. Naylor.

"Now don't you go upsetting yourself any more or making a disturbance about nothing. Doctor Shadbolt's got your watch safe and sound and he's going to bring it back. D'you understand?"

"I want it back before dark. I don't want Henry raging at me another night. And I want it so I can tell the time."

"You shall have it back this afternoon, Mrs. Naylor. I promise you."

She quietened a little. The constable said, "There you are then," as though he had, alone, found a solution to a complicated problem, and with a "Good morning, sir," to Humphrey, put his leg over the sill and dropped down into the road.

"Shut the window. Shut the window," cried Mrs. Naylor. Then, when Humphrey had, with some difficulty closed and clasped it, she reverted to the subject of the watch. "You'll bring it back before dark. Be sure now, before dark."

He promised once more and then let himself out of the house nauseated with shame and very worried. It seemed at that moment that he could do one of two things, both extremely distasteful. He could borrow twenty-four shillings from Doctor Coppard, or he could take the necklet back to the shop and ask to be given his money back. The shopkeeper wouldn't like doing that, and might refuse point blank to do it. More shame. And if he tried to borrow from Doctor Coppard he felt that the old man would inevitably connect the loan with Letty. To Humphrey it seemed so obvious. For four years he had been, or managed to appear to be, financially self-sufficient, and it would surely take very little perspicacity to see what had brought about the change.

He worried miserably all through the morning, trying to decide whether he would rather face Doctor Coppard or the shopkeeper. He had decided upon the latter course and was already feeling pangs of regret at not being able to give Letty her pretty, and altogether suitable, gift when he thought of Plant Driscoll. Not that it would be an easy thing to borrow from him, especially after his lordly refusal of payment; but it would mean that Letty would have the necklet, and that Doctor Coppard's curiosity and disapproval would not be roused. The more he thought of it the more it seemed the one way out of his muddle.

He knew now where Plant lived and who he was. The most casual inquiry made on the morning after dealing with his unexpected patient had revealed that he must be almost the only person in the town who did not know something of Driscoll. Old Duffle — of whom he made his inquiry — had said as he bent over his pestle and mortar:

"Driscoll, why don't you know? No, maybe not, the old Doctor keeps his own horses, enough and to spare. Driscoll has a stable, out Fornham way, just past the fork. Must have been there a year or more. It was a stable, before he took it, but the last man failed. Not central enough. Folks don't want to walk a mile to hire a horse, stands to reason. But he seems to do pretty well. Not that I ever knew anybody go there for a nag. But he breeds too, I believe. What made you ask?"

Humphrey had expected that question and was prepared for it.

"Only that I thought I might hire a horse to carry me home at Christmas and somebody said Driscoll was cheaper than Hewitt. And then I realised that I'd never even heard of the man. Thanks for telling me. I think I'll try him."

"I doubt if you'll find him cheaper. I never heard anybody say so. But I reckon his horses might be better than Hewitt's. Maybe that's what they meant."

CHAPTER
ELEVEN

There was a high wall which began at the fork in the road, and which was pierced, at a point facing the fork, by heavy, ornamental iron gates. But they were padlocked, and behind them could be seen a drive, so covered with weeds that it was as green as the lawns which flanked it on either side. But a little way along the road was another gate, propped open and giving upon a kind of courtyard, surrounded by stable buildings. Beyond them was the back of a house, unpainted, rather desolate looking, with no curtains at the windows and no smoke from any of its numerous chimneys. Humphrey drove in and climbed out of the gig. There seemed to be no life in the place at all. But he found what seemed to be the back door and pulled the bell. For a long time nothing happened and it occurred to him that had he been a man wanting a horse in a hurry this reception would not encourage him to patronise Driscoll again. And his heart began to sink. He put his hand into his pocket where Letty's present lay, all wrapped as the shopkeeper had given it to him. Winter afternoons were short and if Driscoll were out there would be nothing for it but to hurry back to the shop and change this thing which already belonged to Letty for twenty-four miserable shillings. He dared not let darkness fall upon a Mrs. Naylor unsatisfied. She would rouse the street, scandal and disgrace would result. Above all Doctor Coppard would never forgive him for allowing anything to make him behave in so unprofessional a manner.

He had given the bell another tug and was about to turn away, dispiritedly when the door opened and there was the man he had come to see. His hair was on end and he wore a dressing-gown flung round his shoulders over his shirt. The sling which Humphrey had made for his arm was still in place, very grubby now. Altogether he looked rather unsavoury, with his face thickened and blurred with sleep, and full of ill-temper, and Humphrey who had just been longing avidly for the door to open began to wish that it had remained closed. Perhaps the shopkeeper would have been easier after all.

But Plant's expression changed immediately he recognised Humphrey. He looked surprised and pleased.

"Hullo, hullo. The very fellow I've been wanting to see. Come in. It's a bit of a mess, but I've been handicapped. I live alone you see, and with this . . ." he indicated his wrist.

"This isn't really a professional visit," said Humphrey, not wanting any misunderstanding. "In fact I've come to ask you something."

Plant Driscoll's face went blank. And Humphrey remembered the man in the water, the man with the cut hands, and his own suspicion.

"A pretty big favour," he added quickly.

"We're quits then. I have one to ask of you. *Will* you help me to change my shirt?"

"Of course. Is the wrist giving trouble? You should have sent for me. Letty knew where to find me if you didn't."

"Oh, the wrist is as right as a trivet — however right that is. But I daren't take the bandage off, I'm afraid of disturbing the damned thing. So I've been all this time not able to get my coat *on* or my shirt *off*. The coat doesn't matter but of all things I do abominate dirty linen. Don't you?"

Humphrey realised that that was one of the things he had never bothered about much. All his life he had changed his shirt because it was the day for changing his shirt; the garment's condition had been immaterial, and un-noticed. The amount of feeling which this man put into the word *abominate* left him feeling somehow at a disadvantage and he made up his mind there and then to pay more attention to his own linen in future.

"The thing is," he said, "that I've come to ask you to lend me twenty-four shillings until after Christmas. Unless you can do that, and are willing to, I'll have to hurry back into the town and get it somewhere else. If you can — and I swear I'll pay you back immediately after Christmas — I'll help you change your shirt with pleasure. I'm sorry to bother you, and I don't want you to think that it's anything to do with what I did the other night. It's just that I don't know many people and I do want twenty-four shillings in a hurry."

"But of course, my dear man, you can have as much as you like. Look what I owe you. And apart from that, at this moment I'd give twice that to get this shirt changed. Don't look so incredulous. You try wearing a shirt for four days, and filthy to start with! Here . . ." He thrust his free hand into his pocket and brought out a handful of money, gold and silver pieces, and slapped them down on the table. "Take what you want, and welcome. Then unhitch me and lend me a hand. To tell you the truth I was terrified I'd start bleeding again. And another bout of that would about finish me off. I hate all blood, but especially my own."

Humphrey began to untie the sling. "I suppose it was rather remiss of me to let you go off like that. But to tell you the truth both Letty and Mrs. Rowan seemed inclined to make a bit of a mystery about it and I didn't want to push myself forward. I thought that if you wanted a doctor you'd send for one. And until afterwards I didn't know where you lived."

"Letty. That's the new little niece with the eyes," commented Plant, pointedly ignoring the rest of Humphrey's speech. "Ah . . ." he gingerly straightened his arm. "That's a relief. God, it is *stiff*. It won't stay so, will it?"

"Of course not. I'll put you on a clean bandage, smaller. Then you can change your shirt when you want to. It won't hurt. I'd keep it slung for a while, it'd save you knocking it inadvertently. It's doing well. In fact, for an emergency job, it's pretty good. though I say so."

"A chap as clever as you shouldn't be short of money you know. You could have stood over me the other night and said 'Your money or your life' like a highwayman. I'd have paid." He laughed, and the laughter robbed the words of any possible offensiveness. Stretching and flexing his arm he went to a cupboard beside the hearth and opened it. Within Humphrey could see a number of suits neatly hung upon pegs, several shelves of clean linen, and at the bottom a row of well-polished boots. As he watched Plant strip off his dirty shirt and don a clean one he became conscious of something which for four years had been lacking in his life — the companionship of a male person of his own age. He had never noticed it before, he had been busy and happy and, until he had met Letty, would have said that his life had been full and complete. But the sight of Plant's slender, muscular back and the line where his skin changed colour on his neck, brought up vivid, slightly nostalgic memories of his schooldays, of friends with whom jokes and confidences could be exchanged, for whom one felt no responsibility and with whom one did not have to be always upon one's best behavior. For the second time he felt himself drawn towards Plant, wishing for his friendship; but as on a former occasion he had been chilled by the man's own lack of interest, now he was deterred by the memory of his own suspicion. There might, of course, be nothing in it except coincidence. And even if there were more one should not judge without knowing the circumstances. It occurred to him that it would be pleasant to have Plant's confidence, and in return to be able to tell him about Letty, to ask his opinion about the Rowan household.

120

"There, that's better," Plant said. "I even feel less bristly. I did shave — though its *extraordinarily* difficult with one hand — but somehow I always felt bearded and full of lice in that shirt." He picked it up with fastidious distaste and flung it into a corner. "Thanks again. And now we'll have a drink."

He fetched out a bottle of brandy and some glasses. There was no space on the cluttered table and after a little ineffectual pushing he pointed to the scattered money.

"Look how much of this do you want?" His manner of speaking and the way he tried to push the coins aside was a denial of their value. They might have been buttons or a sample of oats.

"Twenty-four shillings. As a loan till after Christmas."

"Yes, I understood that. I meant is that all you want? I mean take enough. I'm flush at the moment. You might send in a belated bill and catch me without a stiver."

"Oh, I shouldn't do that."

"Why not?"

"Because, to tell you the truth I enjoyed working on you the other evening. I was showing off and a man shouldn't be paid for that. I'd always felt . . ." he said shyly, "a little bit on sufferance in the Coffee House. That night when I went to supper — you remember, you were there — half the things they talked about were clean out of my reach, and I couldn't understand their jokes, or play cards . . . so I enjoyed letting them see that there was something I could do."

121

"A very natural feeling," Plant said, handing him a glass. "Oh yes, I remember seeing you and wondering what you were there for . . . Don't take that amiss. I thought you seemed very — superior. Hatton is a nitwit and Everett is a rake and the rest of us are just riff-raff. You did seem rather out of place."

"Out of place, but far from superior," said Humphrey smiling.

The conversation died there, but the ensuing silence was not awkward. After a minute or two Humphrey became aware that the short afternoon was darkening. He finished his brandy with choking haste and stood up. The heap of money still lay on the table and he looked at it with a slight embarrassment. Plant reached out, separated twenty-four shillings from the rest and held them out.

"There you are — and I'm still damned obliged to you."

"I'll bring it back directly after Christmas."

"I shall look forward to that. Good afternoon, Doctor Shadbolt."

"My name's Humphrey."

"Humphrey then. Mine you know."

"Well then, goodbye, Plant, and thank you very much. I hope you'll have a happy Christmas." He said the hackneyed phrase with sincerity. Plant looked slightly surprised, as though the season's nearness had taken him unawares, or as though the idea that he should take heed of it was in some way astonishing.

"And I hope you will," he said pleasantly.

Humphrey slipped the money into his pocket and let his fingers linger upon Letty's present which lay there, redeemed from jeopardy.

In less than an hour he was in Mrs. Naylor's house, the watch in his hand. She received it without a word and laid it carefully on the floor between the two silver-headed canes. Then she stepped back and in the dim light surveyed the arrangement with triumphant satisfaction as though she had just put the last touch upon some intricate and exhausting scheme of decoration.

"I wouldn't give anything else away until I could really spare it if I were you, Mrs. Naylor."

"It's very hard to be poor — after you've kept your own carriage."

He had a frivolous impulse to tell her that at any time, when she found herself really hard up, Pawny Sabberton would give her twenty-four shillings for the watch which lay on the floor and would probably continue to lie there until somebody set a foot on it.

"Well, good afternoon, Mrs. Naylor. Happy Christmas, if I don't see you again before then." One assumed that some of the twists and fantasies of her mental state might be enjoyable.

"I think I shall have a goose. Candles have gone up, you know. They're a terrible price now."

Probably there was a connection but it wasn't worth the bother of sorting out. He felt less patient with her than usual. She had put him in an awkward position and though he knew that it was unreasonable he bore her some resentment.

But when he was out in the street again, with his hand in his pocket, touching Letty's present, he perceived that he had reason to be grateful to her. Until she had given him the watch his desire to make Letty a gift had been vague and indefinite and might have dwindled into nothing because of the difficulties in the way. And certainly in no other circumstances would he have dared to buy anything nearly so expensive. Also the whole business had put him upon a different footing with Plant Driscoll; and that might lead to something, since Plant knew the Rowans so well. Altogether in her witless way the mad woman had helped, rather than hurt him, and he wished he had lighted her fire again for her.

He gave Letty the necklet on the evening of the day before Christmas Eve. There were holly boughs hung against the panels and beams of the Coffee Room and a good, friendly spirit in the place. It was a pity, he thought, looking round, that this wasn't the whole of it; that there should be secrecy and rumours and suspicion.

Letty came, as on other evenings, to take his order, and there was, as there had been ever since the time when he had kissed her, a certain restraint in her manner, a kind of warning in her glance, as though she feared that he might give some sign of his affection in public. At first he had been hurt by it, had thought — didn't she believe me when I said I wouldn't do a thing to displease her? But later on, when he had thought about it, he was pleased. Such circumspection, such a frank desire not to be like Cathy and Susie, were healthy signs, and showed that she was not yet affected by her environment, was, in fact, resisting it.

He said, as she set down his coffee, "Don't go for a minute, Letty," and the old warning flared into her eyes and she began to murmur something about it being a very busy evening, before he had time to finish his little speech. "Look, there's just a small present to wish you a very happy Christmas. I have to go home into the country tomorrow, so I shan't see you again before." He took the paper-wrapped parcel out of his pocket and laid it in her hand.

Everything else was washed away by what he chose to think a wave of childish pleasure.

"Oh," she said, "thank you! That is kind. Cathy and Susie have had such a lot of things." She leaned forward so that the settle screened her from the rest of the room and unwrapped the paper. When she saw the necklet she gave a little cry of pleasure and then quickly cupped the trinket in her hand as though to hide it. "Oh, it's too nice. You shouldn't have given me anything so valuable."

He mumbled out the usual protests about it not being nice enough and the things he would give her if he had his will; but he knew that the present had been successful and was prodigiously pleased that he had overcome the difficulties of obtaining it. The horrible moment when Mrs. Naylor had accused him of theft, and the almost equally uncomfortable one when he had asked Plant for the loan counted for nothing against Letty's frank pleasure, and the thought that his gift had put her on a level with Cathy and Susie — though in a different way. And he was pleased to deduce that nobody else had given her anything.

Presently he saw her, just behind the service door, stop Cathy and show her the necklet and Cathy looked towards his corner and smiled in pleased surprise. Letty did not immediately return to the Coffee Room and when she did she had changed into her childish blue dress, and the necklet was clasped about her slender throat. Her eyes were bright with pleasure, and she looked so pretty, in such an appealing, fragile way, that Humphrey's heart was shaken. The feeling that any man, however rough and crude, must prefer her to either of her cousins, filled him with terror, and a renewed determination to get her out of this place where beauty was so dangerous. He began to think again about Slipshoe Farm and the appeal he would make to his mother.

CHAPTER
TWELVE

In his anticipatory thoughts of that interview he had set up and faced imponderable difficulties, Hagar's opposition, his own half-fearful approach; he had not — though knowing his home he might have done so — realised that one of the most difficult things was to find a place and a time in which to make his bid for his mother's attention.

Hagar was still in the shop when he arrived home on the afternoon of Christmas Eve, and when she had at last locked the door behind a dilatory customer, she went straight into the kitchen to prepare the almost ceremonial supper with which she always greeted his return. By that time his father and both his brothers were in the kitchen too, throwing aside their muddy boots, washing their hands and generally incommoding his two young sisters who were trying to set the table and decorate the place with evergreen. Christmas was a very special occasion at Slipshoe, for even Josiah Shadbolt, whose religion was of the dour and grim variety, felt that joy was seemly and permissible on what he called "the birthday of Our Lord". So the piety which, during the rest of the year lay heavily upon the family, imposing gravity of demeanour, regular attendance at chapel, the mortification of vanity in females, the reduction of high spirits in males, industry and thrift for all, was temporarily lifted and by contrast Christmas was merrier and brighter than in many ordinarily more cheerful homes. In honour of the season Josiah even forebore to display the scar of the wound which his eldest son had dealt him when he forsook the farm, and no reference was ever made during the brief Christmas holiday to that old quarrel which had shattered the family, and still lay, a dark, unbridgeable gulf between husband and wife.

It was the same this year, and the meal, beginning with pork from a pig born and bred within ten yards of the kitchen door, and ending with walnuts and apples from the orchard and a loaf of spiced currant bread hot from the oven, went merrily, with chatter about the animals and last season's crops, a joke or two about Sam, next in age to Humphrey who had begun a sedate walking out with Agnes Carver, a chapel member and therefore acceptable to Josiah, gossip about the shop's customers and news of Mary who last year had taken her place at this table and was now a wife and mother with a home and a fine baby of her own.

Humphrey sat, over-eating to please his mother, listening and smiling as the others talked, and making very little contribution of his own. Home-coming — even in those far-off days when he was a schoolboy — had always been a mitigated pleasure for him. The sense of belonging and of not belonging was very strong. Old ties, rooted apparently in his very entrails, tugged. These were his own people, so entirely his own

128

that he had only to look into the faces of his brothers and sisters to see, beneath the superficial variations, the fundamental resemblances that told of their common blood. But the cleavage which Hagar's will — and that alone — had made in the family fabric had cut him off from his roots, so that returning, he was like a tree, severed and then set back upon its stump, seemingly whole and restored, but drawing no sap, no substance from the soil which had nourished it before. He was even cut off from the normal family intercourse and exchange of chatter, for although there were things which he could have told to interest and amuse them, he was virtually forbidden to mention his new life, since that would draw attention to his alienness and set at least two minds at the table racing back to an old bitterness. So though he could be received back into the family and share, in retrospect, the year's doing, he could never take the family's minds and imaginations into Doctor Coppard's house or surgery, or into any house which he visited.

But these were all familiar limitations, worn smooth and almost painless by the experience of former home-comings. Tonight he was conscious of an even wider gulf, conscious that only twenty-four hours earlier he had been sitting in a place upon which his father would — even if the very worst were not true of it — expect the wrath of Heaven to fall. For what Josiah called with brief condemnation "intoxicating liquor" was sold at the Coffee House and men went there to be idle, to peruse worldly, frivolous literature and to smoke tobacco. Josiah would not have been surprised if the fate of Sodom and Gomorrah had fallen upon the Coffee House, did he know of its existence. *But,* Humphrey thought, feeling a certain shock at the revelation, Josiah would be more sympathetic to the idea of getting Letty out of that place than anyone else he knew. If Hagar could be talked round, Josiah would offer little, if any, resistance. He would speak of Letty as a brand to be plucked from the burning. In return he would expect a strict observance of his rules of behaviour for young girls, but though irksome, they would be harmless. Letty would be perfectly safe here, until such time as he could marry her. If only he could persuade his mother.

But when the meal ended at last, Deborah, his youngest sister, only just fourteen, suggested a game of "Bob Apple" and the kitchen witnessed the annual spectacle of Josiah, serious, gaunt, stiff-jointed from exposure to weather, trying to seize between his teeth one of the apples floating upon a tubful of water — all in honour of the Saviour's birth. And then, abruptly, dignity was donned again, and the father read out of the big worn Bible the story of Bethlehem. Christmas Eve was ended and Humphrey had not had a moment alone with his mother.

In the morning everybody except Hagar was expected to go to chapel. Working class women were, by custom, exempt from attendance at morning service. Sundays — and Christmases — were the only days when working men could give full, leisurely attention to their midday meals and by some curious arrangement which smacked a little of connivance between male creatures and their deity, the women were allowed to perform their devotions over their cooking stoves. But Humphrey, the son of a godly household, would be expected to follow his father into chapel. So it had been on other years.

On this Christmas morning he endured an agony of indecision. The time would have been perfect for a talk with Hagar. The Christmas spirit was abroad, and he knew that his mother enjoyed cooking, especially when some latent extravagance in her nature could be indulged. Over the roasting goose and the steaming plum-pudding he could catch her in a softened mood. But to refuse to go to chapel would be to offend and hurt Josiah who might, in an exasperated moment, refer to "heathen ways of life" and imply that in going to school, in going to Doctor Coppard Humphrey had in fact gone to the devil. And so strong was the moral climate of Slipshoe, that Humphrey was conscious of a truth in this expected condemnation. If he had stayed at the farm he would never have met Letty, never gone to Mrs. Rowan's, never committed the professional misdemeanour of taking Mrs. Naylor's watch, never been forced to borrow from a stranger. Oh, but that was a foolish way of thinking. He must remember too, all the good things he had done, the pains he had eased, the wounds he had healed, the sicknesses he had mitigated or averted. The whole world couldn't be run upon the lines laid down by Josiah Shadbolt and the Old Testament. He returned to the problem of whether or not to accompany his father to chapel. And finally he decided to do so. It was important, after all, to have his father's good favour; and surely, between this time and tomorrow morning an opportunity to tackle his mother would arise.

Hagar herself contrived it. Unexpectedly, almost as though she were conscious that her first-born was making a silent appeal to her she said, as soon as the last fragment of pudding was eaten, "Now I'm going to leave you girls to wash up and I'm going for a walk."

"I'll come with you," said Humphrey hastily.

"I hoped you would. I want to show you the bridge the boys have made between Tug's meadow and the low pasture."

She went upstairs and came down after a brief space, wearing the old bonnet and the old cloak which Humphrey remembered from his earliest childhood. And his heart smote him a little. He had cost her so much, and was about to make an enormous, unjustifiable demand upon her charity; and although his secret fear of her and the fact that she held Letty's future in her hand made her seem strong and established, a bastion to be stormed, it was also true that she was just a hard-working country woman, aged by child-birth and labour, a simple woman, looking forward to a quiet talk with the son whom she must love, since she had sacrificed so much for him. It seemed a heartless, ruthless action — to spoil their short time together by saying what he had to say. But the vision of Letty in the blue dress, the memory of a man's voice saying, "my pretty", obliterated all too easily his vision of his mother as a person also

132

demanding and deserving pity, gentle handling. And Hagar's voice and manner assisted in the banishment of the vision of herself as a vulnerable being.

She stepped out briskly, her shoulders slightly hunched, her head stooped forward, as though taking a walk in the unusual leisure of a Christmas afternoon were just another routine duty to be despatched as quickly, and with as little outlay of physical force, as possible. And she said, as soon as they were out of the yard, "Well, Humphrey, how have you been doing?" in a bracing, business-like voice, as though the life which she had planned, and won for him, had been an errand upon which she had sent him and upon the performance of which she was now demanding a report.

She would have liked to take his arm, to lean against him as they walked, so that she might feel, in warmth and solidity, the physical presence of the one being in the world whom she wholly, unreservedly, loved. But the pattern of her behaviour towards him had been unredeemably cast during the days of his babyhood and could never be altered now. For what had seemed to her to be imperative reasons she had withheld caresses and every sign of loving-kindness from this, her first-born, and the effort had so warped her that the little gestures and inflections of affection natural between mother and son were now impossible. At the same time she had — after a long morning of cooking over a hot stove — suggested this walk because she wanted to be alone with him, because she longed to hear everything that he could tell her about his life and his work, since they were the only things in the world that were completely real to her, and because the memory of this hour spent in his company would remain with her, a source of satisfaction and sustenance until such time as she might see him again.

Of all this Humphrey had no inkling. Racked with nervousness at the prospect of laying his problem and his request before this unsympathetic, intimidating woman, he gave her first what she seemed to demand, a matter-of-fact account of his progress. He made it brief because the bridge, which he felt would be the turning point in their walk was already in sight; and he made it optimistic, partly to sustain his self-esteem, partly to impress his mother, though even as he spoke of the final examination at Midsummer the consciousness that of late he had badly neglected his studies nagged at him. Still, once Letty was safely established at Slipshoe he could easily make up for lost time.

So they came to the bridge and he found himself praising extravagantly the industry and ingenuity which had gone to its making. Sam and Will were Hagar's sons, too. It was quite possible that in her eyes their work was as vital and important as his own. He took, quite literally, her suggestion that they should walk to see the bridge, and never guessed that it was merely an excuse to get him to herself. But even repetitive praises come to an end, and finally he was silent, and Hagar said, "Well . . ." and turned as though to return to the house. Panic came upon him. Now he must speak. Now he must do battle for Letty's sake. He leaned back against the handrail of the bridge and said in a rapid, nervous voice, "Don't go back for a minute, Mother. There's something I want to tell you. Something I want to ask you."

He was surprised to see a defensive, apprehensive look flash into her eyes. It was almost the look of one who was brought face to face with a long-postponed, but anticipated emergency. It was gone in an instant, however, and Hagar folded her arms under her cloak and leaned back against the opposite handrail, her face impassive, her eyes attentive. "Well, what is it?" she asked.

He braced himself, much as he would have done if called upon to plunge into the cold brown water that raced and tumbled under the planks upon which he stood, and began to blurt out the story of his meeting with Letty, his suspicions of the Coffee House, and his plan that she should be asked to come to Slipshoe to take Mary's place. Hagar listened without interrupting, but her sallow face grew a little paler and the lines in it deepened.

When he had finished there was a little silence. Then Hagar said harshly:

"You must put that idea out of your head. You must put all thought of this girl out of your head."

"But that's just what I can't do, Mother. I worry about her all the time. Since the moment I left her at that door I haven't had a really peaceful moment. Until I know she's safe somewhere I shan't even be able to work properly."

"You're in love with her." The sentence came out like a merciless condemnation.

"I . . . I don't know. She's so young."

"Of course you are. Why else should you worry? There's dozens of girls in bad houses all over the world, two more, you say in this very house. You ain't worrying about *them*."

"That's different."

"Of course. You ain't in love with them."

To cut short the argument he said:

"All right. Suppose I admit that. Will you ask her here and take care of her. Just till Midsummer. After that I can arrange something else."

"You mean marry her?" asked Hagar relentlessly.

"If she'd have me."

"If she'd have you!" Hagar spat out the words scornfully.

"Well, she might not. But that isn't important at the moment. Will you do what I asked you. I know it is a lot to ask. But she could work; she wouldn't be a burden in that way. Will you have her here?"

"No. I will not. You must be out of your mind, Humphrey, to ask such a thing. As though I'd help you to your ruin. You know what an uphill job I've had, sending you to school and getting you apprenticed, and all that trouble with your father all along. Now you turn round and ask me to help you to bring it all to nowt. I wouldn't have her here, not to save my own life."

Well, there he had his answer. And he knew from experience the stubborn quality of the woman who faced him. Hitherto her stubborn, iron will had been used to his advantage. Now it was opposed to him and he must accept his defeat. He knew now that he had never really expected anything else.

"All right," he said. "I must think of something else."

"Ah, but that's just what you mustn't do," Hagar said, so quickly and so earnestly that his gaze, which in a momentary distaste he had averted from her stern, unyielding face, was drawn back. Her whole expression had altered, not so much by a rearrangement of the lines and planes of her face, as by a sudden transparency which had come upon it. It was as though a light had been kindled somewhere within her. And her voice held tones which he had never heard before.

"Listen to me, boy. You've fallen in love for the first time. And you've gone a bit wrong in the head, like we all do then. And some of us, with nobody to guide us, do things at such a time that we regret all our life long. Ah, maybe you reckon I'm just an old woman with no knowledge of how you're feeling, but I know better than you think. In your right mind, Humphrey, you'd not be thinking of marriage for another four-five years, when you'd got on your feet and made your way; and then you'd choose a likely girl, not a little doxie from a brothel. Love, when you're young and fresh to it can make you like you was bewitched. But it'll go over and the thing to mind is that you don't do something crazy while the bewitchment is on you. You mustn't do anything about this girl — leastways only one thing. If you fetch her away and make yourself in anyway responsible for her she'll have a hold on you and you'll marry her and go like a horse with a hobble through the rest of your days. Do what I tell you, now. When you think about her think to yourself that you must fight this thing like you would a bodily sickness. Keep out of her way, do your work, work extra hard so you go to bed tired. And that'll pass. I promise you that. That's the right way, the hard way." She paused and looked at him with shining, earnest eyes. Then she suddenly looked away, over his shoulder, across the field to the line of elms that marked the boundary of the pasture. "There's another way, quicker and easier, the surest way for a man too. Maybe thass a funny thing for me to be telling you, but you're young, and I do know. Lay with her a few times. That'd get her off your mind."

He was unspeakably shocked. The suggestion, made by implication had been foul enough when made by Doctor Coppard; coming from a woman, his mother! it was immeasurably more so. He was still goggling at her, with so many words of repudiation, rebuke and horror thronging upon his tongue that he could not say anything at all, when Hagar looked back at him and said quite gently:

"But the hard way's best in the end. Nobody's hurt."

By that time he had decided to say nothing. There was no point in argument or discussing the subject further. He would ignore everything except the fact that he had asked her to assist in the rescue of Letty and that she had declined to do so. He set his mind against the idea that — apart from the refusal — his mother had tried to be helpful; he would not admit that there was a word of wisdom in anything she had said. She had refused to help Letty. She had refused point blank.

She hadn't even said, I'll ask your father, or I'll think about it.

And with that thought there returned to him the revelation of the previous evening; the idea that his father might help.

It would be very difficult now that his mother had set herself against the plan; but Josiah could be stubborn too, and in this case, if he could once be persuaded that a moral obligation was involved, he might be moved to action. Hagar had defeated Josiah over the matter of Humphrey's career, but Josiah had been handicapped because he could not bring God into the argument. Here he would have God for an ally, surely.

Of course it would mean that Hagar would always be against Letty, but the rest of them would be kind, and even Hagar must melt before that innocent, fragile charm. And — his mind swerved nimbly — if he could once get Letty away from the Coffee House perhaps it wouldn't matter if she didn't settle at Slipshoe; Mrs. Rowan would be angered and cast her off, and if she didn't like the farm she might take kindly to the next thing he thought of, like Miss Pendle's for example. The thing was to get her out of that house before its atmosphere of slipshod comfort, false good-nature and easy morals had begun to corrupt her. He felt that he could not bear to go back to work knowing that nothing had been arranged.

Unaware of the full extent of the cruelty of what he was saying he turned to his mother and spoke.

"The thing you either couldn't or wouldn't realise is that an innocent girl, hardly more than a child, is living in moral danger. None of the rest, my feelings, or my plans, is important. But I think Father would understand. I shall go back and ask him whether Letty may come to stay."

Hagar said quietly, "Don't be a fool, boy. You know what he'd say."

"He'd say yes, if I could convince him that it was the right thing to do."

"He'd say yes . . . but he'd make a condition. He'd take her in, and a hundred more like her, if you'd come back and work on the farm." It was Humphrey's turn to look startled. Hagar studied the effect of her words with something like sour amusement. Then she said in a slow, dry voice, "He's fifty years old and he believes that God favours the just; and he's only had one set-back in all his life. That was when you didn't come back to take your place as his oldest son. He's never forgiven me for what I did over that . . . but he'd forgive you quick enough. He'd take you and your Letty in, and say that the mills of God grind slowly but they grind exceeding small."

She brought the last words out with a sneer, looking at him mockingly, sure, so sure that upon the question of his career at least their minds and wills were united, expecting to see him blench and wince, thrown into a panic of recantation. But in Humphrey's mind a red flower of madness began to bud. If that were the price . . . if that were the only way . . . and what a triumph over this sneering taunting woman who in the same breath had called Letty evil names and then suggested that he should put her to the very use from which he was agonising to save her.

"All right," he said breathlessly, "if he makes that condition I'll accept it." He made as though to rush towards the house, and as he did so, under the heat and the passion and the despair something entirely irrelevant, something sweet and seductive stirred. He saw himself making a sacrifice of his career for Letty's sake, and his reward. He saw himself tanned with the sun, weary from honourable toil coming back through a sunset glow to rest in Letty's arms. The ageless delusions of rural peace and plenty, the invincible pull of the soil seduced his mind and his reason. Everything became all at once very simple. The hay was fragrant; the wild roses wreathed the hedges; his peasant blood rose triumphant.

He felt his mother's hand upon his arm, painful, compelling. She swung him round until he faced her, and he saw that her face was alight again, transparent, utterly transformed.

"You don't mean that. Say you don't mean it, Humphrey. You must be mad."

The red bud flowered, brave and reckless.

"But I do. If Father will take Letty in I will come back and work for him."

Behind the madness hope stirred. Now she would say that to save him from striking such a bargain she would take Letty in. But Hagar made no such capitulation. She held on to his arm and slowly her face darkened until it was again a dull, clay-like mask, chiselled into severity.

"I can see," she said, after a pause during which she swallowed with difficulty several times, "I've got to make things plain to you. This girl has driven you daft. And you're willing to chuck away all I've done and schemed for you. You've got to be brought to your senses." She spoke as though the means for compelling the return of sanity were there, ready to her hand. Yet she hesitated. And when she spoke it was pleadingly:

"Humphrey, give up. Go back to your work and everything you've worked for. The girl will manage and you'll forget her. I can't have her here because that'd commit you and I *know* that in time you'll thank me for not doing what you want. But above all don't go to your father. Don't chuck away everything I've tried to do for you. I hev slaved and pinched to save you from muck on your boots . . . don't come back to it now."

She saw by his face that she had failed.

"You're still in a mind to ask him? And to come back?" As he nodded she put her thin, work-scarred hand to the high close collar of her shabby dress and pulled at it as though she were choking. "Very well then. I'll tell you the truth. You can't come back here, Humphrey, and take the place of his eldest son, because that's just what you ain't. 'Longside of what I've tried to do for you there's been the idea that Sam must hev his due. Sam's younger'n you, but he's the first Shadbolt, and he must hev the farm. Can you understand that?"

"You mean . . . that I . . . am illegitimate?"

"You was born in wedlock," said Hagar quickly. "I saw to that. I married Josiah for that, and for no other

142

reason. And I managed so there was no talk and no noddings of heads. But from the very first I made up my mind to get you off the farm, both for your own sake and for the rightness. Sam ain't as dear to me as you are, he never was. But the farm is his. I never wronged Josiah, I been a good wife to him . . . and I won't hev Sam wronged, neither. And what wrong I did you I've done my best to make up for. I stood up for your schooling against Josiah and that's the only time I crossed him and he took it hard, things've never been the same between us since. I opened the shop, so there was never any doubt about whose money was spent on you, and I've skimped and slaved. Not that that mattered," she lifted her chin and looked at him defiantly, "I chose what I did. And now, when all seemed set to go right with you, you come and say you're willing to chuck all for the sake of a little hussy. 'T'isn't to be borne." The lifted chin began to quiver and for a moment Humphrey feared that his mother was about to cry, she who had never shed a tear that he could remember. But she steadied herself again. "I'm telling you all this, which I thought never to tell anybody to make you see reason, lad. Even if you don't mind spoiling everything I've worked for and want to ruin your whole life, you can't come back here because you don't belong. And you mayn't come between Sam and his rights. There's another reason too, why I'm telling you this . . . to show you I know what I'm talking about when I say love drives you crazy. There wasn't anybody to talk sense to me, so I mucked up my whole life, all on account of love." She brought out the word with supreme contempt. "Somebody else was crazy with love, too. But what I said to you just now was true then, just as it is now. He had his way with me and that was the end of that. A right good cure . . ." Something very like humour flavoured the last bitter words. Then, with another change of manner and voice she put her hand on his arm again, gently this time, and said:

"Thass a shock to you, no doubt, to hear that you're not of Josiah's getting. But don't take that to heart. Take to heart the rest of the things I've said to you, and go back to your work and leave this girl alone. 'Tisn't even as if she was crazy for you. Let her go her way and you get on and do the things I planned for you since you was in your cradle."

Conflicting, unrelated thoughts beat, like converging arrows upon the surface of his mind. The realisation that he was illegitimate, the knowledge that his last hope of installing Letty at Slipshoe was gone, the recognition of the fact that Hagar's disillusioned advice was the result of experience . . . there were all these to think of; and there was curiosity, and a sense of wonder that this ordinary, matter-of-fact woman had held her secret all these years; and there was humility too, for there gleamed here and there through the bare outlines of her story, the light of a great, self-sacrificing love, and of an unflinching integrity.

Mingled with all these thoughts and feelings, touching them all there was an awkward embarrassment. He felt oddly ashamed, almost as though Hagar, in telling him the truth, had at the same time thrown off her clothes and torn off his. It was in fact curiously like the shame of nakedness; he would have liked to run and hide himself. But he could not even turn away from her, for her hand still lay upon his arm and her grey eyes were looking at him seriously and tenderly, without a shadow of embarrassment which he himself was feeling. So, clumsily, since it was the first gesture of fondness that he had ever consciously made towards her he moved his arm until her hand lay between his sleeve and his body, clasped in a warm, reassuring pressure, and although his tongue felt wooden he forced it to speak, kindly.

"You've given me a lot to think about. And I promise that I will think about it and not do anything . . . rash." Even at this moment he could not renounce all thought of Letty. "About . . . about what you've just told me . . . I don't want to make you talk about it, but I would just like to know . . . who was he?"

"Your father. There's no reason you shouldn't know. His name was Henry Ackroyd. His people were up at the Hall, and I was parlour-maid there. They've gone now. They had another place somewhere in the South. And that was a good thing, because you turned out the spitting image of the old man. If they'd stayed somebody might hev noticed." The glint of humour with which she looked at him was surprising, almost shocking.

"And . . . and what happened?"

"With us, you mean? Oh, he come home from the army one time. It was summer, and we both went crazy, like I told you folks do. Then his regiment was sent to the West Indies and I married Josiah right quick. He'd

145

asked me a lot of times. I was lucky that way, I suppose." She spoke in a flat, unemotional voice, as though that far-away summer, that ill-fated love had been experienced by some other woman, barely known to her. And indeed the pretty, laughing, high-spirited, love-dazzled girl who had crept out to meet her lover in the summer dusks had been dead, and buried for more than twenty years. Even the road backward through the mind was closed, she had closed it herself, refusing to be weakened by sentiment and memory. If it had remained open, so that now she could have groped her way back and known again how it felt to be young and in love, could have lived in the memory of just one evening when the hay was sweet in the fields and the ditches frothed with meadowsweet and the woods arched cool and dark over the lovers, she might have turned to her son and spoken more kindly, less wisely. But the summer tide had run out and the rocks were bare. What Hagar knew for truth — that lust is easily satiated, longing capable of being overcome — she had passed on to Humphrey. She had exposed her own folly to save him from his. There was no more to be said. Even Humphrey was silenced by the thought that love could vanish so completely, leaving so little trace. So they crossed Tug field in silence, and half way across Hagar withdrew her arm. The habit of twenty years was not to be broken. But next morning, when Humphrey was preparing for his ride back to Bury, she chose her moment and slipped into his hand two guineas, instead of the one which was customary. He stood looking at the coins for a moment, thinking that now he could easily pay Plant what he had borrowed, and wondering at the same time what motive had prompted his mother's generosity. Could it be penitence? And if so, for what? Making him a bastard, or refusing Letty a home? Riding back along the familiar roads he reflected that it was strange that now, knowing his mother's past weakness and present obdurance he should feel, for the first time in his life, a really warm affection for her.

CHAPTER
THIRTEEN

As soon as Letty came through the doorway between the Coffee Room and the kitchen he saw that she was wearing a new dress. It was the clear bright colour of an unripe apple, and trimmed with bands of velvet in a darker shade. The absence of the little white ruffles at neck and elbows made her look older, and without at once seeing the reason he thought, Letty's growing up. When she came to his table, with her usual smiling welcome and a question about the happiness of his Christmas upon her lips, he saw that she was wearing a necklet of large green beads and that ear-bobs swung from the tiny ears. Her brown hair was drawn up to the top of her head, and from there to the nape of her neck fell in a cascade of curls; her lips and cheeks were coloured pink and her face filmed with pearly powder. She looked very pretty, and entirely unlike the pitiable little waif on the coach. But the change was not pleasing to him. Nor was it reassuring. After the first greetings he said almost spitefully:

"More decorations, I see. Christmas present?"

Her eyes darkened a little, but she said quite happily:

"Yes. One of the girls' friends brought us all the same. Susie's is blue and Cathy's is pink and mine is green. Don't you think they're pretty?"

"And you've had your ears pierced."

"Yes, Cathy did them for me . . . on a cork, with a darning needle. I was horribly scared, but it didn't really hurt much."

"Which friend was it?"

Letty said, a little reluctantly, "Well . . . it was Taffy."

"But I thought you didn't like him. You said he was horrible."

"I know. And I hadn't even tried to be nice to him. I was right ashamed to see that he'd brought me just the same present as the others."

"So then you began to be extra nice to him to make up I suppose."

Letty looked stricken, but not for the reason he imagined.

"Well, no. I'm funny that way. I can't just like anybody all of a sudden. I didn't really want to take the things but Cathy and Susie said it'd look rude. And then this dress came home late on Christmas Eve, it's my aunt's Christmas present, you see. And they did match . . . so . . ." She let the sentence trail away and then added with what was either a disarming ingenuousness or a subtlety too deep to be believed, "I thought I'd change over and keep my blue . . . and *your* necklet for best."

He was moved, and remorseful. It was as though he had given a child a toy and then rebuked it for accepting another toy from somebody else. Poor little

149

girl, so very innocent, so untroubled by the dark thoughts which haunted him. And she'd never had pretty things . . .

"Well," he said handsomely, "I'm sure you look very beautiful, very beautiful indeed, Letty."

She smiled, her happiness restored. But as soon as she had gone, as soon as the visible evidence of her childlike innocence was removed, he began to worry again. The idea of anything which that man Taffy had chosen and paid for and handled coming into contact with Letty was repulsive; the fact that he had treated all the girls alike was ominous; and so was the gift of the dress which lent such a spurious maturity, the piercing of the ears, the new way of doing the hair. Obsessed by the idea that the Rowans were all bent upon forcing Letty into one particular pattern, acceptable and valuable to themselves, he could see signs of pressure and collusion everywhere. He could even imagine that Mrs. Rowan had mentioned to Taffy the colour of Letty's new dress. And now, of course, he could no longer comfort, or fool himself with the idea of taking Letty to Slipshoe. Unless he could think of yet another scheme she must remain here until Midsummer. And so much could happen before then. Already she *looked* just like the others.

He carried this unpleasant thought about with him for a day or two, and it was in his mind when, on New Year's Eve, he walked out to Plant Driscoll's farm to return the twenty-four shillings. It was an evening of hard frost, clear and windless, and he was young and

150

strong enough to find it stimulating. He meditated, as he strode along, the possibility of discussing the matter — cautiously, of course, with Plant; and decided that if circumstances seemed favourable, to endeavour to bring the conversation around to the subject of the Coffee House.

Tonight there was no waiting. Plant himself, elegantly clad in a red velvet dressing gown, with speckless linen showing at breast and wrist, came to the door and his dark, monkeyish face brightened with pleasure at the sight of Humphrey.

"There's nobody I'd rather see," he said warmly. "Fancy your venturing out on such a night! Come in and let's shut the door, for God's sake. As you've probably noticed, I've got a cold."

He hurried back to the stove where a great red fire was burning, and, mindful of his linen, stirred something that was brewing in a pan. "You're just in time," he said. "I've got a gallon of rum punch and nobody to help me to drink it. Best thing in the world for a cold — or is that blasphemy in your ears?"

"Colds are a puzzle," said Humphrey seriously, taking off his coat and looking around the kitchen which had been thoroughly cleaned and tidied since his last visit. "There are palliatives, but I never met anybody who knew a cure. I always take onion gruel. I daresay what you've got there is just as good, and it smells nicer."

"It should, it's full of good stuff," said Plant, withdrawing the pan from the heat of the fire and taking up a beautiful ladle with a long handle of black whale-bone and a bowl of chased silver. Once again Humphrey's heart warmed to him and he was reminded of happy moments at school when boys who had been home, or stolen into the town had come back with stores of indigestible food and had, with their friends, devoured the most incredible mixtures. There was some echo of those times in this, with he and Plant tasting the scalding mixture and pronouncing upon its goodness. Again he thrust away the thought of the man in the water.

"How's your wrist?" he asked.

"Oh, practically well," said Plant pushing back his cuff and revealing the thick red scar. "Well enough to use, anyway. I cleaned out my sty," he indicated the kitchen, "and I did a job of work. That's how I caught this cold. I do abominate cold weather, don't you?"

"If you keep this room as hot as this and then go out you will catch cold," said Humphrey, easing back his chair.

"My cherished dream is to keep this room as hot as this and not leave it between the end of October and the first of May," said Plant with a grin. "I've even got my bed in that corner. I can't bear to leave the fire."

"But you must go out sometimes — with your job."

"My job?" Plant's voice was vague, but his glance was sharp.

"The farm . . . the horses."

"Oh. Why yes, of course. I have to go out. There's a man and a boy or so, but they need looking after."

One of the silences which seemed bound to fall between them fell then. Plant huddled close to the fire and cuddled his glass, as though even within the radius of heat his hands were still cold. Humphrey sat wondering how soon, if ever, he could bring up the subject of the Coffee House. Then he remembered the reason for his visit and took from his pocket the twenty-four shillings.

"I mustn't forget why I came. There it is, and thank you very much. If ever I can do you a favour, believe me I will."

"But you have done me a favour already. Why don't you put that back in your pocket and call it a fee and forget all about it. It's your due."

Humphrey looked at the money and was tempted. It would pay for twenty-four visits to the Coffee House, which meant twenty-four glimpses of Letty. But that wouldn't alter anything. If it had been twenty-four pounds it would have been enough to buy one's self-esteem.

"No," he said. "I explained that, didn't I?"

"You know," said Plant, "you are a peculiar fellow. Your voice becomes quite reverent whenever you mention money. Anybody'd think it was holy."

"Not holy — just important." He thought — I'd like to tell you just how important it is; but the time did not seem quite ripe. He laid the money on the table, since Plant made no move to take it. The silence fell again.

This time Plant broke it, and with the very words which Humphrey had wished he would use.

"Have you been to Mrs. Rowan's lately."

"To the Coffee House; yes."

Plant laughed. "A nice distinction! She'd appreciate that. She does so enjoy the difference between her front door and her back. Back in the autumn a couple of fellows I know made a bet — just an ordinary wager with one another — and when they next met, in the Coffee Room, the loser went to pay the winner across the table. And would you believe, Mrs. Rowan pounced on him like a tiger. 'If that's a gambling debt,' she said, 'kindly settle it outside. I don't allow gambling on my premises.' And the same night, or early the next morning, she took fifteen pounds off Chris Hatton, playing Faro."

He laughed and Humphrey managed to smile. Plant refilled the glasses.

"She's clever," he said. "Too clever to be comfortable. She did me a very dirty trick once, and in such a way that I hadn't any redress. I never forgave her. And that's odd. Because since then she's done me a number of *good* turns and if she'd been a man I'd have balanced one against the other and called it quits long ago. But being outwitted by a woman — that does rankle." He drank deeply and then stared at the fire, scowling, while Humphrey sat forming and discarding sentences which might bring him nearer knowing what it was he wanted to know. Before he could find one which invited information without too much exposure of ignorance and inexperience Plant turned in his chair and looked into his face.

"Look here, you're a good chap and I'm obliged to you. But we don't know one another very well, and I don't want to offend you. So I'll ask you a question

154

before I say any more. What exactly are you aiming at with regard to Letty Rowan?"

"Ah," said Humphrey, "now you have asked me something. And an exact answer is very hard to give. I don't . . . like her being there. I've hated it from the first. I've made two attempts to get her away. But it's difficult to know what to suggest and they're kind to her, and there are times when one wonders whether it's all just imagination and rumour — what they say about the place, I mean. I feel that it isn't the place for her, but I'd be damned if I could prove that it wasn't. You know it better than I do. What would you say?"

"It depends upon what I asked you just now. Your intentions with regard to the girl."

"Oh," said Humphrey eagerly, "I'm serious. I . . . I suppose I'm in love with her." Two glasses of rum punch made it easier to speak of one's feelings. "The devil of it is that I can't even think about marriage until after Midsummer when I've passed my examination. And what worries me is what might happen between now and then."

"Then I'll tell you this — but mind, it's strictly between you and me. As I said, you're a good chap and I owe you something. Also, as I said, Ma Rowan once made a monkey out of me, and if I can save her from doing the same with you I'd derive a certain *pleasure* from the process." He tested the heat of his mixture, refilled the glasses, and put the pan a littler nearer the full heat of the stove and then lay back in his chair.

"I went in," he said, "on the night that Letty arrived. They'd cleaned her up a bit and lent her some clothes,

155

Cathy told me. Apparently she arrived looking like a waif, unexpected and unannounced, and they'd all set about making her feel at home. In a *way* — in fact I might say as long as she is having her way — the old woman's heart isn't bad, and I think she was genuinely sorry that the girl had got so low before coming to her. So she was making a fuss of her and trying to draw her into things and pressing food and drink on her. And then all at once the child was roaring drunk. Quite maudlin. She suddenly turned to Mrs. Rowan and made a speech about how kind she was and how different from what she'd been led to expect; and then she went on to say what she *had* been led to expect. Her papa had evidently summed up the situation with more accuracy than charity and said enough about Aunt Thirza to make the girl keep away even when he was dead and she had nothing but her needle between her and starvation. She spoke so passionately about how she'd struggled to keep herself that it'd have been quite touching if it hadn't been so damned funny. All this pouring out into Mrs. Rowan's startled ears, and Cathy and Susie standing there hearing themselves described as whores. Luckily we were all good friends there that night and we laughed it off. Finally Cathy took her and put her to bed, still raving on about keeping herself respectable and how she'd rather die . . . and so on. Mrs. Rowan said she'd feed her up for a week, give her some money and ship her back to London. I think she was disappointed in her apart from the ranting; she said she was undersized and seemed dim-witted. But next time I went in there she still was, brightened up and settled in like a stray cat. And I asked her about her — a bit maliciously I admit, just to remind the old woman of that delightfully frank speaking we'd all so much enjoyed; and she said she hadn't given up hope. Letty had met a young gentleman on the coach and had taken a fancy to him, and he'd been in during the week and she'd made a few inquiries and — saving your presence — he wasn't in a position to marry; and it was the first step that counted. She'd an idea that with a little encouragement he'd put Letty on the right road." He surveyed Humphrey's horrified face with some satisfaction. "Well, next time I was there was the night you went to supper and I looked at you and thought — again saving your presence — that you didn't seem bent on seduction. But it was nothing to do with me until that night when you sewed me up so nicely and didn't ask a lot of damn-fool questions. And the pair of you did look rather touching, coming in hand-in-hand, you know. I was pretty far gone and a bit sentimental perhaps. I thought then that if I ever had the chance I'd drop you a hint, so here it is. Once the deed is done you'll find that she'll rig up some scheme for keeping you away from the Coffee House. And Letty'll go gay on the rebound — the way Cathy did. Susie was that way from the start. Well, now you know."

"And it's worse than I thought. Cold-blooded and deliberate and filthy. It makes me feel utterly ashamed. I'd like to wring her rotten neck for her."

"We all feel that way at times. I have a soft spot for Cathy, as doubtless you know. And she's treated Cathy abominably. Cathy had a baby, you know, from what seems to have been a genuine love affair; before my time, but I've heard about it. Mrs. Rowan put the baby out to nurse, though Cathy was dotty about it. It has a good home, nice clothes, goes to school now and everything, and Cathy sees it two or three times a year. But she lives under the perpetual threat that if she puts a foot wrong in any one particular the brat'll be in a Foundlings' Home before she could blink and she'd never see it again. That keeps Cathy very tame."

"She's a devil," said Humphrey solemnly. "And what is it all for? She's got a good business. I thought round about Christmas time what a nice, happy, sound concern it could be if it were all like the front . . . Why does she bother with all the rest of it?" He remembered, unwillingly, incongruously, Mrs. Rowan's expression of weariness on the night of Plant's accident. "She doesn't enjoy all these shifts and schemes and rumours, does she?"

"Our old friend, money. And, I think you're wrong. She does enjoy it. Pitting her wits against the world."

"Well, they're pitted against me, now. After what you've told me I'll get Letty out of that place if I have to go as a day-labourer to do it."

"Labourers don't earn much," said Plant gravely. "But I do agree that if you want Letty in *status quo* so to speak you'll have to do something, and sharp. I know by what Mrs. Rowan says about her improved appearance and so forth that she's getting a trifle impatient with you. A little more shilly-shallying and you'll find yourself supplanted. Other tactics will be

158

tried. Plain rape by Taffy I shouldn't wonder." He watched the effect of his words.

Humphrey jumped from his chair and began to stride about the room.

"It's this damned question of money," he said jerkily. "I've tried other means, got Miss Pendle to say she'd take her, begged my mother to give her a home. If only I could get hold of some money I'd make a place for her. But I've no hope of having any till after Midsummer."

Plant's manner suddenly ceased to be sympathetic. "That's all nonsense," he said curtly. "No man need be without money in this world unless he chooses to be."

"That's nonsense if you like," Humphrey retorted. "I don't *choose* to be without money. But I *am* without."

"I didn't say wishing for it would get you any. Have you ever tried to make some?"

"Counterfeiting, you mean?"

"Don't be pedantic. Making — earning — wringing it out of something or somebody."

"And how could I do that?" Humphrey asked. "I'm busy all day. I suppose I could drive the night-soil cart. God knows I would if that'd solve the problem."

"Would you really?" asked Plant with interest. For a moment his dark, prematurely-lined face took on a look of wonderment, not untouched by wistfulness, such as an atheist might wear as he listened to a mystic relating some spiritual experience, or with which a person stiff and immobile with age might watch the nimble antics of a playful child. But it passed and the expression of watchfulness and caution returned. "I wasn't suggesting

159

anything so extreme, or so unremunerative," he said. "In fact, I haven't suggested anything yet, have I? But I might. Let me fill your glass; and then, if you can manage it, sit down and be calm. There's nothing to be done tonight, but we might think of something. You're young and strong and don't mind the cold . . ." He laughed as he enumerated the unremarkable qualifications.

"Who's going to pay me for that? And what could I do between say, nine o'clock at night and six in the morning, except be a footpad?" He spoke more lightly than he would have done in a state of cold sobriety, but the motive behind the words was genuine. He was saying aloud, encouraged by rum and a sympathetic listener, the things which he had been turning over and over in his mind since November.

"There's nothing in footpadding," said Plant gravely. "It's overcrowded and dangerous, and this isn't the locality for it. And you needn't think," he said, reverting to his curt way of speaking, "that I'm going to suggest any sinecures to you. If you want money I can show you how to make some, but it means doing what you're told and keeping your mouth shut. Think that over."

"I take it that it is illegal."

"That depends entirely upon how you look at it. A good many reasonable people see no harm in it at all; but technically speaking, yes, it is. You may have observed that lawful ways of making money are few and slow, especially when one is otherwise occupied during the money-making hours of the day." He grinned. Then, with deliberation, he took from his pocket a

160

handful of money and counted out on to the corner of the table a quantity of sovereigns and half-sovereigns, at the same time sweeping away the shillings which Humphrey had laid down. "Look, there's twenty pounds. If you like it's yours, on account. Suppose you sit there and think just exactly what you would and would not be prepared to do for it, while I gather some supper together. I've been off my peck with this cold on me, but talking to you has given me an appetite."

He took a clean cloth and some good cutlery and silver from the table drawer and set the table neatly, leaving the money where it lay with the cloth folded back at that corner. Then he made one or two shivering journeys into the larder and brought back a cold fowl, bread, butter, cheese, which he arranged upon the table with finicky neatness. Humphrey watched idly. He had already reached his decision and chosen the words in which to convey it. He dared not look at the gold coins shining upon the corner of the table behind the fold of the cloth. He wanted, needed them so badly, and he wasn't sure that his answer would be sufficiently satisfactory to bring them into his possession. Nor dared he think about the story Plant had told him. So he sat and wondered why Plant, with all his fastidious ways and all his money, should choose to live in the kitchen of this sizable house, and wait upon himself.

"There," said Plant, "it's ready. Rather meagre, but then I wasn't expecting a guest."

"I've made up my mind," Humphrey said. "I'll do anything you like to suggest provided it doesn't injure anybody. It may sound offensive to say that I stop short at murder, because it sounds as though I credit you with wanting me to do murder, but when I say it I just mean that, short of murdering or injuring anybody there's nothing I wouldn't do, and gladly, to earn that twenty pounds."

"Well, that's frank and very satisfactory," Plant said. "I won't ask you to murder anybody. In fact I prefer to do my own murdering." He laughed and the sound fell a little unpleasantly on Humphrey's ears. "All right then, put that in your pocket and pull the cloth straight and I'll tell you what I want you to do." He began to hack inexpertly at the fowl in a way that neat-handed Humphrey found difficult to watch. As he hacked he said in an almost elaborately casual way: "In return for your crediting me with planning a murder I'll credit you with double-dealing, and warn you here and now that it wouldn't be good for your health." Involuntarily Humphrey looked at the scar, now fully exposed because Plant had pushed back his cuffs before taking up the carving knife. "Not that I worry much about that. I take it you're a man of honour and that you'll earn your money."

"If you have any doubt about it you'd better take it back now," said Humphrey angrily.

"But I haven't. I assure you. And now I'll tell you what I want you to do. Three times a week — you can suit yourself most of the time as to what days of the week — I want you to come here, get in a gig and drive to destinations I give you and deliver certain goods. On other evenings, but not more than once a month, though pretty irregularly because so much depends on

162

the moon and the weather, you'd have to be prepared to work hard and fast for an hour or so, unloading similar goods. And that is all."

"Contraband goods?"

"As you say, contraband goods. I buy and distribute practically anything in that line, but mostly brandy, tobacco and tea. I'm pretty far inland and the goods have changed hands several times by the time I get them, and the biggest profits go elsewhere. All the same, it's a paying game, the best I've found so far, and I've tried several since I was thrown on the world to make my own way. And it isn't particularly dangerous in these parts, the Preventive Force is small and inactive. The Riding Officer is new to the area, and some smart fellow took him to Mrs. Rowan's and introduced him to Susie, so we always know when he's riding this way. I have a circle of the most fantastically respectable clients, and I never take a new one who isn't properly introduced. In fact I have reduced the risk to the minimum. But I can't go out six nights a week myself. I've had partners before." He shook his sleeve over his wrist. "But they haven't been the kind of person I liked to work with. You and I could get on well, I *think*. But if you've any doubts, if you *felt* you'd do anything and now don't feel so wholehearted, this is the time to say so."

"I haven't. I don't know exactly what I expected you to ask of me, but I can assure you I was prepared for worse. In fact I think the tax on tea is criminal. If the people who make laws could come round with me for one day and see what joy and comfort a cup of tea is to all women, but especially the poor who have few comforts, they'd take the tax off tomorrow. D'you know, I know several poor old creatures who go out, whatever the weather, to collect the *tea-leaves* from better-class houses. The damned stuff is brewed in the parlour first, then in the kitchen, and if there's a good-natured maid she'll save the leaves to give away. Anybody who smuggles tea is a public benefactor."

"Well, you see one in me, and that's the first time I've ever been called that," said Plant, amused. "You should put your poor patients in touch with Trinket Ted. He calls here twice a month with a tray of rubbish and fills up his jacket. A cunning device. A kind of jerkin made of thin stuff, stitched into partitions so it's a whole series of pockets. He fills it up with tea at three shillings a pound and sells it for fourpence an ounce. It pays him better than pins and bootlaces, and at that is cheaper than the shops. But that, of course, is just a piddling little business. The real money is made on brandy and tobacco and soft goods like gloves and laces. But customers do like deliveries to be regular; they like shop service at cheaper prices, that's the whole of it. And having lost my last partner and cut my wrist and then got this cold I'm in a devil of a muddle. I'd want you to start right away."

"I'll start tomorrow night."

"I'll work out a round journey. There's Major Ayres at Euston, the Reverend Tomber at Barningham, Mr. Orchard at Livermere Parva that I know of, all outstanding; and I can work in some more." He was thoughtful for a moment, drawing on the cloth with his fork. Then he looked up. "There's one thing we haven't thought about. Suppose you're wanted, professionally, in the night and you happen to be working. It's entirely your affair, of course, and you must make your own arrangements; I can't do that for you. But I don't want old Coppard howling after you and tracing you here. You see that, don't you?"

It was the situation which Humphrey had been facing since he announced his willingness to drive the night-soil cart.

"People don't *often* send by night, expecially in winter. And I'll stick at home closely on the nights when you don't want me. Between nine and eleven, if Doctor Coppard wanted me badly he'd send to the Coffee House; he knows I go there, and I'd say I'd been there and was called away from there. After eleven he'd look for me in bed — but calls after eleven are rarer; and if one came I should say that I'd already been called to Mrs. Naylor. She's quite crazy, and if he did ask her next day, which I don't think he would, she'd say I was a good boy and proceed to sing him a hymn. It doesn't sound anything like foolproof, but as you say, it's my risk. The one thing I can promise is that nobody shall ever trace me here."

"That's all right then. For the rest your profession serves our purpose. It's natural for you to be driving late at night. Well, do we go into partnership?"

"Please," said Humphrey. "It's the kind of thing I've been longing for. I can't tell you what a weight you've taken off my mind. The twenty pounds will enable me to get Letty out of that place, and that's one thing I've wanted to do ever since November. By the way . . . how long will it take me to earn that much? How much can I count on in a week?"

"It varies," Plant said. "I'll work it all out and let you know. A lot depends upon the amount of stuff we shift. The last fellow I had was a poor tool, and with winter coming on I refused several would-be customers. We could expand. Anyway, don't worry about money. I'll let you know when that's worked off and you let me know as soon as you need some more. I suppose you'll get the girl away at once? I *rather* look forward to the day Mrs. Rowan tells me of her loss. I'll feel even with her at last."

"You won't have to wait long," Humphrey assured him. "I shall start finding a place first thing in the morning."

CHAPTER
FOURTEEN

He had imagined that all that stood between him and the fulfilment of his scheme had been his lack of money, and he had been completely certain that with twenty pounds in his pocket and the prospect of earning more as he needed it, he could find a home for Letty within an hour. But a full two hours — more than he could legitimately filch from his round of duties, was expended on that first day, and Letty was still homeless, save for the Coffee House.

He had tried reputable houses first. There were seven known places in the town where respectable widows or spinsters eked out a pitiable income by receiving lodgers. Between his professional visits he contrived to call on four of these ladies during that first day. Three of them had no room vacant at all, and the fourth did not take females. It had caused trouble in the past, she said darkly.

So when he presented himself to Plant, ready to undertake his first attempt at contravening the customs, the establishment of Letty in a safe and happy home was still — as it had been since November — a dream.

For a little while on that night of frost-bound darkness he forgot Letty and his self-assumed obligations. The gig was ready in the yard, its load concealed under an ordinary carriage rug. Plant, huddled against the cold in so many clothes that he was shapeless, helped to harness an almost-too-fresh horse to the vehicle, and gave and repeated a number of instructions. Humphrey, climbing into the driving seat, so ordinary, so like the one he mounted every day for out-of-town calls, thought — and now I'm smuggling; I'm putting myself on the wrong side of the law, and if anything goes wrong with me old Sir Silas Pridworth, whom I bled this morning, will sentence me to transportation at the very least. Apart from that thought, which was fantastic, the whole business was reassuringly, almost disappointingly tame. Like most other schoolboys of his generation, Humphrey had taken an avid, if surreptitious, interest in the exploits of Beddoes and Skipper and the notorious Throston gang, and the word "smuggler" had evoked a vision compounded of cut-throat blood-thirstiness and romantic adventure. That it should have boiled down to an arrangement between a man with a cold in his head and a medical apprentice trying to earn an honest penny, seemed to be a negation of those schoolboy excitements, and brought him face to face with the realisation that most of the things which seemed romantic to those who read or heard about them had been just part of the day's work to those who took part in them. And it was conceivable — though highly unlikely, and he hoped it would never happen — that, given bad luck and a bloody end, he might be written of as Humphrey Shadbolt, the notorious Doctor-Smuggler. It was absurd. But what a story it would make. Without being, in essence, a story at all. Nevertheless, when at his first place of call he had lifted the rug from the casks and bundles in the back of the gig, he did touch the unrealisable reality of romance. The load *smelt* of the sea, of far places, strange happenings, of daring and outlawry. And this is me, Humphrey Shadbolt, lined up with Beddoes and Skipper and the Throston gang. Yes, Doctor Shadbolt; no Doctor Shadbolt; Humphrey, hand me that scalpel; gentlemen, we have here a specimen . . . Nobody had really lived until he had lived two lives, each sharpening and ridiculing the other.

But the houses at which he called to deliver his goods were perfectly ordinary, undistinguished from those to which he might have been called professionally, and the people who received and paid for them were perfectly ordinary too, just like the people who would call him in to lance an abscess, set a bone or deliver a reluctant baby. They might be the very same people — and with that in mind he kept his hat well down over his eyes and his scarf, justified on account of the cold, well up over his chin.

When, during the early hours of the morning, he returned to Plant's farm he did experience a sharp, unreflective feeling of danger. Suppose the excise men had ambushed themselves in the yard. "I was called to Euston and hired this horse and gig." That was what he must say. But the thought, which should have been a comfortable one, brought a feeling of shame with it. There was something particularly despicable in using an honourable profession as a cover for a nefarious undertaking. He hoped he would never be driven to use it.

Next morning Mrs. Gamble, calling him with a can of hot water for shaving, found him difficult to wake, and all through breakfast he had to fight a tendency to fall into sleepy silence, and to yawn. It was eleven o'clock before he was fully awake and capable of devising a time-saving shift or two which would allow him to proceed with his hunt for accommodation for Letty. He set about the business doggedly and managed to visit two of the remaining reputable houses before he returned to the house for his three o'clock dinner. One of them had changed hands and had reverted to being a family residence; and in the other there were no rooms to let.

After dinner he went to visit a country patient, and when he came back it was twilight and Mrs. Naylor had sent one of her urgent messages. He swallowed a cup of Mrs. Gamble's perpetual brew of black tea and went out again, first to the mad woman's and then on to the last house on his list. The landlady there was closing her business on account of her age. He pleaded with her; the young lady for whom he was seeking accommodation, he said, would give no trouble, need no attention, would even, he promised desperately, do some shopping and help in the house. But the landlady was firm, saying plaintively that she'd always intended to retire when she was sixty and enjoy the feeling of having her home to herself. "Thirty-eight years I've had other folk in and out of my front door, and I'd like to have it to myself for my last years. If I took your young lady it wouldn't be the same, not like I've hoped for."

Humphrey went home to supper and then across to the Coffee House.

He now knew the worst, the full and horrible truth about Mrs. Rowan, and though it was policy to maintain friendly relations with her until Letty was safely out of her keeping, it needed a great effort to reply to her smiling greeting and remarks about the weather without betraying curtness. And when Letty came to his corner his ordinarily muddled feelings of love and longing and admiration and responsibility were further complicated by a sick embarrassment as he remembered the thing that Plant had told him. And it was maddening to think that after weeks of abortive planning each scheme beginning "If only I had the money . . ." here he was with twenty gold sovereigns in his pocket and still no nearer finding Letty a home.

As he drank his coffee and watched Letty moving about the room, and looked at Cathy with new, sympathetic eyes, he began to dwell upon the possibility of installing Letty in one of the two better-class inns. It was not a good plan. An inn wasn't the place for a young girl to make her home; and an inn was public; there'd be little to prevent Mrs. Rowan from following and accosting Letty if she felt like doing so. And inns were public in another sense too. Hotbeds of gossip. It would soon get about that Letty was there and that he was concerned. Oh, why couldn't there be some nice, discreet, motherly woman who would take a girl in and look after her and make a home life for her. There must be dozens such in the town.

Mr. Bancroft broke in upon his unhappy meditations, and it occurred to Humphrey that the schoolmaster might know of a likely place. The question threw Mr. Bancroft into such profound thought that it was left to Humphrey to pay for the coffee and brandy that had been ordered. The results of the meditation were not very gratifying, one by one Mr. Bancroft named the landladies upon which Humphrey had already called.

"I've been to them all," he said disconsolately when the list was finished. "It does seem stupid, doesn't it? There must be dozens of suitable places."

"Must be," Mr. Bancroft agreed. "But you can't very well go knocking at doors of private houses on such a quest. Might be offensive. Of course in the poorer parts it'd be all right."

Instantly Humphrey began to run through his mind the names and locations of some of his less-well-to-do patients. Most of them lived in squalor and discomfort, and many were undisguisedly dirty. But there were exceptions and he might even find a place where it would be possible for him to add some comforts to the room Letty would occupy.

Comforting himself with this possibility he went home and to bed early and slept like the dead.

Through the next day, and the one following, he pursued his quest. Many of the small houses were overcrowded already; some, which he had thought tolerably clean and comfortable when called to them to visit a patient, were now revealed as palpably unsuitable backgrounds for Letty. There was a good deal of sickness in the town, too, and he began to be the victim of a nervous fear lest he should install her within range of some contagion. And once he found himself confronted by something even more repulsive than a case of bilious fever. The woman of the house had begun to leer, he thought, as soon as he spoke his opening words, and that made his manner lose all composure. When he had explained what he wanted she attempted to reassure him. "Why, yes," she said heartily, "I'll put her up. And everything'll be all right; you can come when you like and stay as long as you like. I ain't one for questions or gossip."

That well-intentioned speech made him shocked and angry, and set him miserably wondering whether more respectable women had formed a similar opinion of his errand, and whether that accounted for his many refusals. Perhaps it did look rather odd, and perhaps he should have implied that Letty was his sister, or cousin. But then he hoped that she would stay in the place he found for her until Midsummer, and after that he hoped to marry her. Well, one could marry one's cousin, and in future Letty should be his cousin. He wished he could have started all over again with the word cousin well to the fore in every interview.

CHAPTER
FIFTEEN

During this busy, harassed and so far as Letty was concerned, unprofitable week, he drove out with two more loads of contraband. The journeys were completely uneventful, and the thing he found hardest to do was to keep awake in the gentle swaying gig behind the steadily plodding horse as they moved through the cold starlight from point to point of an itinerary previously carefully planned out by Plant. Sometimes he could only keep awake by thinking of Letty, and by this time such thoughts had become as monotonous as a treadmill; for his own sake he longed for some new element to arise in the situation; if he could only find the promise of a place for her with what delight and relief could he dwell upon that, and plan.

He found it by accident, a full fortnight after he had begun his search. He had been out to one of the Bradfields to set a broken leg, and in Southgate Street, as his horse eased down to a walk upon the short hill before the Horse Market, he saw a quantity of poor, shabby furniture being carried from a little house and loaded upon a handcart.

He had never noticed the house before, but now, with the handcart and the crowd of interested neighbours blocking the road as an excuse, he checked his horse and looked at it and was instantly, poignantly aware of its charm. It was small and poor, with larger houses, also shabby and fallen from a higher estate, pressing upon it on either side. Its woodwork was unpainted, scaly with dirt and neglect and some of its window panes were broken and stuffed with rag and paper. But it had an intrinsic attractiveness. There was just one gable facing the street, and the lower window of the two visible ones, protruded on little wooden legs and was paned, where it was not broken, with thick, greenish old panes of bottle glass. The doorway was set back, deep in the front hall, and had a cosy, almost a secret look. It was a dear little house, Humphrey thought.

Before he had completed his survey the crowd had moved back and the man with the handcart had shoved it an inch nearer the gutter, calling with cheerful respect, "There you are, sir, room enough now." Humphrey clicked his tongue and his horse moved on, breasting the slope. But at the top he checked him again and asked of a stout woman who was watching the house-moving from her own doorway:

"Could you tell me, is that house to let?"

"Thass right, sir. They're being put out. They ain't paid no rent since Michaelmas."

"Who's the landlord?"

"The same as mine, sir. Mr. Stubbs of Risbygate."

"Thank you," said Humphrey and rode on. But the little house haunted him. A picture of it, small and detailed as the tail end of a book, with its one gable, its odd little window, its deep secret doorway, hung at the back of his mind like a back-cloth. Half way through his supper he knew that the little house had arrested his attention and attracted him, because it was offering him the real answer to his problem. If he could hire it and furnish it it would make a perfect home for Letty until he could marry her; and then he could live in it too. He could make it more and more comfortable and beautiful as he earned the money. He had the usual young-lover vision of the loved woman going lightly and happily about her little household tasks. He had the hearth-building impulse which men have known since time immemorial.

As soon as supper was over he walked into Risbygate and found Mr. Stubbs at home. The house, Mr. Stubbs said, was already half promised to somebody from the country who was coming to see it tomorrow, market day. The rent was three and sixpence a week, and it was a good house, though it'd been shockingly treated by the last tenants.

"I only saw it this afternoon," said Humphrey dolefully. "I came as soon as I could." Without guile he put his hand into his pocket and touched the money which he had carried there ever since Plant had given it to him. In his penury he had thought gold invincible, but in his hands apparently it lost its virtue.

"If you're really interested in it," said Mr. Stubbs, "and cared to make up your mind now, and paid a month's rent in advance . . ."

"Oh, but I am. I will."

"And the repairs ... This man who's coming tomorrow is very handy. He was going to see to them himself without bothering me in any way."

"Oh, I'll get them done," said Humphrey eagerly. "I may not be very handy and I haven't a lot of spare time, but I'll see that it's properly repaired."

"That's all right then. I expect you'd like a lease, proper fashion. Say for a year?"

"Oh, longer than that."

"Two years then ... with an option. Very good, sir, I'll see about that in the morning."

"And I pay the rent now. And ... would you mind if I had the key? I would like to look inside it."

"The key isn't here just now. Look, I'll have the key and the lease here, ready for you to sign, tomorrow midday. How'll that do?"

"That'll be splendid," said Humphrey. He walked home on air, a householder.

Next evening, in possession of the key and armed with a candle, he visited the house; and except for the fact that its strange charm laid hold upon him even more powerfully as soon as he crossed its threshold, he would have thought himself properly fooled. As it was he saw why Mr. Stubbs had withheld the key until the rent was paid and the lease signed. The place was as dirty as Mrs. Naylor's and far more derelict, for the state of her premises was due to neglect and decay, she had never wantonly destroyed anything. This little house had been savagely used. Even the kindly candlelight revealed its wounds. He walked over it, mourning for it, cherishing the sentimental idea that the little ill-treated place had issued a wordless appeal to him as he halted by it, had trusted him to rescue it. To such a mood the crumbling plaster, the broken floorboards, the cracked hearths, the sagging ceilings, the unhinged doors could only be an incentive, a challenge willingly taken up. He was appalled but not discouraged. He communed with the house, like a lunatic, as he moved through its four small rooms; he promised it restoration, cleanliness, beauty. For almost an hour the purpose for which he had taken the house was pushed into the rear of consciousness; and, although he was not aware of it, the relief from the nagging round of Mrs. Rowan-Letty-get-her-away-from-that-place acted like a tonic upon him. He felt young and vigorous again, no longer undermined by sleeplessness.

But Letty was not easily usurped. As he closed the door behind him and thriftily pocketed the end of the candle, he began to wonder how soon the restoration of the house could be effected and whether Letty would like it as much as he did. The susceptibility towards women which Doctor Coppard had noted and slightly deplored, had at least made him very observant of them, and one of those observations influenced his thoughts now. He had absorbed the idea that to a woman a home of her own was a thing of paramount importance and preciousness. He had heard his mother say to his eldest sister, "This is *my* house; when you have one of your own you can arrange it as you like." And that was because Mary had altered the position of some cups on the kitchen dresser. He had been in more

178

than one house where a man had died and the widow's first question, asked through tears, had been, "Shall I be able to keep my home?" Even Doctor Coppard, a far from sentimental man, would excuse Mrs. Gamble's occasional lapses and ill-humours with the remark, "After all, it isn't as though it were her own house." So it seemed reasonable to suppose that Letty, sharing with other women this passion for a home, would be delighted by the arrangement he had made, and as he walked back towards the centre of the town he toyed with the idea of going straight across to the Coffee House and imparting the news. His heart beats quickened as he thought of it, and for a while he knew nothing save joyful excitement and a feeling of triumph. But as he neared Mrs. Rowan's house doubt and caution assailed him. It wasn't — and there was the whole crux of the matter — as though Letty had asked him to find her a home. In fact the proposition he was to make was rather a delicate one; it might involve some plain speaking and some persuasion.

Then he remembered, not without relief, since it shifted the decision from his own will and laid it upon circumstances, the state of the house. Suppose Letty asked to see the place now, and was revolted by it. By far the best thing to do was to get it put in order and prettily furnished as well as his means allowed and then take her to see it and present her with it. And then if she raised any demur against leaving her aunt, her so kind aunt, he could say what he had to say in the privacy of his own, her own, their own house.

So he sat that evening in the Coffee House, cherishing his secret, and then went to bed early because he was still in arrears with his sleep.

He was kept too busy during the morning of the next day to do anything about the business of mending and decorating the house; and afterwards he was grateful that he had not been able to go along and engage a bricklayer and plasterer in the first thoughtless flush of excitement; for round about midday the thought occurred to him that in so small a town a person so well known by name and sight as he was could hardly exert and interest himself so obviously in such a matter without attracting undesirable attention. Even hiring the house had been a little rash, though he had given Mr. Stubbs to understand that it was for an acquaintance, not for himself; and though he had paid the rent and signed the lease that could be explained by the pressure of time. But the rest of the business had to be handled more carefully. Reluctantly, since his instinctive desire was to oversee every detail of the work and to take part in it himself, he decided to ask Plant's help as a go-between, and resolved only to visit the house under cover of darkness.

Plant, amused, a little bewildered, at times a little scornful, agreed to help on condition that he might also conceal his movements.

"If the plot hatches and you get the girl away Ma Rowan will be out for your blood — but that's your affair. I don't want her after mine, I tell you frankly. So don't, if we meet in her place at any time, come galloping up to me with questions and instructions. The less, in fact, that we're connected in public the better."

"What could she do to you?" asked Humphrey curiously, remembering that Mrs. Rowan had said that Plant never told her anything.

"She could lock the door on Cathy. Cathy likes me well enough, but I'd weigh very light against that brat of hers."

"I see. I'll be very careful."

"That's right. I've always found not letting the right hand know what the left is up to a pretty safe rule. I'll put the work in hand for you and let you know when it's done."

It was just bearable to leave the repairs and the painting to underlings and intermediaries, but when it came to furnishing the place it was different. No other person's taste and judgment could be trusted. But he was very careful, buying one thing at a time, and patronising as far as possible shops and workrooms in the villages he visited. For anything he bought in a place where he was known he gave specious, unnecessary explanations. Hagar Shadbolt would have been astonished to know how many birthdays she celebrated in the last fortnight of January and the first fortnight of February, and how much her son expended in gifts for her. The expense staggered Humphrey, who had hitherto dealt in pennies and shillings, and to whom twenty pounds had seemed inexhaustible wealth. But Plant was sympathetic and obliging, and advanced a further two pounds without quibbling.

At last the workmen had finished, and a wagon, ordered by Plant, had collected the pieces of furniture from their various storage places. And there came an evening, one of those February evenings bloomed with the immanence of spring when Humphrey was able to go into the little house and set it out for Letty to see.

In the joy of possession and achievement he forgot, or chose to ignore that he had not yet broken news of the project to Letty, and that once before he had shied away from doing so, giving the state of the house as his excuse, and that now there was no excuse. In fact his mind, weary of gnawing worry, leapt over that inevitable interview and browsed in the pastures of dreams come true. He was sure that Letty would like the little house as much as he did, that she would come to live in it willingly, gladly; and that eventually he would come to live there too. Moving about the three apartments which he had been able to furnish — the quiet parlour at the back of the house, the unexpectedly spacious bedroom above it and the kitchen which he had equipped from memories of Slipshoe, he dared to look back to that meeting with Letty on the coach in a November afternoon and reckon with modest pride his achievement.

He dwelt on the memory of the three past months with satisfaction. He did not know that they had aged and altered him. He had shaved each morning without noticing the lines which worry and perplexity had graved in his face; he had put on his clothes without observing that over-exertion and lack of sleep had stripped flesh from his prominent bones. Old Doctor

Coppard had noticed the change and attributed it to the hard weather and hard work in the winter bout of ailments, and had paused in his own busy round to concoct an agglutinant of gum Arabic, cassia and comfrey in which he put faith in all wasting conditions, and Humphrey swallowed it meekly, even gratefully, because he also believed in it and hoped that it would enable him to work for nineteen hours for three days of the week without feeling too much strain. Apparently such faith had been justified.

The worried lines smoothed out from his face as he walked his domain, trying a piece of furniture now here, now there, using his handkerchief as a duster to brush away some lingering dust or the mark of a greasy finger. The change in the place was incredible, and though the furniture was oddly mixed he regarded it all with equal approval. Two irreconcilable motives had influenced his purchases, the thriftiness which upbringing and long habit had made a part of his very blood, and a romantic extravagance evoked by the thought that Letty would handle and look at and live with these things. And the motives had scored alternate victories; after a fit of extravagance he would turn cautious; having been cautious he would become spendthrift, and as a result Letty's bedroom had a silk-curtained four-poster standing upon a worn and threadbare rug, and a travelling theatrical dressing table, fitted with every device for the safe transport of every imaginable cosmetic, which an actress, temporarily out of funds, had sold to a second-hand dealer and which was now confronted by a plain white wooden milking stool as a seat. In the parlour there was a sofa covered with worn but beautiful brocade, but the table was a dealtopped one whose painted legs protruded incongruously from the folds of an Indian shawl which Humphrey had chosen for a tablecloth. There were no pictures or ornaments, because he fancied that Letty might like to choose them for herself, but there was wood in the shed and coal in the cellar, candles and groceries in the kitchen cupboard. He flattered himself that he had thought of everything. He had even instructed Plant to instruct his intermediary to instruct the workman in charge of the job to see that the well was cleaned out and a new rope and bucket fitted. When he had finished his arrangements and rearrangements inside the house he went out to look at the well.

The garden was bare and desolate, but the heaps of mouldering rubbish left by the previous tenants had been cleared away, and in the spring the place could be planted afresh with flowers and young fruit trees. The well was satisfactorily put in order; in fact for a job so little supervised the whole thing had been well done. He thought that, looking up at the back of the house in the moonlight, and felt grateful to Plant and whoever it was whom Plant had employed. Then he saw, at the bottom of the house wall, under the parlour window, a patch of whiteness, and thinking it was a piece of paper or rag overlooked in the clearing, went to pick it up and found his hand touching the cool, drooped heads of a clump of snowdrops.

Snowdrops! His mind jolted. On Monday he was due to go to Cambridge again. The flowers reminded him

184

because the front path of the house where he lodged there was lined with them, and his landlady, seeing him off on that grey November morning, had said cheerfully that they would be in bloom when she saw him again. Now he looked down at the vague white patch, reckoned the date and realised that he would have to go to Cambridge on Monday. This was Thursday. Tomorrow he must drive a load out for Plant. Then on Saturday he must install Letty in the house. She must be there safe and contented before he went away.

A wry, acid little voice which of late had occasionally made itself heard in his mind asked why, since he had planned to get Letty out of Mrs. Rowan's clutches and the house was now completely ready for occupation, the sight of the flowers and the realisation of the need for action within forty-eight hours should have been such a shock. And he knew then that he dreaded the moment of utter frankness which the revelation of his project must entail. He wanted to get Letty out of the Coffee House, but he didn't want to talk about his reasons. He wanted to pick her up, just as one would a doll which was in danger of being trodden on, and put her in a safe place.

But Letty wasn't a doll. Dolls were for children.

He stopped, and with quick rough plucking movements of his hands gathered a bunch of the snowdrops, bruising and dropping almost as many as he culled. They should stand on the parlour table and wait until the night after tomorrow, and then Letty should see them.

CHAPTER
SIXTEEN

On Friday, before going out to Plant's place, he went into the Coffee House and was bold enough to make a bid for Letty's attention without the pretence that he had come just to drink coffee.

"Letty, there's something very special that I want to show you. Ask your aunt if you can come out tomorrow evening for an hour. I'll call for you at the back at about eight o'clock."

"I'll ask. But I don't think she'll let me. Saturday's very busy, you know. And somehow I haven't done anything right this week at all."

"What do you mean? Have you broken something, or offended her somehow?"

"I don't know," said Letty in a sudden rush of confidence. "No, I haven't broke anything. But everything I do or say seems to be wrong."

"Would you rather I asked her. I will."

"Oh no. Anybody'd think I was afraid of her. I'll ask, but I don't think she'll let me. Are you taking coffee?"

"Not tonight. I haven't time. But I shall expect you to be ready tomorrow at eight o'clock. And if she doesn't let you come I shall tackle her myself."

Letty's eyelashes met and mingled and slowly untangled themselves and revealed a glance which there was no understanding. Her lips curved in a perfunctory smile as she said "Goodnight" and turned away. There was something dispirited about the set of her shoulders, from behind, and he had a feeling of the unwilling satisfaction with which one greets proof of an evil prognostication coming true. Now, he thought, they're getting tired of deceiving her and are changing their attitude towards her — or else she's seeing through them at last. And she's miserable, poor little Letty. He would have minded more but for the thought that within twenty-four hours she would be cut adrift from them for ever. But for the thought of the house in the background, ready, waiting, he would have known an uprush of anxiety for fear that Letty would do anything to restore herself to favour. Tonight he was armoured against dread. But he couldn't allow Letty to walk away so miserably. He caught up with her and said, "Cheer up, Letty, you'll like what I have to show you, I promise you." She gave him another polite, perfunctory smile, but no interest or curiosity lightened her eyes.

He walked out to Plant's farm thinking that God had been exceptionally good to him after all. He had learned of Mrs. Rowan's foulness on the very night when he had become equipped to deal with it; and he had the house ready for Letty at the very moment when she had ceased to be enamoured of the Coffee House. Things had worked out so well that one could only recognise and be grateful for Providential intervention.

Letty went to ask leave to walk out with Doctor Shadbolt hoping that Aunt Thirza would reply with an unequivocal "No." She asked, not because she wanted to go for a walk or to see anything that he might possibly show her, but for two reasons of her own, widely diverse. She was deeply sentimental about Humphrey; his original act of kindness and his subsequent behaviour had inspired her gratitude and, in a way, her respect. If she could have paid off her debt to him by any act of service she would have done it gladly, but his obvious desire to serve her made her uncomfortable, more indebted and conscience stricken. Conscience stricken because it seemed to expose a fault in her very nature that she should regard his touch and his kiss with the same distaste as that with which every other man in the world — save one — inspired in her. It made her quite sick to think that once out with him, away from the protective company of other people, he would again say that he loved her, and attempt to kiss her, and that she would be obliged to repel him. But she was driven to ask for leave to go with him because not to do so would seem so mean after all his kindness to her, giving her food on the coach, giving her the necklet, making her look important by saying that she had saved Plant's life . . .

Her other reason for asking was even more confused. She had been long enough in the Coffee House and knew enough about its standards to understand that a girl's worth was measured by the amount of masculine attention she could attract. That had never been stated, either frankly or by implication, but it touched and coloured everything in the Rowan household. One's underclothes, for example, might be a mass of tatters, but money could always be found for ribbons, new dresses, things which men could see and admire. Cathy, in every possible way, was superior to Susie, kinder, more industrious, much more sensible, but Susie held sway in the house and was her mother's favourite because she took more trouble to please and attract men.

Letty knew that she could have as much attention as she chose, and a good deal of the superficial part of her nature longed for it; yet the slightest advance from any customer, either at the back or front of the house, filled her with terror and repulsion because it roused again the slavering, red-eyed beast which lurked in the tangled undergrowth of childhood memory. Humphrey's touch and kiss, even a certain look in his eyes, could stir the same repulsion, but not quite the same terror because she felt him susceptible to her will; added to the repulsion however was a sickness of self-hatred rooted in a tenderness that was not sufficient, a gratitude denied and a genuine feeling mocked by a false one.

But to the Rowans Humphrey was a man, a follower, an admirer, and she knew, obscurely, that the invitation to go out with him would give her standing in their eyes. Aunt Thirza might not allow her to go, but she would be pleased to know that she had attracted the invitation. Letty knew that on the former occasion she had been gratified, though obdurant.

So she chose a moment when her aunt and both her cousins were present, and then made her request, feeling some of the satisfaction of a known miser who makes, publicly, a single generous gesture, or of a pervert who is once in the position to say — you see I am quite normal. But behind the satisfaction lay the hope, almost the comfortable certainty that her aunt would refuse to give permission.

She was disappointed. The crescent smile curved Mrs. Rowan's upper lip and her voice was gracious as she said that Letty might go. The girls began to discuss what she should wear, for although she now had several dresses her outdoor clothes had not been replaced. Cathy offered her fur cape, Susie a pair of gloves. They were, just as she had anticipated, pleased with her; and she tried to conceal her disappointment and her creeping sick dread behind an affectation of pleasure.

When she had gone to bed Mrs. Rowan said, "Well, we'll see what a moonlight walk will do!"

They walked through the churchyard and emerged into the lane at its lower end. The moon had risen, and against the luminous sky the leafless trees looked like black lace, sequinned with stars. They spoke very little, Letty because she was shy and ill-at-ease, Humphrey because he was filled with tremulous excitement. It had all been so easy at the end. Letty had been ready punctually and they had come away, closing the door behind them. She would never go back. Ever since

November he had been planning and scheming for this moment. He had thought of it so often that the words "get her away from that place" had taken on the tasteless smoothness of a well-worn proverb. And now he had done it. Here they were, walking through the moonlight to the place which he had found for her. He had won. He had staked everything that mattered to him, his profession, his reputation, his safety, even his sleep — and he had won.

There now remained just the business of making Letty see things from his standpoint, but at the moment that seemed easy. He felt that he had an ally in the little house. No woman could see it, he thought, and not want to own it. He was content to walk in silence, with Letty so close beside him on the narrow footpath that the soft fur of her cape rubbed against his elbow and he could smell the faint sweet perfume which, had he but known it, arose from Susie's scented gloves.

But Letty found the silence oppressive, although she could not, for some time, think of any light, chattering thing to say. Half way down the short hill she did speak:

"What is this that you want to show me?" and even then the words didn't come out right. They sounded rather peevish and demanding.

"You'll see," said Humphrey happily. They were near enough now to their destination for him to see the window protruding over the path, its panes glittered with moonlight.

"We're there," he said, as they reached it, and there was a catch in his voice.

"Are we going to see somebody?"

"No. Nobody lives here yet. But it's all ready to live in and I thought you'd like to look at it." He took out the key and fitted it to the door.

"But we can't go in somebody's house when they aren't there."

"This house we can," said Humphrey as the door swung back. "I know the man it belongs to." He stepped down into the long passage which led from the front door to the parlour at the back, and reached out a hand to guide Letty in. This time her recoil was unmistakable.

"I mustn't go into an empty house with you. And in the dark. It would look bad."

"Nobody's looking," said Humphrey. "And I've got candles. Letty, surely you aren't afraid . . . of me."

He felt so sure that everything would be all right in a moment that he laid his hand boldly on her arm and pulled her down into the passage and pushed the door closed. Then he lighted a candle and said, "Come along, it's this way. Now stand there a moment, I want to light up this room so that you see it properly."

"Don't leave me in the dark," said Letty, quite vehemently.

"All right. Here, you hold this and stand there for a moment. I'm only just going into this room." He gave her the candle and opened the parlour door.

He had set the candles ready, two in little blue china sticks on the mantelpiece, two in pewter stands on top of the cupboard, and two more in rather thin, battered silver ones on the table, flanking the snowdrops in the tumbler of water. He wanted the room to strike Letty in its full perfection, so although impatient of the delay, he waited for a second until the candles were burning clearly, looking about the room as he waited. It was beautiful. It hadn't got dusty and the flowers hadn't withered. It looked just as he had wanted it to look. He went to the door and found Letty pressed up against the passage wall, the candle held out stiffly before her.

"There's a funny feeling about this house," she said. "I don't like it."

"Ah, you wait a minute. Now . . . *look!*"

She stood just inside the doorway and gave a rapid, searching glance about the room as though she were looking for something unusual and peculiar, not ordinarily found in parlours. Failing to find it, she looked at Humphrey doubtfully, questioningly. He was staring at her with an expression of fatuous pleasure and anticipation.

"Well," he asked, "what do you think of it?"

"You mean the room? The whole room?" He nodded. "Oh, it's nice. A nice little room." She gave a slight shudder. "Isn't it cold, though."

"It hasn't had a fire for some days. But that's easily remedied."

He reached down one of the candles and tilted it to the paper and sticks which he had put ready in the grate.

"You mustn't light other people's fires," said Letty uneasily.

"This fire I may." He was tempted to tell her the truth then, but the success of his plan depended, he felt, upon her showing some admiration and enthusiasm for the house. But of course she couldn't do that while she was worrying about their right to be there.

"It's quite all right, Letty, honestly. Nobody'll mind us being here. Nobody'll come." A long tongue of flame began to lick at the wood and he rose from his knees.

"Try the sofa, Letty. It's very comfortable. And a pretty cover, don't you think?"

"Yes. It's very pretty." She stayed in her defensive, dubious attitude just inside the door.

He opened the cupboard. "Look. Everything to hand." He displayed the tea-set which he had chosen. It wasn't new, there were only four cups left, and one of those was a little chipped, but it was made of thin fine china, white, with a full-blown rose painted on the outside and a bud on the inside of each cup. The teapot was round and low and fat, a comfortable shape, and had roses on each side.

"There's tea and everything in the kitchen," he said. "When the fire is brighter I'll make you some tea. It'll be a change for me to wait on you."

"Oh, I mustn't stop," said Letty quickly. "I've got to be back in an hour. Aunt Thirza was very firm about that. And now I've seen . . . what you wanted to show me I think we ought to go."

"But you haven't seen half. Come and look at the kitchen."

He took up a candle and went to the door. Letty drew away as he passed her, and then, dubiously, fearfully, as though she were humouring a dangerous lunatic, followed.

194

"You see, everything clean and bright. And a big window. It looks out into the garden . . ."

"Yes, it's very nice," Letty agreed, looking round and noticing nothing.

"And now I'll show you upstairs."

Letty said sharply, "I'm not going upstairs!" Her eyes took on an expression at once startled, suspicious, and scared, but her mouth set in a line of derision as though, when it opened again it would be to say, "I'm not such a fool as that!"

It took a second or two for the significance of her refusal and her expression to reach his innocent, romantic, absorbed mind. When it did he was shocked.

"Letty darling . . . surely you don't think, you couldn't think . . ." He saw suddenly that this whole scheme for surprising her had failed. The happily planned, carefully cherished secret must now be revealed, not as a climax to a mounting scale of excited, envious admiration — (Who does this lovely little house belong to? You, darling, you!) — but as an antidote to a horrible suspicion.

He said in such a gruff, short way that Letty might have been justified in thinking him angered by her refusal to accompany him upstairs:

"Come back into the sitting-room. I've got to tell you something."

"I'd rather go home. You can tell me on the way back."

"I want to tell it to you here. Letty, don't look so frightened. Have I ever done or said anything to frighten you? Don't look at me as though I were Taffy.

Now you sit on the sofa by the fire and I'll sit here. No, sit down properly, as though you were at home. This is your home, Letty. Your very own. I got it together for you. The house and everything in it is yours. It's all ready to live in as you could see by the kitchen. All you have to do is to stay here and I'll go back to the Coffee House and fetch anything you want brought away, and explain to your aunt that you're not going to live there any more."

She looked at him as though she had been pole-axed. Apart from stunned stupefaction there was no expression on her face at all. He had expected surprise, some protest, some incredulity, and was prepared to deal with any, or all of them. But the dumb blankness of her face found him at a loss because it gave no clue to her feelings and offered him nothing with which to deal.

"I've given you too much of a surprise. I'm sorry, darling. I thought a *happy* surprise couldn't hurt anyone. You're not going to faint, are you? Would you like some water?" Only syncope, he thought, could account for that utter blankness, for the deadliness of her pallor. She shook her head.

"No, I'm all right." She paused. "But whatever made you think of doing anything so crazy?"

"Do you think it was crazy? It isn't really, you know. Look, Letty, you know, in your heart, that the Coffee House isn't the sort of place that you should be living in. You knew that from the first. You asked me whether it was a respectable place when we were talking on the coach. I couldn't say anything about it then because I couldn't think of anywhere else for you to go. But as soon as I could I offered you to go to Miss Pendle's, and that wasn't very suitable. Since then I've thought of lots of other things, and then I saw this house empty, and that seemed just right. You can live here and just spend the time as you wish and be happy and independent. And you needn't mind about Mrs. Rowan," he went on, as Letty did not answer, "I'll go back and put things plainly to her. And if she did come after you, you could lock the door and refuse to let her in."

"But why should I do that? My aunt's always been very kind to me. Whatever would she think?"

Now, he knew, was the moment to tell her what Plant had said. By exposing Mrs. Rowan he could justify his own apparently preposterous suggestion.

"She may seem to be kind to you . . ." he began, and the next words stuck in his throat. He couldn't look at Letty and tell her that shocking and appalling thing. The very thought of it smirched her innocency and — in a subtle way — insulted his manhood. As though they were not people at all but one insentient tool with two halves, a male and a female.

"She may seem to be kind to you, but she isn't the proper person for you to live with, and her house isn't the proper place. You *know* why, Letty. You said yourself you didn't want to be like Cathy and Susie, and you must see that unless you get away that's what you will be, in the end."

"I shouldn't. I'd never be like that. And they know it now. They've been very good to me, very understanding. And you see things differently when you live with people and find out how good and kind they are, though their ideas are different. I can live with them and keep myself to myself. And it isn't for me to set myself up in judgment when they've been so good to me."

He recognised this new tolerance as a seed of eventual corruption. She was looking at him earnestly now, really believing what she was saying, believing that she could go on living in that house and remain unsullied. The candlelight touched her long lashes and thin, smooth childlike brows with gentle gold, and he thought that he had never seen her look so innocent and young.

"But think, darling. Wouldn't you like to live here, in your own house, and lead your own life. I'd see you never lacked for anything. I'd look after you so carefully. I'm sure you'd be happy."

Her eyes looked — there was no other word for it — trapped, like those of a person who has suddenly become faced with a situation of the most intolerable embarrassment, and can see no way out of it.

"You mean . . . I should live here . . . all alone?"

"For the time being, yes. Later on, when my articles are run out . . . and if you ever felt that you could . . . we could get married. But that's all a long way off and you needn't let it affect you now. Just be guided and persuaded by me and say you'll stay. I'll make a cup of

198

tea and leave you with it while I go for your things and tell them at the Coffee House."

With quite startling suddenness tears filled her eyes and began to spill down her face.

"Darling," he said, "why are you crying? What is there to cry for? I want you to be happy. I wouldn't make you cry for all the world."

"I know," she gulped. "That's why I'm crying. Because you did it all for me and you want me to stay and I can't."

"Why not?"

"I daren't."

"Because of Mrs. Rowan? I'll settle her."

"No, not that. I daren't stay here alone. I've never gone to bed in a house all by myself. I daren't do it. I shouldn't dare go to bed or put the candle out. I never did dare to be in a house all by myself after it was dark."

"But you could lock the door. And there're neighbours both sides. There's nothing to be frightened of, darling."

By this time she was crying violently, like a terrified child.

"Don't make me stay. I daren't. Sometimes I'm right scared to go upstairs when all the others are in the kitchen. I wouldn't stay in a house by myself all night, not for a hundred pounds."

"But what are you frightened of?"

"I don't know. I'm just frightened. I'm sorry. It's a nice little house and I know you meant it all for the best, but I daren't stay all by myself."

"All right, of course I couldn't think of making you. Look, darling. Suppose tomorrow I find a little girl to live with you and help with the work and do the errands and sleep here at night . . . then will you come?"

Letty drew in her breath and checked her sobbing. "I'll think about it. I'll see."

He chose to ignore the inconclusiveness. "I'll take you back now. You'll know not to mention the plan, won't you. And tomorrow I'll call for you at the same time and bring you here — to stay."

"All right. You aren't cross, are you? You've been so kind to me. I don't want to make you cross."

"I'm not cross. I'd never be cross with you. I am a little disappointed, but I suppose one night won't matter. And it'll all be arranged by this time tomorrow."

He rose and blew out all the candles save one which he saved to guide them along the passage. The little room receded into a dusk made rosy by the firelight; the bowl of snowdrops was just a pale blur upon the dark surface of the table. A sense of having failed in what he had made his mission oppressed Humphrey, and he said again, this time to himself, that everything would be all right tomorrow.

Letty walked ahead of him along the passage and halted just inside the door. He blew out the candle and stood the stick down and was about to reach out for the door handle when something happened. His arm, stretched towards the door, seemed of its own volition to curve and draw Letty nearer. The warmth, softness, frailty and closeness of her went to his head. The evil thing which Mrs. Rowan had planned clamoured in his mind, overpoweringly suggestive.

His whole body seemed to move towards her under the thrust and pull of a force he had never experienced before, and which was at once terrifying and delightful. All that was gentle and romantic and sentimental in his emotion towards her deserted him. His mouth moved savagely against hers and he clasped her brutally, as though by mere pressure he could attain some degree of the unity for which his whole being clamoured.

For Letty the moment was one of horror made manifest. The same hot, searching mouth, the same hard groping hands, the same grim deadliness of purpose. It was useless to scream, the child had screamed, piercing agonised screams whose sound had never wholly died away though the thing had happened years and years ago. Struggling was useless too. It only resulted in more hurt. Just bear it, bear it, try to take your mind away, try not to notice, not to feel anything. The end would come, it had before. And this wasn't some strange dirty man, it was Humphrey, usually so kind. Stay still, try to take your mind away, try not to feel.

The mad, ravening moment passed and instantly the violence of his feelings was diverted into shame and self-hatred. It was assault, nothing less. Letty's closed mouth, trying to avert itself, her stiff, unresisting yet unyielding body made his action an assault. He dropped his arms to his sides, drew a deep breath, and said:

"Oh God, Letty, I *am* sorry. I don't know what came over me. I must have gone mad. Letty, I'll never do it again. You must try to forgive me. It's just that I love you so very much."

She said nothing, but he heard the door handle rattle as she fumbled with it. He reached over and turned it for her. She slipped past him into the street and began to walk away, rapidly. He locked the door and hurried after her.

"Letty, please, you must listen. I wouldn't hurt you for the world, you must know that. I just went mad for a moment. I'm so sorry, I just can't tell you. I hate myself. Do please try to forgive me." His voice was piteously humble.

"All right. Don't talk about it."

"But I must. There's tomorrow to think of. Look, Letty, for God's sake don't hold that against me and let it upset our plan. I daresay you think I'm no better than the others, but at least I do love you, and I swear that that sort of thing'll never happen again. I didn't know I was such a beast, but now I do know and I'll be on the watch. And listen, I'll have a serving girl there for you tomorrow night if I spend the whole of tomorrow looking for her, and I'll just walk as far as the door with you and never come into the house unless you ask me to. Letty, if I thought that after this you stayed in the Coffee House because you felt you couldn't trust me, I should go utterly crazy. I couldn't bear it. Do please promise me that you'll stick to our arrangement and be ready when I come for you tomorrow night."

"All right," Letty said again. She walked even faster.

"And you will forgive me?"

"Oh, yes."

She didn't want to talk about it or be reminded of it. She walked so quickly through the churchyard that she was almost running. All she wanted was to get into the Coffee House once more and feel safe. When they reached the back gate she opened it and would have been inside before Humphrey could stop her, since he dared not now put so much as a restraining finger upon her, but he cried out "Letty" in a voice of such agony that despite herself she halted.

"You know that I'm sorry and I didn't mean any harm, don't you. And it'll all be right tomorrow. The girl'll be there. You won't let it make any difference, will you, Letty?"

"No," she said.

"And do you forgive me?"

"Oh yes."

"Goodnight, then . . ."

"Goodnight."

There safe at last! She ran across the little cobbled yard and flung herself into the kitchen and burst into a flood of hysterical tears.

"Why, Letty," said Mrs. Rowan. "Whatever's the matter? What has happened?" She offered her shoulder as a refuge, and across Letty's bowed head she and Susie exchanged significant, satisfied glances.

Humphrey went home in a mood of self-disgust, self-reproach and self-hatred which lasted until well on in the next day and gave him the worst night he could remember. Every vestige of common sense deserted him, until finally he was accusing himself of luring Letty into an empty house and there attempting to rape her. After that his self-esteem could sink no lower and very gradually the tide of feeling turned. He hadn't hurt her, and she had forgiven him and had said that she would come out again, so she wasn't very much frightened either. That was one solace. Later on in the day he found it possible to think that he must remember it when he was inclined to be intolerant — as he now saw he had been in the past — of other men's conduct. That kind of thing could happen almost against one's will — and if Letty had made one responsive gesture . . . He thought that several times with a feeling of thankfulness that thanks to her restraint he had been saved from behaving even worse than he had; and then all at once it evoked a different feeling. The idea of Letty, loving and responsive, was almost unbearable in its loveliness.

He saw that he was at his best when he had something to worry about and to work for. He must take himself in hand. He'd get Letty installed and then settle down to hard study and keep his mind occupied until he had passed his examination.

In this mood he visited the local Poor Farm and picked out from a proffered dozen of little starvelings a serving wench for Letty.

CHAPTER
SEVENTEEN

He was in the kitchen of the Coffee House just before eight o'clock. He had suddenly remembered, in the middle of the afternoon, that he had not told Plant of his impending absence for a week, so now he hoped that Letty would be able to come out directly, and that would give him time to deliver her at the house, return and pick up her luggage and explain to Mrs. Rowan — which might be a lengthy as well as unpleasant business — walk to Southgate again and then go out to Plant's farm.

But Letty was not, as he had hopefully anticipated, dressed and waiting for him. There was nobody in the kitchen at all. The whole of the back of the house seemed curiously quiet and deserted, yet he had a feeling, disconcerting because it was so unreasonable, that his arrival and entry had not been unobserved. There were so many doors opening into the kitchen, and some of them had little glass panes set in them so that the passages and apartments beyond might borrow a little light, and although he had heard no door close softly, and seen no shadow behind the panes, he felt that he had been watched for and that now, in some hidden region, his coming was being announced.

He dismissed it as fancy and stood for a moment intending, if no sign of life became apparent, to call Letty by name. But before he could do so one of the doors opened and Mrs. Rowan came into the kitchen. She was wearing her black dress and the little white cap with the black ribbon in it, and looked just as calm and dignified as usual, and as gracious; but he knew the moment he saw her that his simple pleasant plan for walking Letty away from the Coffee House was not going to proceed without some difficulty. Oh, if only she had agreed to stay in the little house last night. That was the God-sent chance, and perhaps it was too much to hope for to think that it might come again so soon.

"Good evening, Doctor Shadbolt," Mrs. Rowan said in an ordinary voice. "Just come in here for a moment, will you? I want to talk to you."

To say that Letty can't go out two evenings running. Well, he would plead, make his forthcoming absence an excuse, get round her somehow. Quite cheerfully he followed Mrs. Rowan into a small room opening from the kitchen, a room he had never seen before, a dismal airless little apartment furnished with a sofa, a hard upright chair and a table which took up too much of the scanty space.

"Sit down," said Mrs. Rowan, pointing to the sofa. She took the chair which gave her the advantage of being able to look down upon him. She folded her hands in her lap and proceeded to look down upon him, calmly, speculatively, and for such a long time that he grew nervous and was himself driven to break the silence.

"Are you going to say that Letty can't come out tonight? I know I took her away last night, and that you're busy. But I have to go to Cambridge tomorrow and I'll be away a week . . . so I thought . . . I mean I hoped that you wouldn't mind, just for once."

She did not reply immediately, but continued to study him as though he were a specimen of some strange creature which she had never before encountered, and about which it was essential that she should learn all that her eyes could tell her. At last she said, in quite a gentle way:

"Doctor Shadbolt, you must know that I can never allow Letty to be alone in your company again." She waited and watched the effect of that sentence, while Humphrey, knowing that something had gone badly wrong, felt his face begin to redden and his heart quicken at the prospect of a quarrel. It was only a little premature, but he had meant to face Mrs. Rowan when Letty was safe in the Southgate house; at the moment she was still in this one, and that made everything very different. "I'm astonished," Mrs. Rowan went on, "that you should dare come here this evening at all. I can only assume that you trusted to Letty's silence. I may tell you that Letty has no secrets from me, and that I have heard all about last evening's events. Does that surprise you?"

It did. Her opening sentence had warned him, but not of that. He could imagine her finding out, guessing, suspecting; but that Letty should have *told* her . . .

"What did Letty say?" he asked, forming the words clumsily because his mouth had gone dry.

"She told me everything. She came in last evening in a state of complete collapse and told me about your astonishing attempt at abduction. I'm not easily shocked, Doctor Shadbolt, but when I think of my trust in you, and of Letty's youth, and of the really appalling results which might have arisen, I must say I am filled with horror. At the same time, I can't help wondering *how* you dared to take such a risk with your own reputation. One would have thought that if you had lost all respect for Letty's you would have been careful of your own good name."

His face was flaming by this time, and his discomfiture was increased by the realisation that he must be looking the very picture of guilt-discovered, the would-be seducer exposed. At the back of his mind he knew that Mrs. Rowan's attitude was false to the core, that the feelings she was expressing were all assumed, that in a few words he could, in turn, unmask her, and that, above all, he was innocent of the charge she was pretending to bring against him. Any one of these factors, steadily considered, was sufficient to steady him and give him the advantage, but for the moment he could not avail himself of any calm thought because the attack had been so sudden and he could not help wondering about Letty. Had she misunderstood his motives, in spite of his explanations; or had she blurted out the simple straightforward story which Mrs. Rowan had promptly seized upon and twisted? And what was Letty thinking of him at this moment. If she believed her aunt there was little wonder that she was prostrate with shock. But thinking wasn't going to answer Mrs.

Rowan or restore him to the appearance of self-respect. He must say something quickly. And he, like his accuser, must remain calm and in possession of his temper. He said quietly:

"Did Letty tell you *why* I proposed that she should leave this house and allow me to look after her?"

Mrs. Rowan raised one hand slightly and flicked it, palm uppermost in an outward direction, as though brushing away a trivial irrelevance.

"Oh that!" she said. "Some nonsense about my house not being a fitting place to live. Don't mistake me, Doctor Shadbolt, I do not resent that. I know what is said of me, and I might not blame you for subscribing to the general belief, even though you have been made free of my house and should, perhaps, know better. No, what I resent is the hypocrisy of your behaviour. Had you offered the child an alternative form of a respectable home with respectable people I should have believed in your good faith — though I should have resisted your action and deplored your credulity. But to say that my home is not the place for Letty, and then to attempt to establish her in your house, as your mistress, does seem to me to be a piece of sorry humbug."

Anger began to replace discomfiture, but he forced himself to speak calmly.

"Mrs. Rowan, you should know which of us is given to humbug. Before ever Letty came into this house I knew that it wasn't the proper place for her; and she knew, or suspected it, too. Weeks ago I did offer her the alternative of a respectable home in a respectable house, but it involved an employment for which she had no taste, and by that time you had so worked upon her that she no longer thought a change desirable. Since then I have tried repeatedly to find her another home, and I have failed, so I made one. There was never at any time — and Letty must know that, however much you have confused her — any suggestion that she should be my mistress. The thought never entered my head. You invented it so that you might turn Letty against me and pretend that *you* were protecting her from *me*. Not that any of this matters now. I've found a little companion for Letty, and now I have come to take her to the house. With, or without, your permission, Mrs. Rowan, I intend to do that, tonight."

Their eyes met in a long, combative stare. Humphrey's were angry and challenging, Mrs. Rowan's almost expressionless, and when she spoke her voice was flat and without emphasis, rather as though she were being forced to pursue a subject of which she had tired.

"I see," she said, "that I shall have to speak plainly to you, Doctor Shadbolt. Letty is my niece — so far as I know she has no other living relative. I am her guardian and she is a minor. Neither tonight nor at any other time shall I allow her out of this house without the company of one of my daughters. I *forbid* . . ." — she did stress that word, and repeat it — "forbid you to make any further attempt to talk to her or to see her. Have I made that plain? I want you to go away from my house and to keep away. If you do that I promise you that no word of last night's escapade will ever reach the ears of the town's gossips. But if you persist in this insane notion of removing Letty from my care I shall see that news of it gets abroad, and you must see that such a report would injure you, perhaps irretrievably."

"But I don't mind who knows that I tried to take Letty away from this place," Humphrey said. "You may print it in the *Post* for all I care. Most people would agree that I was right to try to remove an innocent young girl from a brothel."

He used the word deliberately, hoping that it would sting Mrs. Rowan and rouse her to some display of feeling which would shatter her intolerable assumption of superiority. But she only said:

"Would they? I should say that it was far more likely that people would ask why you should bother to take a girl out of a brothel in order to make an attempt on her virtue. In fact, isn't it the clearest proof of my integrity that before you could seduce my niece you must first remove her from my establishment?"

The argument was propounded gently, with no obvious sign of triumph, but the cold logic of it was triumphant and left him speechless. Properly handled — as he knew it would be — last night's story could be made to redound to Mrs. Rowan's credit and to his disrepute. And oddly enough the bitterest thing about the prospect of the story being bruited abroad was the fact that, as an abduction, it had been unsuccessful. She could, if she liked, make him look a fool as well as a knave. He saw all at once how it was that men cleverer and more experienced than himself had met their match in this really horrible woman. The idea that he, too, had been defeated by her fanned his anger, but still he controlled himself, and resisting a strong impulse to shout at her all that Plant had told him he said, as calmly as he could:

"Before I made any bargain of that nature, Mrs. Rowan, I should want to see Letty, and talk to her, *alone*. Can I do that, now?"

"Letty is in no condition to see or talk to anyone. But I assure you that we talked the whole thing out last night when she returned in a state of pitiable distress, and she said repeatedly that it was her wish not to see you again. You *must* realise, Doctor Shadbolt, that if Letty had seen eye to eye with you either about this house or about your intentions she would, at this moment, be in the house which you offered her last night. It may be very distasteful for you to accept but, it is a fact, Letty trusts me and distrusts you. You'll do no good by seeing her. Let the thing end here, and be thankful that it has ended in this manner. On the whole, you know, you've been far luckier than you deserve."

"I mean to see Letty," he said stubbornly. "Since my reputation seems to depend upon your charity I might as well risk it further. Either I see Letty now or I raise such a row in this house that the constables'll come running."

Mrs. Rowan regarded him with eyes infinitely experienced and gave a little short sigh. But she rose to her feet.

"A pot-house brawl of the kind you threaten would be the very worst thing for Letty in her present state.

212

You may see her. You may ask her whether she wishes to live in your house or mine, and whether she wishes to continue friendship with you. But you will kindly accept her answer as final and not attempt any argument or recriminations. She isn't very robust, as you surely have seen for yourself, and last night's business has upset her seriously. Come this way." She led the way back into the kitchen and up the stairs, through a labyrinth of little passages to a landing upon the left of which a door stood ajar. She pushed it wide and said, "Letty, are you awake?"

Letty's voice, gentle and drowsy, said, "Yes, Aunt Thirza. Come in."

Mrs. Rowan stepped into the room and Humphrey followed. There was a narrow bed covered with a patchwork quilt and with a high pile of pillows against which Letty relaxed like a doll which some child has put, open-eyed, to sleep. Her face was very pale, her eyes wide open and extraordinarily dark and set in a stare. Her brown hair poured sleekly down over her shoulders, and her hands lay motionless upon the cover of the bed. The neck of her nightdress ended in a little frill at the throat, and her shoulders were covered by a white shawl.

"Now there is no need for you to upset yourself, Letty. You've only to answer two questions," said Mrs. Rowan. As she spoke she stepped to one side of the bed and Humphrey, who had been behind her, stood revealed in the light of the three-branched candlestick which stood on the chest of drawers. He saw Letty's face change — horribly. She had been staring at her aunt with eyes which were wide open and yet slumbrous, her whole face relaxed and peaceful. At sight of him her face seemed to shrink and stiffen and her eyes filled with fright.

"Oh," she said, "you promised! You said you'd explain."

"I tried," said Mrs. Rowan smoothly, "but Doctor Shadbolt couldn't believe that you didn't want to see him. So I thought the best thing was for you to tell him so yourself."

It was one large, rather awkward body, half man, half boy, which stepped a pace nearer the bed, and it was one voice which said, tenderly, tentatively, "Letty," as the one body moved. But there were three Humphrey Shadbolts in the room. There was the lover, aware of the shining hair, the sweet line of the throat above the little frill, the soft immature swell of the bosom where the shawl fell away. For him it was a moment of pangs and dreams. There was the bothered young man with a mission, hastily mustering his arguments and wondering how much he could say that would convince the girl's mind without causing a nervous upheaval. And there was the professional man taking note of the things which were familiar and unmistakable.

It was he who spoke. "You've been giving her opium," he said accusingly. Mrs. Rowan raised a shoulder, unperturbed, weary.

"I gave her Doctor Bulmer's Blue Pills. A reputable anodyne and sedative."

"Not in excess."

For the first time Mrs. Rowan allowed her voice to sharpen.

"Really, Doctor Shadbolt, this is beside the point. I hadn't the advantage of medical advice, I simply did what I could for a girl who was in a state of nerves. Will you, before we are all in a similar state, say what you want to say and have done?"

The bothered young man came to the surface and said:

"I want to talk to Letty alone."

But he was summarily dismissed too. Letty gave a kind of moan and moving one hand as though it were very heavy, reached for Mrs. Rowan's skirt. "Aunt Thirza, I don't feel well enough to talk to anybody."

"Not to me, Letty?" asked the lover. "I don't know what they've told you or what they've said against me, but if you'll think back, Letty, you'll know that there's no reason to be afraid of me."

Without giving Letty time to reply, Mrs. Rowan said:

"Will you answer Doctor Shadbolt's questions, Letty, if I remain in the room?"

Letty seemed to brace herself. She pulled herself higher against the pillow and spoke in a firmer voice.

"I'm sorry about last night, but I don't want to talk about it any more."

"Listen, Letty. There's a little girl in the house now, getting everything ready for you, so you wouldn't be alone. I've got to go to Cambridge in the morning, and I shall be away for a week. I should like to think you were there before I left. If you can't walk I'll fetch the gig and drive you there. I won't attempt to come inside the house until we're married, and I'll marry you whenever you like. Does that convince you that anything she has said about my intentions is a foul lie? Letty, are you listening? You know why I can't leave you here, don't you? I don't want to upset you by going into it . . . Will you trust me and come away, *now*?"

The trapped desperate look which had been upon Letty's face the previous evening was there again. And as on the previous evening it presaged tears. They stood, like thick glass for a moment before the dilated pupils and then began to spill down her face.

"You both say such horrible things about each other," said Letty brokenly.

"Don't shed a tear over what is said about *me*," said Mrs. Rowan in quite a humorous voice. "All you have to do, Letty, is to decide whether you would like to live in the house Doctor Shadbolt took you to last night . . ." — she managed somehow to say the words so that the innocent, well-meant, happy little house became the abode of unmentionable evil — ". . . or to stay here with your cousins and me. That is simple, isn't it? Which would you rather do?"

For answer Letty began to sob. Through the sobs they could hear some words, "always so kind" and "hurt feelings".

"I've tried to be kind to you, certainly. But I assure you that if you desire to go, child, my feelings will suffer no hurt." Letty shook her head, so that some tears fell from her cheeks and eyelids like raindrops, and with one hand she pointed to Humphrey.

"Darling," he said quite violently, "it isn't a question of hurting my feelings: it's a question of what's best for you. I suppose I shall have to say it! I've tried not to. But it's the only thing that will make you understand. I can prove to you that all this kindness means nothing, and that she meant ill by you from the very first. And it isn't something I made up or imagined; it's a fact. Letty, you know Plant Driscoll . . ." He was past the point where one could consider the matter of petty ethics and pause to wonder whether what he was about to say was a breach of confidence, a thing dishonourable in a gentleman. The slight hesitation after the mention of Plant's name had nothing to do with that, for just then he would have said and done anything in the world to bring Letty to a clear sense of her own danger. Nevertheless, he did hesitate because to repeat what Plant had said shamed him; the words he must use were so crude and the whole thing seemed to reduce him from the status of an individual human being into a blind phallic tool.

So, as he spoke Plant's name the embarrassed scarlet which had been in his face once that evening and died away again, returned, and his voice faltered. He had no chance to observe the effect which the two words had upon Mrs. Rowan, he was looking at Letty. And as he braced himself to plunge on with the horrid disclosure and encouraged himself with the reflection that he had tried everything short of brutal frankness and now must resort to that, Letty began to cry in loud wild sobs and to beat her hands and throw her head from side to side against the pillows.

"Don't say it! Don't say it! I don't want to hear any more. Aunt Thirza, please take him away. I'm ill. My head has started again. I shall go mad. You'll drive me mad between you." She interspersed the words with demented cries and wild gestures which had in them the essence of madness. Mrs. Rowan, after a brief struggle, managed to get both Letty's hands within one of her own. With the other she tugged at the bell rope which hung beside the bed.

"It is obvious that this interview must end, Doctor Shadbolt. Be so good as to step outside. Letty, Letty, you really must control yourself. You'll do yourself harm. There is no need for this display. Lie down. Be still. I've rung for Cathy. Hush, hush, dear! They'll hear you downstairs."

Humphrey got as far as the door. Then, desperately, he turned.

"Letty, I'm going now. But I'll come back at the end of the week. When you're better, think things over. And remember everything shall be just as you want it to. And remember the house is ready and waiting for you. Goodnight."

He doubted whether she heard or took any notice. With a feeling of heavy defeat upon him he walked to the end of the landing. Cathy Rowan came running up the stairs, holding her long skirt knee high and panting as she ran. She passed him without seeming to see him and went in Letty's room, from which the sounds of sobs and cries, dominated by Mrs. Rowan's calm voice, still issued. In less than half a minute Mrs. Rowan came out and closed the door and stood on the landing smoothing her hair and resettling her cap.

"Well," she said, "that gives you your answer, doesn't it? Now I hope you will see your way to striking our bargain. You leave Letty entirely alone and we allow all this unhappy business to drop into oblivion."

Rage almost choked him.

"I'll never do that, Mrs. Rowan. I've failed with Letty tonight because you've poisoned her mind and drugged her body until she is almost demented. But I know why you got her here in the first place, and I know why you encouraged me to visit your house. And I warn you that if I come back at the end of next week and don't find Letty in a better state of health and of mind, I'll make public what I know. I'll start another inquiry. I'm far from finished, I assure you."

"I don't like being threatened," said Mrs. Rowan slowly. "But your threats are very empty. Letty came here because she was destitute, and I encouraged her friendship with you because you were the only man she seemed to like and to trust. Bad judgment, but she is very inexperienced. Why do you think that I should mind all that — and last night's sequel — being made public, Doctor Shadbolt?"

"Because your story isn't true. I can prove, by what you said yourself to a third person, that you picked on me to play a part in a very dirty game. With that, and with what I have seen myself of your establishment, I think I can make a case. Nobody else has ever been at the back of your house without a good reason for keeping silence about it. I have no such reason. Nothing matters to me now except Letty."

"If you intend to base your case on anything Plant Driscoll — I take it he was the *third person* you mention — has said about me you will make a fool of yourself. I can't imagine Plant giving evidence against me at a Church inquiry. No, I think not." For the first time in all the evening the crescent showed on her lip and she smiled, slowly, sardonically.

"He could be made to," said Humphrey recklessly.

"And you think you have the power to make him turn against . . . an old friend?"

"I know I have."

There was a short silence.

"Ah well," said Mrs. Rowan at last, "those who live longest see most, they say. We'll hope that when you return you will find Letty in good health and good spirits and in a mind to listen to your proposals. I'll see what I can do."

She began to walk swiftly down the stairs. Humphrey followed her, suddenly light-hearted. That last speech had been one of capitulation and promise. He'd made her see reason. The evening hadn't been entirely wasted.

CHAPTER
EIGHTEEN

As he walked out to Plant's farm he cherished his sense of triumph over Mrs. Rowan because it lay comfortably over the raw wound of the memory of Letty. Occasionally, however, the salve failed and painful thoughts attacked him. There was no doubt that he and Mrs. Rowan had been fighting for the possession of Letty just as two dogs might fight for a bone, and in the process it was the bone which had suffered. However, that was over now. Letty would recover from the effects of Doctor Bulmer's Blue Pills and find that her aunt had gone over to Humphrey's side. She would no longer be tugged in different directions by her fatal gratitude for kindness and her fear of hurting the feelings of those who had been kind. It was a thousand pities that the situation hadn't been clarified earlier. He should never have attempted to fight Mrs. Rowan with craft, he should have tackled her openly. On the other hand, there had been no point in making an enemy of her until he had somewhere for Letty to live, and he'd only had that since last evening.

It was rather unfortunate that his interview with Plant should come so soon after his match with Mrs. Rowan, for he was feeling raw-nerved and reckless, and Plant chose to be awkward.

The friendship for which he had hoped from Plant had never really come to anything, and their partnership in business and their collusion over the house had, in a peculiar way, made them less rather than more intimate. Over the house Plant had certainly been helpful and active and efficient, but rather in the hope of confusing Mrs. Rowan than of aiding Humphrey, time after time that truth had been made clear; and over the business of the smuggling Plant seemed under the recurrent necessity of showing that he was the master and Humphrey his man. Humphrey recognised the position and was willing to accept it unquestioningly, but Plant, rather as though he doubted his own ascendancy, emphasised it with ways that were maddening because they were so petty. And what Humphrey had come to tell him on this Sunday evening offered him an opportunity for asserting himself.

"I think you might at least have had the grace to give me a *little* longer notice," he said, when Humphrey had explained his forthcoming absence. That was reasonable enough, and Humphrey was apologetic.

"I know. It was very remiss of me. But I didn't realise it myself until Thursday."

"Thursday! Then why the hell didn't you tell me on Friday? You were here then."

"I know. I suppose I was thinking about something else. I am sorry. I should have told you about these visits to Cambridge in the first place."

"The devil you should! Before you'd taken the job. Before you'd taken the money."

"I know," Humphrey said for the third time. "But it's only five nights, I'll be back on Saturday, and I'll drive every night in the next week, if that will make up to you."

"Oh," Plant said, with irony. "Only five nights is it? And you'll be back on Saturday. Fat lot of good that is to me. I've a load coming in on Friday night. What about that?"

"Couldn't it be arranged for Saturday instead?"

"Loads," said Plant, with weary patience — explain to the child once more — "come when it's convenient for somebody slightly more important than you, my dear Humphrey, to send them. And you may remember that when I engaged you I did *mention* that loads arrived and had to be unloaded."

"That's true. I'm afraid I didn't think. And now I don't know what I can do about it. You see I have a lecture on Saturday morning. And I have so few, every minute in Cambridge is important to me."

"Lectures helped a great deal when you wanted money, didn't they? It's no use, Humphrey. The load comes in on Friday. And I told you that unloading is the trickiest business of all." He added with exaggerated thoughtfulness, "Maybe that's why you're shirking it."

"I am not shirking anything," said Humphrey rather loudly. "Are you sure they wouldn't hold the load back till Saturday? It doesn't seem so much to ask. Have you never asked them to alter a date?"

"Your ignorance is only exceeded by your egoism. The load will arrive on Friday and you will be here to help handle it. I don't let my partners just walk away when there's work to be done."

"No. They don't walk away, do they?" asked Humphrey. He looked at Plant's wrist as he spoke. Then he raised his eyes and saw that Plant's face had changed colour. A deep feeling of satisfaction settled upon him. It had, really, been a shot in the dark — or in the dusk — but it had gone home. And he'd known for some time that there was a flaw in Plant. He dabbled in a dangerous business, but he didn't enjoy danger: he did reckless, ruthless, criminal things, but he did not do them with the ease of, say, Mrs. Rowan. There was in him a streak of weakness as incongruous as his fastidious linen in the kitchen. He wouldn't be too difficult to handle, especially by anyone as desperate as Humphrey would be, if it ever came to the point.

"Not with thirty pounds unearned," said Plant, recovering his equanimity, plucking out the barb and returning it. "Not to mention certain favours. One would have thought that in a man of honour the matter of getting that house seen to would have inculcated some feeling of obligation."

"I'm not denying my obligation. I'm acutely aware of it. I merely asked whether the load couldn't arrive on Saturday. The fact is, Plant, you're so used to dealing with slippery people that you suspect slipperiness where it doesn't exist. I'll be here on Friday night since it's so important, and the day can't be altered."

224

"Then why all the jabber?" Plant asked sulkily. "And don't, for God's sake think you're doing me a favour. It's to your interest to get the stuff in and out again. With Letty Rowan round your neck you'll need money, won't you?"

At any other time Humphrey would have said that Letty was not yet "round his neck", told some part of the story, and given some idea of the position. But he thought that Plant's attitude had been, though not unjustified, too readily and too fully antagonistic, and he felt disinclined to talk to him.

"What time do you want me here?"

"About nine. I never know quite when they'll arrive, but it's best to be on the safe side."

"Very well, I'll be here at nine. And I'm sorry I didn't tell you sooner, and I'm sorry that I shall be away for the four nights."

"All right. Another time give me a word of warning." He brushed the whole thing aside. "Have a drink before you go."

"No thanks," said Humphrey.

Afterwards, walking home and reverting to his thoughts of Letty and Mrs. Rowan and his own behaviour last night, he was sorry that he had refused the drink. Among other things which the past three months had taught him was the virtue of alcohol as a softener of hard circumstance.

CHAPTER
NINETEEN

Next day he went to Cambridge — for the first time unwillingly, feeling that in the disturbed state of mind and feeling which had developed since his last visit, serious attention to lecture and study would be impossible. He had previously been conscious of the gulf that existed between this enclosed, academic world and himself, the outsider, and now it seemed to widen to absurdity. On other visits he had felt strange, seated among young students who had never served an apprenticeship, never risen at dawn to deal with a difficult confinement, or ridden ten miles in the rain to set a broken limb; but that had been only a difference of approach, of timing. Now he would, he felt, be wholly apart, marked by the experiences of the last weeks.

But he discovered, with astonishment and relief, that Cambridge had learned a magic all her own by which to focus the eyes anew, to remit, absolve and absorb. After his first lecture he emerged into the quiet grey street and realised that for a full two hours he had not once thought of Letty, or Plant, or the little house in Southgate. For an enlightened moment he acknowledged the power of thought over that of emotion, and while

the moment lasted everything save his profession —
and all that it implied — seemed a little tawdry, a little
unreal. He saw that this was his real life; the
dispassionate acquisition of knowledge, the equally
dispassionate business of putting such knowledge into
practice. And some rapidly maturing facet of his mind
presented him with the startling idea that his failure
both to leave Letty alone and to manage her
satisfactorily had its reason in his own nature and
personality; the very qualities which would, in time,
make him a good doctor, were against him as a knight
errant. Plant now, if he ever found himself in such a
situation, would deal with it without muddle or
distress.

But later on, after some hours of hard reading, he
experienced a revulsion of feeling and paid for his lapse
into academic detachment. As soon as he had blown
out his candle Letty seemed to be in the room with
him. Her pathetic smallness, her innocence, her awful
susceptibility to kindness, the soft sheen of her hair, the
flutter of those long lashes — each little detail of her
personal appearance and of her personality assaulted
him so sharply that he felt he must rise and make his
way, there and then, back to the Coffee House. It
seemed incredible that he should ever have walked out
of the place with nothing decided, nothing resolved. A
week was a long time, and in her unstable state of mind
and health she would be putty in Mrs. Rowan's hands.
Yet what could he have done more than he had done?
He'd offered to carry her out of the house — and she
had begun to cry; he'd offered to marry her and she

had cried harder. And he hadn't left her without a refuge, the house and the little maid were there waiting for her. For the first time since she had entered the Coffee House it was her own fault if she stayed there . . . The first time? What about Miss Pendle's?

There was no end to the tangle of thought. He fumbled about in it until he was exhausted and then fell into troubled sleep.

Once or twice during that curtailed week he experienced again the refreshing sensation of living in a cool and orderly world where emotion was of less importance than the process of thought. But such moments always passed, and when he boarded the coach to take him back to Bury he was wholly Letty's. Every landmark along the road reminded him of her, and when the coach halted in the inn yard at Newmarket the memory of her was so sharp and the anticipation of seeing her again so exciting, that he could not swallow the food with which his landlady had provided him. After one dry, choking mouthful he tossed the remainder to a prowling mongrel dog in the street, and then leaning against the wall, fell into a dream and saw himself, young, untouched by anything but tepid pity, walk about the yard and debate the wisdom of sharing his staypiece with the girl in the coach. It seemed such a small beginning!

At Bury he slipped down and made his way out of the "Angel" yard by the back gate, thus avoiding the Abbey Hill where there was just a chance that he might be seen by Doctor Coppard or Mrs. Gamble. The lane brought him out into a narrow street, and a turn and a few steps found him opposite the Coffee House door. And there was the young man, now beginning to be worried, leaving Letty with her hand on the bell-pull; he stared at them, knowing now that they had started something that was going to lead to that frantic little scene in some room hidden away by the placid front of the house.

The door was open, but the Coffee Room was empty of customers. Cathy was there alone, laying out a fresh consignment of papers and periodicals upon the centre table. Her back was towards him and she did not look up as he entered. He was glad that he could ask his first question concerning Letty of her; he had always liked her best of the three Rowan women, and since hearing her story had chosen to believe that she had once been like Letty — a Letty whom no one had succeeded in rescuing.

He said, "Hullo, Cathy," and with a start she turned and looked at him. Her trained, ready smile did not brighten her face, nor did she speak. He was abruptly reminded of people whom he had seen in houses where someone had recently died. She looked stern and bleak, as some bereaved people did; not broken, hardened, determined to go on with life but knowing that there would never be any sweetness in it again. He was so surprised to see such an expression on her face that his eager question concerning Letty's well-being died on his lips and he asked instead:

"Is anything the matter, Cathy? Has anything happened?"

"I thought you weren't coming back till tomorrow."

"I altered my arrangements. Cathy, you don't look like yourself at all. What's the matter?"

"Nothing. Letty's all right, if that's what you want to know." She brought out her cousin's name with an expression of supreme distaste.

"I'm glad to hear that." He was glad, but he was disturbed by Cathy's look and by something brittle and strained about her manner. Had something happened to her child? Impossible to ask, of course.

"I'd like to see Letty."

"She's at Depden."

"At Depden! Whatever for?"

"Mother thought the country air would be good for her health." Something quite appalling in its ferocity flashed into Cathy's eyes.

"Her health? Was she ill, then? After I'd gone?"

Cathy looked at him with what would have been venom had it not been oddly tinged with contemptuous pity. It was as though she were finding him guilty of some vile crime, but at the same time excusing him because in committing it he had injured himself.

"You needn't worry about her health," Cathy said, with a faint, ironic emphasis on the last word.

"Whereabouts in Depden is she?"

"If you've got any sense you won't go running out there. Though why I should bother to tell you that I don't know. All right, she's at Mulberry Cottage. Go on, chase after her and see what good that does you! Let her finish off what she's started. And when you see the little . . . tell her from me . . . tell her I hope . . ." The message was never given, for as Cathy chokingly sought for words a gentle cough sounded from behind the door which stood half-open to the kitchen. Cathy's eyes, showing a great deal of white, like those of a frightened horse, turned in that direction. She ran her finger along the inside of the necklet that encircled her throat and then walked out of the room.

Humphrey stood staring after her for a moment; then he turned and hurried out into the street. He knew in which direction Depden lay, somewhere off the turnpike on the west side of the town, but he had no idea of its distance. Hewitt would know that, however; and he'd hire the best horse in the stable and ride hard. With any luck he'd be able to see Letty for just a minute and still be back to keep his appointment with Plant at nine o'clock.

Hewitt had no horse of any kind. There was a wedding in a village three miles away, and every horse he owned had been hired to carry guests. The livery-keeper was sufficiently apologetic and concerned to set professional jealousy aside and mention his rival, Driscoll.

"I don't know what his horses are like, sir. Poor old screws I've been told. But you'd find one to get that far I should reckon."

"How far is it?"

"Matter of seven or eight mile. Might be more. Say nine or ten to be on the safe side. And the road's bad."

It was striking six as he left the livery stable, and for a moment he considered, in his desperation, the possibility of sneaking into the yard of Doctor Coppard's house and taking one of his horses. But

Davie would certainly be pottering about at this hour, and the risk seemed too great. Much as he hated the idea of asking another favour of Plant, it seemed the only thing to do. If the livery-keeper had slightly over-estimated the distance — as livery-keepers were inclined to do — and Plant lent him a good horse, he could still see Letty and be back on duty by nine o'clock. He began to hurry in the direction of Plant's farm.

CHAPTER
TWENTY

Plant, with the facility of his kind for ignoring any unpleasantness which they have themselves originated, greeted Humphrey with geniality. It vanished abruptly when Humphrey announced his intention of going to Depden and asked for the loan of a horse. It was quite clear that at the back of Plant's mind lingered the idea that Humphrey was set on evading the unloading, and having kept the letter of his promise by returning from Cambridge now intended to avoid the performance of it by riding to Depden and losing himself in the wilds.

"Now look here," he said, "we've had this out once. I want you here from nine o'clock onwards. What *is* the point in coming back from Cambridge to do a job and then dancing off to Depden. You couldn't possibly be back here in time, and even if you were you'd be too tired to be useful. This is a job, not child's play."

"But I'm anxious about Letty. I left everything in a muddle when I went away, and then I come back and find she's been pushed off to Depden. And there was something very queer about Cathy just now, when I saw her. Something isn't right there, and I want to know what it is."

"Maybe I can tell you, if you'll stop bellowing about Depden and stamping about like a horse with the itch. Letty and Cathy had a flaming row. I went in on Tuesday morning. I didn't see Cathy, but Mrs. Rowan told me. She sent Letty away to stop her and Cathy tearing one another's hair out."

"But what conceivable reason could they find for quarrelling?"

"God knows! Some typical woman's nonsense about who had the last new bonnet and who should have the next. Nothing for you to bother about. And your Letty's all right. I know the old dame she's with. Years ago she lived with the Rowans — proper old dragon. So make yourself easy."

"Cathy didn't look or sound as though the quarrel had been trivial. She was very fierce — and tragic, almost. She was just going to say something to me about Letty when she heard somebody in the kitchen. Look here, Plant, let me take a horse and go to Letty and get the whole story. I'd be back, I swear."

"I've got enough to worry about," Plant said savagely, "without having to fret my guts as to whether you'll be back in time or not. You're here and here you'll stay until that load is in. After that you can take a horse and ride to hell if you like. I'm sick to death of all this talk about Letty, Letty, Letty. It's time you learned to keep women where they belong. We'll get this load safely disposed of and then, if we *must*, we'll consider the temperamental upheavals of the Rowan household."

Later on Humphrey remembered that contemptuous dismissal of the apparently irrelevant.

Plant grew more nervous, more easily exasperated as time wore on. More than once he said that he must keep sober, yet he drank a good deal and was offended by Humphrey's refusal to drink with him. Nine o'clock came, half-past, and ten. Plant looked at his watch at frequent intervals, but when Humphrey once looked at his own he snapped, "Oh yes, probably you could have gone and got back. But I didn't know they were going to be late, did I?" Humphrey did not trouble to deny that that thought had been in his mind.

Finally Plant seemed to find Humphrey's outwardly calm demeanour irritating. "You do realise, I hope, that we've got to work fast. It's all very well for you to sit there like Buddha, but you might understand that we're vulnerable as long as that stuff is in the yard. Nobody'd ever find my store, and the odd cask going out could be explained at a pinch. But it only needs somebody to watch the wagon in and pounce ten minutes later and we'd be . . ." He snapped his fingers.

"That'll never happen to *you*, Plant," said Humphrey. "It's the unforeseen danger that overtakes us, and you seem to foresee them all."

"Oh, I admit that," said Plant, with a sudden disarming frankness. "I happen to have some imagination. But that's an advantage in the long run. I foresee things and I guard against them." As he spoke he put his hand inside his coat and Humphrey saw that he wore a belt, incongruously inelegant, strapped over the top of fine cloth trousers, and supporting a pistol and a knife. He thought again of the man who had had his throat cut, and the fact that Plant seemed to have lost a partner at about the same time as the man lost his life, and he thought that it was no wonder they quarrelled if they spent many hours like this together.

Plant looked at his watch again. Then he got up and opened the door of the cupboard which he used for a wardrobe. The shoes had been taken away so the floor was bare, and between the shelves of linen there was a narrow dark aperture, where the whole of the space where formerly the suits had hung from pegs had been pushed away. Out of the space came the scent that he remembered, the only breath of romance left to the smuggling legend, the scent of tarry twine and sail-cloth, tobacco, rum, and salt water. He forgot that he and Plant had been saying unfriendly things.

"Oh, that's very cunning," he said. "I thought you used the ordinary cellar."

"Too many people would think that. This is the main chimney stack of the house. That's why I can't have a fire in any other room. I had this," he tapped the cupboard back which served as a door to the hiding place, "specially made. It's three inches thick and backed with felt. It wouldn't sound hollow if it were tapped."

He stepped back into the kitchen and looked at his watch and sighed. And then, although Humphrey had heard nothing, he said:

"Ah! Here they are. Come on now . . ."

236

They snatched up their lanterns and hurried into the yard. A wagon was just turning at the gateway. Plant went straight across and closed the gate behind it, shooting home the bolts.

It was an ordinary, rather smallish wagon, loaded with hay which was roped down at the back and the front. It was drawn by two horses which, as soon as they came to a standstill, fell into attitudes of weariness, their heads drooping, their hides steaming into the cold air. The man who held the reins seemed to share their exhaustion. He sat slumped in his seat with his shoulders slouched forward, his chin lowered on his chest and hardly any of his face visible. Another man sat beside him, muffled in a thick red scarf. He looked wakeful and alert. As Plant held up the lantern and the light fell on their faces Humphrey could see that this one, at least, was sensible of haste and urgency. But it was to the other that Plant spoke.

"Hullo, Jeremy. You've brought help, I see. I'm glad of that. Did you have a good journey? Hop down. I've a hot drink waiting for you. You two go inside and swallow it while we get the hay off."

The driver lifted and slightly turned his head. The face thus revealed was pale and curiously dull looking. He did not speak. The more lively fellow beside him did move, and as though wakened by the movement, the driver said:

"Hullo, Plant."

"Come on, come on," said Plant, cheerily, but with a rousing note in his voice.

Very, very slowly, like someone walking in his sleep, the man got down from the wagon. The one with the red scarf skipped down nimbly, alighting on the same side as the driver and standing close to him with what Humphrey thought an oddly protective air. Plant must have noticed it too, for he said sharply:

"What's wrong with you tonight, Jeremy. Have you been drinking?"

"He's all right," said the driver's mate, a little truculently. "He's just dead beat and perished of cold, ain't you, Jeremy?"

"You're new, aren't you?" Plant asked.

"New to you, maybe. But I know my job. We'll go and get this drink you spoke of. We'll be thawed out by the time you've got the hay off." He put his arm through that of his companion and led him away. The driver was either drunk or very cramped, his legs seemed to move reluctantly.

"They've both been drinking," said Plant savagely. "Fat lot of good they're going to be. Come on, let's get the ropes off."

He strode away to the rear of the wagon and Humphrey got busy with the forward one. The knot yielded easily, and he went round to the other side of the wagon to pull the rope free from that side. Plant was still fumbling with his, grunting and cursing with impatience.

Humphrey's rope came free and he coiled it tidily and laid it aside, just as the loose end of Plant's came whizzing through the air, missing his head by a fraction of an inch.

"D'you want to blind me?" he called.

Plant said "Sorry! Pitch the hay to the back and then we can roll the barrels out on to it. We've got to save ourselves as much as we can. We've got to do it alone to all intents and purposes . . ."

They began to strip off the protective layer of hay. The air was filled with its dust and with its desiccated fragrance. Humphrey was up on the hub of the front wheel on his side of the wagon, and had grasped what he thought to be the last armful of hay, since in collecting it his fingers had brushed against some hard substance, when he heard Plant emit a strange sound, something like that which a man might make if he seized something and found it to be only just short of red-hot. And in the same instant he found himself seized around the waist from behind, thrown from his precarious perch on the hub of the wheel to the ground, and then pinned down by the heavy pressure of someone's knee in his stomach, and beaten over the head with something heavy.

For a second he thought that Plant had run round the wagon and attacked him, but there were sounds of struggle on the other side, and as he heaved and writhed and twisted and fought for a hold on the arm which rose and fell above his head he knew what had happened. The hay at the back of the load had hidden more than contraband.

The man fought in silence, and with an utter ruthlessness. Humphrey, spreadeagled upon his back, with only his arms to fight with, and with his head full of blackness, shot with scarlet flashes, felt that this was the end of Humphrey Shadbolt. The man would either kill him or batter him into unconsciousness and then hand him over to be hanged. Once he succeeded in getting a grip of the fellow's collar, but he only leaned back a little and deflecting a blow from Humphrey's head, brought it down on his elbow instead, so that his fingers opened in a spasm of pain. Fighting in this position was useless, the man had every tactical advantage. All at once he ceased to resist the pressure of the knee, ceased to fight for a hold on the punishing arm. He lay limp. The man gave him one more blow on the head, waited a cautious second, and then, with a little satisfied grunt, shifted his position and prepared to get to his feet. The next instant Humphrey had him by the throat.

He had had, in the past, many a friendly tussle with his brothers and with boys at school, but he had never before fought anyone in anger or fear or with the desire to inflict real injury. Now, as his hands closed about the warm, pulsing, sinewy throat he knew that he must squeeze to hurt, squeeze until the man was senseless. If the man had stood still and allowed himself to be half-throttled Humphrey could have judged the effect of the pressure and let go in time. There was a place where far less than fatal constriction resulted in the stoppage of blood to the brain and a brief insensibility. It had been pointed out to Humphrey as a useful expedient in dealing with dangerous lunatics, or as a merciful one in operation cases when opium and alcohol had failed.

But the man, not knowing into whose hands he had fallen, resisted strongly. He kicked and flailed about with his arms. And the big hands moved deliberately, coolly, knowledgeably into position. The man tried an old trick and brought up his knee, sharply. Humphrey was hurt. Pain and anger became all at once a blind, atavistic lust to kill. He clung on to the man's throat as though he were drowning and it the only thing to which to cling.

The result was almost frightening in its effect and completeness. The legs and arms ceased to thrash, the head fell backwards, the whole heavy body turned into a dead weight, held upright by the killing grip about its neck. A little guggling sound, as though water were being shaken in a bottle issued from somewhere within the man's chest. Then that ceased. But it was thirty seconds later before sanity returned to Humphrey. When he did, and he had laid the man gently down — collapsing like a heavy bundle of clothing — he knew that he, too, was a murderer. There was no doubt at all in his mind; the fellow was dead.

Ungovernable nausea came upon him and he held on to the wheel of the wagon and was sick. As though from a great distance he could hear sounds of struggle going on on the far side of the wagon, and was astonished that the fight should have lasted so long. It seemed an endless time since he had heard Plant cry out. He knew that he must go to Plant's assistance; and when the next spasm of sickness had spent itself he stood for a second, wiping his mouth and gathering strength for the effort. As he did so a shot rang out, startingly loud and close. The tired horses, stirred at last from their apathy, jerked forward, and as the wagon moved he had a clear view of the yard.

A lantern, kicked over in the struggle, had ignited some of the hay, and by the light of the flames Humphrey could see Plant lying huddled on the ground, with his assailant bending over him, a smoking pistol in his hand. And beyond this fantastic, fire-lighted scene he could see the tall, stockade-like fence which enclosed the yard. Two impulses, comic in their divergence, came to his dizzy brain — one, to run forward and see what could be done for Plant; the other, to run to the fence and climb it. There'd be no time to fumble with the bolts and bars of the gate, but if he could swarm to the top and drop over — unobserved — there might be a chance.

At that moment there came a shout from the kitchen. Looking in that direction Humphrey saw the man who had worn the red scarf come bounding out. Just within the door, quite visible in the light, was Jeremy, bound immobile to a kitchen chair by means of the red scarf. But it was not until afterwards that Humphrey realised that in that moment his mind had absorbed and retained that picture. He saw only the man. And knew that now he had two enemies. Now he would be killed, or hanged. There was no hope at all.

Yet he acted as though hope were high. Launching himself forward he flung his weight against the man who had shot Plant and threw him face downwards to the ground, at the same time hitting him as hard as he could with his bare clenched fist on the base of his skull. Then he made a run for the fence and leaped at it like a cat. He was on top and astride it when the man who had run from the kitchen fired at him. He felt a thud on his shoulder, but no pain then, and as he dropped to the ground into the road he knew a momentary hope that the bullet had, by some freak of chance, been deflected. But before he had taken many steps he could feel the blood running down his back and knew that he had been hit.

Pursuit, he knew, was imminent and inevitable. The man who had come from the kitchen might halt for a moment to estimate the damage done to his comrade, but that was slight, and the chances were that within a few minutes they would both be out in the road, one casting in one direction and one in the other, and each well able to overtake a fugitive who had been beaten about the head, bruised in the stomach and shot in the back. Concealment, not flight, seemed to offer the best chance. So he crossed the road, clambered up the steep bank which bounded it and slithered down into the deep moist ditch on the other side. Then, down on his hands and knees, he began to crawl in the direction of the town.

After a few yards the nausea came upon him again and he lay on his face and vomited. The location of the wound became pinmarked by searing pain, and despite his professional self-assurance that if his lungs had been injured he would have known some inconvenience in breathing, and if his spine had been touched either movement or thought would have ben impaired, he became conscious of a layman's superstitious fear of a wound that could not be investigated. He might be bleeding to death. Records proved that it could be an easy and painless way to die. He might die in this ditch. "To die in a ditch" was an ominous phrase and one often used by Josiah Shadbolt. It was the logical and inevitable result of idleness, ungodliness, wastefulness and levity. To die in a ditch meant to be friendless and outcast, without resources. For a few moments he lay there, supine and despairing — aware, with an odd abruptness of the stigma of his birth, seeing himself as a bastard who had, despite certain advantages of upbringing, justified every prejudiced foreboding. He had wasted his opportunities, been dishonest and deceitful, lecherous and unscrupulous, he had taken to a life of crime and was now going to die in a ditch. A few weak tears crept down his face to mingle with the streaks of blood from the wounds in his scalp and the smear of vomit and the mud upon his face.

But it was impossible to review his life of crime and folly and failure without thinking of Letty, and all at once she was there, just as she had been, so short a time ago, in the Cambridge bedroom. Then he had contemplated deserting her by letting himself die . . . and Letty, it seemed, did not intend to let herself be deserted, either for one cause or the other. He became so sharply aware of her that a flood of male possessiveness and lustful power rose in him. He knew that he was not going to die here; he was going to reach the one person who could help him, extract that help by some means and go, tomorrow, to Depden. Out of the sinister, charmed circle of Mrs. Rowan's influence he could bend Letty to his will. He would take her away and they would start a new life together.

He raised himself and began again to crawl along the ditch.

It seemed a long time before any sound of pursuit reached him. He heard the sound of footsteps and voices and immediately lay flat. The men — they were holding together — stuck to the road, though at intervals they mounted the bank and held aloft the lanterns they carried. They passed him, went on for about a hundred yards and then came back.

"Well, we got Driscoll, and that's the main thing," said one voice.

"The other one killed Pete; I'd like to have got him," said the other.

"I'd say I did. I hit him smack atween the shoulders."

"No matter. We'd best not waste any more time. Get back and report to the Riding Officer . . ."

The voices trailed off in the direction of Plant's farm. Humphrey crawled on for another five minutes, then, cautiously, he emerged from the ditch and began walking with the best speed he could muster towards the town. He swayed as he walked, reeling like a drunken man from one side of the road to the other. His head throbbed and he was obliged to breathe in rapid shallow gasps because a full breath increased the pain in his back. But he knew where he was going and was determined to reach his destination. Doctor Coppard would be angry beyond all description, he would be so disgusted and so disappointed and so furious that only the sheerest desperation could make tolerable the prospect of facing his disgust, his disappointment, and his fury; but at least he would not let one bleed to death. And once the bullet wound was dealt with one would, in part, be one's own man again.

Once he reached the outskirts of the town he went warily, ready to direct his reeling progress into a garden or doorway at the sight of any human being. But he met no one and no one overtook him. The citizens of the little town kept early hours during the winter and, though here and there a window was still lighted, nobody was abroad.

CHAPTER
TWENTY-ONE

Doctor Coppard himself would have been abed an hour earlier, but he had been called to a case at nine o'clock and, returning at half-past the hour, and finding a good fire burning, had sat down to enjoy a final pipeful of tobacco and fallen asleep. As he had told Humphrey some weeks before, he was beginning to feel his age and to rely upon his assistant to keep the practice going. The past few days of unaided work had exhausted him, and he had fallen asleep before the pipe was well alight. Humphrey's first desparate peal of the bell failed to rouse him, but the second — or the opening of Mrs. Gamble's door above, brought him to his feet with a start. He shuffled into the hall, calling upwards as he did so, "It's all right, Mrs. Gamble, I'm still up. I'll go."

He opened the door, expecting to see some white-faced, breathless messenger gasping out some list of horrifying symptoms, making some demand for immediate effort upon his part, and he braced himself to meet an emergency. He opened the door upon Humphrey, who should have been at Cambridge, and Humphrey was, at that moment, a more horrifying sight than the old man had ever seen upon his doorstep before. But the calm manner, result of many years of unhurried self-control, held. Doctor Coppard reached out an arm, an arm against which many a pain-crazed woman, many a frenzied child had leaned, and caught his apprentice. "Why, Humphrey," he said, "what brings you back? What has happened to you?"

"I've been shot. In the back. Bleeding prof-profusely. Please help me . . . do something . . ."

"Of course, of course," said the old man, calmly but breathlessly. He let Humphrey lean against him, but at the same time he pushed the door closed and turned the key again. "There now, hold up. Just a minute. Ah, that's right. Lean on me. Now, this way. There, now you can lie down . . ."

He knew, by the smell, that he was in the musty little surgery, lying on the high, hard, leather-covered couch upon which patients lay for the performance of emergency operations. Standing by this very couch he had lanced his first abscess . . . oh, years and years ago. The dread of pursuit, the sense of the need for caution, left him; he was home, in safety, in good hands. The tautened will relaxed; a great feeling of peace flooded over him. The black leather sofa expanded, growing wider and blacker until it engulfed the whole world.

"I saved it to show you," said Doctor Coppard, rolling the bullet around in a little china dish. "The luckiest one I ever saw. One-eighth of an inch innards and it'd have shattered your spine, my boy. Now don't try to talk. You've been bleeding like a pig. Lie still and relax for a bit. When you feel a bit better I'll be interested to

248

know who shot you, and why and what happened to your head, and all about it."

"I ought to go. I might be . . . followed," said Humphrey, his white lips scarcely moving.

"Well, the door's locked," said Doctor Coppard comfortably.

But although he spoke calmly, almost lightly, as though assuring a child that some dreaded, half-imaginary assailant was safely excluded and his place of refuge invulnerable, that was only because for forty years he had been combating other people's terror. He was now frightened himself. The high colour had drained from his plump cheeks, leaving them like suet, streaked with little congested veins; and his eyes were anxious. A feeling of the most complete compunction came upon Humphrey. He put his head in his hands and groaned.

"Why should you be followed, Humphrey?"

"I'd better not tell you, sir. It'd be better if you didn't know anything about it. I've done the most terrible things anybody could do. I ought never to have come back here, and I wouldn't but for that bullet. I knew I shouldn't get far with that in me. I've utterly disgraced you . . ."

"What have you done, Humphrey?"

"I've killed a man."

The words seemed to hang on the air for a long time.

"Across at the Coffee House?"

"No. An excise man. Since Christmas I've been working for a man who handled contraband. Tonight there was a raid. We were tricked. I killed the man who set about me." He held out his hands and looked at them as though he expected to see blood on them. "There's no excuse for me at all, sir," he said dully. "I killed him, deliberately."

"And the others are after you?"

Humphrey nodded.

"Then we mustn't sit here talking about it. Whatever you've done, Humphrey, they shan't hang you if I can help it." He thought for a minute, and as always when he was thoughtful, his hand went to his chin. Tonight the mottled old hand was trembling, and compunction struck Humphrey again. He got to his feet, and though the sudden movement made him dizzy, he concealed it by hanging on to the back of a chair.

"You have helped, sir. I'd rather you didn't do any more. Unless you would just let my mother know. She'll hear soon enough, but if you could just tell her how sorry I am for making such a mess of things. It's no good my writing, you see. She can't read."

"Oh, of course, of course. I'll see to that. And, my boy, you'll want some money." He shambled quickly across the room and unlocked a drawer, and came back without closing it again, and held out a netted purse with gold gleaming within its meshes. "There's about forty pounds, all I have in the house. Oh, take it, take it for God's sake! I meant to give you fifty pounds when you finished your articles. I should have thought — I didn't realise. Why didn't you ask me for money, Humphrey. I suppose it was for money . . ." he broke off. "You do look shaky. You'd better have some brandy. Coffee would be better, but there's no time. Sit down

250

again. That's right. Now drink this while I go and put the horse in the gig. I'll drive you to Kentford, and you can catch the coach from there. We'll go at once. They won't think of looking for you at Kentford . . ."

"I don't want you to incriminate yourself by helping me, sir. I'm not worth it."

"That's for me to say, isn't it? Besides, who's to know? And what else can we do? You're in no state to ride, and you wouldn't get far, running. You just sit still and drink that and stay as calm as you can, while I get the gig ready."

The old man had reached the door before Humphrey remembered.

"I've got to go to Depden before I go away."

"To Depden? In heaven's name, why?"

"Letty's there. I've got to see her. I've got to take her with me — if she'll come."

"Now that is nonsense. There's no time. And you'll have enough to do getting yourself to London and keeping yourself alive. You can't have a woman hanging round your neck. You forget all about her, Humphrey. I'll let her know you're all right, if that's what you're worrying about."

"I've got to see her," Humphrey said stubbornly. "Before I went to Cambridge I asked her to marry me, and she's had the interval to make up her mind. Besides," he went on, his voice rising to a high wild note, "everything I've done has been to get her away from Mrs. Rowan. If I leave her now it'll all have been wasted and I'll have ruined myself for nothing. Sir, you must see . . ."

251

"Don't get excited," said Doctor Coppard sternly. "Very well, we will drive round by Depden. It's a waste of precious time, but I don't suppose they'll look for you there. Finish that brandy and then walk, very steadily, out to me. I'll be ready."

It was like dying, Humphrey felt when he was left alone; like performing, slowly and consciously, the act of dying. He looked round the familiar (and, now that he came to leave it, well-loved) room, where he and the old man had spent so many hours, and his awareness stretched to all the other rooms in the house, to the kitchen which always smelt of good cooking, to his own room upstairs with his few precious possessions. There were things he would have liked to take with him, but he could not spare time, nor could he face the stairs. Outside there were the streets which were almost as much part of him as the house; he'd never tread them again through the wintry murk or the summer sunshine. And there was his mother, to whom all this would be worse than any bereavement, because it would shame her. And Josiah would say, "If the boy had stayed where he belonged this would never have happened!" What could she reply to that? After all she had done, all she had sacrificed, she would be left with nothing but defeat to add to the weight of the dark secret which she had carried for so many years. He mustn't think of her.

There was only Letty now. And why *only* Letty? He had, quite deliberately, and knowing what he did, thrown his career, Doctor Coppard, his mother and everything he knew and cherished into the scales

252

against Letty's well-being. He shouldn't grudge them, now. Shouldn't pity himself. The truth was that he had wanted to have everything, to stake all he had, but to win the gamble and avoid paying. It hadn't turned out that way. So he mustn't think *only* Letty, he must think, there is *still* Letty. It was true that on the last occasion when he had seen her she had shown no sign of affection for him, and had implied that she didn't want to see him any more. But then her mind had been full of Mrs. Rowan's poison, and Mrs. Rowan herself had been in the room, casting her blighting influence over everything. It would be different now. Letty would have had time to think things over and to realise that he was the only friend she had in the world. She would go with him into exile and they would make a new life together.

As he set down the glass and began to move feebly towards the yard his vivid, limited imagination ran ahead of him, promising good things. Already he could see himself with a post as ship's surgeon. Shipowners were not particular as to qualifications or antecedents, too few real doctors wanted to go to sea. He'd earn money by plying his trade, and come home at the end of each voyage to a little house where Letty was waiting.

Doctor Coppard was not quite ready. It was a long time since he had harnessed his own horse and the animal, resenting his unfamiliar hands had been as awkward as possible. The old man was completely breathless, and when the gig-lamps shone on his face Humphrey could see that the suetty colour had been replaced by a deep scarlet, and that beads of sweat stood on his forehead and upper lip. Compunction smote him again.

"Why don't you go to bed, sir? I can drive to Depden and then on to Kentford and get somebody to bring the gig back. And that wouldn't involve you. They'd think I'd just taken it. They might make things awkward for you."

"You're not in a fit state to drive," said Doctor Coppard shortly. "You'll inflame your wound and take a fever. You shouldn't even be on your feet. There, that's done. Get in and lean back. I put a rug there, folded thick. Make yourself comfortable and stay as still as possible. Which way out is this blasted place? West? It would be! Worst road in Suffolk."

He climbed up beside Humphrey and spread another rug across their knees. Then he fumbled for a moment, and Humphrey saw that he had laid his heavy old-fashioned pistol in the slack of the rug on his lap. He reached out and grabbed it.

"I appreciate that, sir. But if we're stopped you must give me up. Bury needs *one* doctor, you know."

"It's losing its best one. I'm an old man, Humphrey. I'm a *very* old man. All last week I was thinking . . ." He broke off and slapped the reins across the horse's back. "Now, you awkward bugger, put some of your prancing to good use. And you, Humphrey, don't talk for at least half an hour."

But within ten minutes, as soon as the hoof beats had ceased to echo back from the closely packed houses and were falling soft and flat on the open road between the fields, he began to ask questions.

Gradually, by answering them, and explaining his answers, Humphrey told him the whole story. When it was all told, down to the last trivial detail, Doctor Coppard said, "It's a mystery to me. It sounds like a bewitchment. When I think that three months ago . . ." He did not elaborate, but added with bitterness, "And now here we are, running from the hangman. It's terrible, Humphrey. God knows you've suffered, and will suffer enough without my saying anything to hurt you. But I feel compelled to say that I think you're making a mistake in seeing the girl again. And if she goes with you it'll be the worst thing that could happen. I'll say nothing against her; maybe she's harmless enough in herself, but it looks to me as though, for you, she is the instrument of a bad fate. There are people like you, you know. And the devil of it is that from what you say she doesn't even seem to love you."

"That's very hard to judge, sir. She's so young. And I've never really had a chance to make her understand. But she'll know now. She's had time. And if we get away together everything will be all right. At least . . ." He forced himself to say the things which he felt must be said, though his throat thickened and his ears and his eyes went hot. "Not all right. I've messed up everything and made a shocking bad return for all your kindness."

"There's something a little wrong with kindness which doesn't beget confidence. I've failed you somehow, Humphrey; that's a fact for *me* to face. But it's too late to think about that now. Listen, when you get to London go straight to Staff Lane. It runs down

from the Strand to the river. There's a Doctor Shillito
there. Tell him I sent you and that I'll write him a letter
by the next post. He'll take care of you. He was a friend
of mine years ago. You can trust him."

CHAPTER
TWENTY-TWO

They reached Depden in the thick darkness, long before the first sign of the winter dawn, and were faced with the problem of finding, in the sleeping village, a house which they knew only by name.

"There's always somebody awake in any community of more than twenty people," Doctor Coppard said. "Somebody's always got a sick cow or a child with toothache." But they passed through the little village without seeing a light or any other sign of life, and at last the old man began looking about for a gateway in which to turn. When he had found it and was guiding the gig through the rutted mud, a dog, somewhere in the yard behind, sprang out to the full length of his rattling chain and began to bark ferociously. Doctor Coppard leaned over the side of the gig and made snarling, hissing noises which provoked the dog to frenzy, and within a minute or two a faint golden light was kindled behind a window in the dark bulk of an almost invisible house, and then a window creaked and a voice, the human counterpart of the dog's for ferocity, shouted "Who's there?"

"I've lost my way. I'm looking for Mulberry Cottage," Doctor Coppard called back in a reassuring voice.

"Then you ain't far lost," said the man more amiably. "Go back to the Green and you'll see it, just alongside the pond."

"Thank you very much. I'm sorry to have disturbed you."

"So long as you ain't arter my fowls thass all right," said the man. The window closed.

"Now," said Doctor Coppard, when they had found the cottage, "I'll go and rouse the girl and bring her out to you. She'll be warm enough, wrapped in this rug for a few minutes, and it'll save you moving about."

It was impossible not to be touched by this further evidence of the old man's consideration, but Humphrey pushed back the wrap from his knees and began to heave himself out of the gig.

"It'd be better for me to go, sir, and for you to stay here with the rug. You mustn't make an invalid of me."

"Well, don't be long. It's a long way round to Kentford from here, and the horse'll be far from fresh. And remember, you're not to get excited. You'll need all your strength before you get to London."

He felt very feeble and dizzy now that he was on his feet again, and that alone, since he had never failed anything in all his life before, was enough to give everything an air of complete unreality. Half way along the path he paused and leaned for a moment against the crooked, gnarled trunk of an apple-tree whose shape was etched darkly against darkness. And during that moment it seemed as though he were moving through the mazes of a nightmare; that everything which had happened since he had boarded that coach in November was part of a wild and terrible dream from which he would wake presently, whole in body, untroubled in mind, happy Humphrey Shadbolt, without a worry in the world except the passing of a simple examination at Midsummer.

But there, just ahead of him, was the squat dark shape of the cottage, and under its roof Letty lay sleeping. And though everything else might seem unreal and partake of the quality of nightmare, Letty was real enough and dear enough to outweigh any regrets for an innocent and untroubled youth. Everything that he had done had been done for Letty's sake and for her sake he would make this last effort.

He straightened himself and walked the rest of the path. A chill, desolate wind was abroad, and as he fumbled his way into the little porch which sheltered the front door and mustered his strength for urgent knocking, the wind moaned around him, crying with a lonely lost voice that told of all the sorrows in the world, presaging ill. No one answered the knocking for a long time, and complete despair came upon him as he thought that Cathy, for some reason of her own, had deceived him. The cottage was deserted; the whole time-wasting journey had been made in vain.

Into such a mood the sound of Letty's voice from just above his head, a voice thick with sleep and shaky with apprehension, broke like sunshine, like the singing of celestial choirs.

"It's only me, Humphrey. I'm sorry to disturb you, Letty, but I've got to see you at once."

There was a perceptible pause. Then Letty asked, cautiously, "Did my aunt send you?"

"I haven't seen her. Cathy told me where to find you."

"Cathy!"

"Letty, please come down and let me in. I've got a lot to tell you, and not much time. Letty, it's urgent or I wouldn't have come at such an hour. Please hurry."

She did not answer, but he knew that she had withdrawn from the window, and presently he heard the sound of bolts creaking back on the inner side of the door, which opened, and he saw an old, old woman, wrinkled and bowed, with one hand on the door handle and the other holding a drooling candle. Just behind her stood Letty in a defensive, unwelcoming attitude, also holding a candle and clutching a long dark cloak over her nightgown.

Then he saw Letty's face and everything else was blotted out. Made sharp and avid by absence and imaginings, his eyes dwelt upon the dear familiar outline, the features — common to the whole human race — yet in their arrangement so peculiarly and eternally Letty and all she stood for. There was the physical emanation of the force which had upset the whole pattern of his life, which had effortlessly and irrevocably devoured everything that he possessed, so that in its absence he had stood in a formless void alone with a moaning wind, and now, in its presence found himself whole and restored. Letty, sanity, vigour, happiness.

He wanted to move forward and take her in his arms, to bury his face in the hair that poured over her shoulders and so stand, without thinking or speaking, until his starved senses had taken their fill of her nearness, her warmth and sweetness, her very existence. But as though aware of his need the old woman thrust her withered frame forward and said in a cracked but determined voice, "You can come in. But you got to behave yourself. This is no time of night to get a girl from her bed."

"I know. I'm sorry. But my business won't wait." As he stepped into the cottage Letty moved away and he saw that the front door gave directly into a low wide room, sparsely furnished. There was a round table in the centre and Letty took her stand on the further side of it. The old woman closed the door behind him and then came close to his elbow.

"Well," she said, taking charge of the interview, "what's your business? A fine time of night to get folks up, I must say."

"Letty," he said piteously, "I must see you alone. I've things to say to you that I can't say in the presence of another person."

"Anything that ain't fit for my ears ain't fit for hers, thass a certainty," said the old woman.

"Have you come to apologise?" Letty asked coldly. "Because I'd like her to hear that. She may as well know the truth. She's heard all the lies."

"What lies?"

"The lies you told Aunt Thirza about Plant and me. The lies that made Cathy go for me and got me sent out here."

"I don't know what you're talking about, Letty. What am I supposed to have said?"

"You know," said Letty, ominously.

"Upon my soul I don't. And, anyway, I haven't come to apologise for whatever it was. I've come to tell you what has been happening, and to ask you . . . Letty, I must see you alone. I'm in a hurry, and what I have to say is important."

The bleak, bewildered, inimical little mask with which Letty confronted him did not soften.

"Unless you do say that it was lies, and let her hear it, I don't want to listen to anything else. I was sent out here in disgrace, and she's treated me as though I'd done something dreadful. And it was because of something you said. There's no sense," she went on hastily, cutting short his splutter of protest, "saying you didn't. That night after you'd gone Aunt Thirza took Cathy in the next room and they talked and talked. Cathy cried and carried on like anything. I listened as much as I could, and I know that it was all on account of something you said about Plant and me. I couldn't hear it all, but that much I did hear, and then afterwards, when Cathy went for me like a fishwife and said dreadful things to me, I knew what it was you had said. I don't see why you should; I never did you any harm. And I'd like you to take it all back now, in front of Mrs. Shaw."

The faintest glimmering of understanding dawned upon him. Knowing Mrs. Rowan, he could guess at the form the lie had taken. But why? What point had she gained by setting Cathy and Letty at loggerheads.

"What is it that I am supposed to have said about you and Plant?" he asked patiently.

"You should know. That I'd taken Plant away from Cathy. That Plant and me were . . . that we had . . ." The painful colour flooded her face. She turned abruptly to the old woman. "You know what it was, and so does he."

"I know what I was given to understand, dearie."

"And I can guess. Letty, it isn't true. You must believe me. I've come here tonight at the risk of my life to talk to you. I've no time to waste on this other business. If you'll send Mrs. Shaw away I'll tell you exactly what it was I did say to your aunt, and why Plant's name was mentioned. Then perhaps the way will be clear for me to say what I came to say."

Something flashed into Letty's face and was gone. But she turned to the old woman and said, "Please, Mrs. Shaw, leave us for a few minutes."

"I'll be in the kitchen. But you'll be all right. I know a gentleman when I see one," said Mrs. Shaw placatingly. She shambled away. Humphrey pulled a chair from under the table and sat down heavily.

"Now listen, Letty. This isn't a nice story, and I've kept from telling you lots of time when I ought to have spoken out. Some weeks ago Plant Driscoll told me — and I've no reason to think he was lying because he'd nothing to gain by it . . ." In as few and unhurtful

263

words as possible he told her, ending with the threat of exposure which he had made to her aunt. Letty listened attentively, but not wholeheartedly; and as he watched her carefully for signs of shock or repulsion, he gathered the impression that she was hearing the story not as a whole thing, important in itself, but as part of something else, as though she were fitting what he was saying together with something else she knew, or guessed, or had wondered at. But so long as she did not give way to hysteria, or cry that he was a liar, or shrink from him on account of his postulated part in the affair, he was not concerned with what she thought of the story; and as soon as it was done he hurried on — "So you see, Letty, darling, that is why I couldn't leave you to go back there or get into her clutches again. That's why I'm here now. I'm in trouble, serious trouble, and I've got to get away and hide myself in London, but I want you to come with me." Something else stirred in her face then, something that made him rush on with hasty explanations. "It may not sound very promising, asking you to come away with me when I'm running for my life, but thanks to Doctor Coppard I've got a good start, and have a place to go to. I'll be able to look after you properly. I'll get a job as doctor on a ship and start earning money right away. I'll marry you the moment you want me to, or if you don't want that I'll look after you as carefully as though we *were* married. I'll devote my whole life to you. Only I can't give you any time to think it over any more. You must come straight away. If you don't they'll catch me.

264

Doctor Coppard has the gig outside, and he'll drive us to Kentford in time for the first coach to London."

Either his manner had convinced her of his truthfulness, or something of what he had said had fitted into the puzzle she was turning over in her mind, for her attitude had altered. She no longer looked at him with enmity. Her face wore its old trapped look of puzzled, agonised indecision. Sweat broke out all over him as he realised that he must do more persuading, more convincing. And time was running out, precious and irreplaceable as life-blood. He opened his mouth to speak but Letty forestalled him.

"Maybe it was all as you say," she said dubiously. "Though why should she tell Cathy that Plant and me . . . and then send me out here. It doesn't make sense. None of it makes sense." Then she looked at him with a flash of interest for his personal problem. "And you . . . why are you running away? What's happened to get you into serious trouble?"

"It was to get the money for the house and furniture," he said, gladdened by the shifting of interest. Now surely she would understand. "Knowing what I did — what I've just told you — I had to find you some other place to live. And to get the money I went to work for Plant Driscoll. He dealt in contraband and I helped him. Tonight, while we were unloading a wagon full of smuggled stuff we were raided. I killed one man and another shot me in the back. But I got away. Now do you see why I'm in a hurry. Letty, I am hurt; I really don't feel well enough to argue, and there isn't much time. If they catch me they'll hang me for certain. Will you just go and put on all the warm clothes you have and come right away. I have some money, I'll buy you everything you need in London." He got up from his chair and went towards her as he spoke the last words, intending to put his arm around her shoulders and lead her to the door, and to deal with any protests which the old woman might raise, and stand at the bottom of the stairs while she dressed, and lead her out to the gig. And in the fraction of a second, in the silence between his last word and the next which fell from Letty's lips, he had time to think that it hadn't all been vain. A few weeks ago he had set himself the task of getting Letty away from the Coffee House, and he'd done it. He'd had to lie and deceive, break the law, connive at murder and commit it, he'd had to shed his blood and flee for his life, but he had won.

"And Plant?" Letty asked. "What happened to Plant?"

Blind, unsuspecting, he blurted out the truth.

"He was killed, Letty. One of the men shot him."

She drew a noisy, gasping breath and her hands, which had been holding the edges of the dark cloak, fell to her sides and then came up again, reaching for the back of a chair. The greenish pallor of her face — one of the things about her which had always had power to move him and make him yearn to cherish and protect her — deepened until her face looked like an ill-bleached cloth. And out of it her great eyes looked like those of a stricken animal. Humphrey thought, unwillingly, irrelevantly, that the curious sorrow which

266

they had always held had been the shadow, the forecast of what was in them at this moment.

Touched to the heart he went towards her, his arms held out, ready to comfort and support, his hands curved to touch her with the oldest form of comfort, used before suffering had words.

"I'm sorry, Letty. I shouldn't have blurted it out like that. You always liked Plant, didn't you? I should have remembered that. I'm so sorry." A recollection of a phrase which he had found to be of comfort in many a death-visited house came to him. "He didn't suffer, Letty. He was shot dead in the middle of a fight. He didn't suffer at all." As true, or false, as it usually was, as such statements could ever be. For who could know which was preferable, the slow small doses of death or the bitter gulp taken suddenly?

"Don't," said Letty, shrinking away from his hands. She moved round the chair like a blind woman, reached for the edge of the table and slowly, slowly lowered herself into the chair, put her elbows on the table and buried her face in her hands. The cloak fell to the floor and he lifted it and laid it over her shoulders. Then he waited a moment, helpless, and impatiently aware of time's passing. Presently he said tentatively, "Letty . . . we can be sorry about Plant later. Just now we have to think of ourselves. We must get to Kentford in time for that coach. Unless," he added deliberately, "you want me to be killed too."

She lifted her face. There were no tears on it. It was dry and bleached and shrunken like a piece of old weathered wood.

"It's perfectly clear now," she said in a small, astonished voice. "She did it. Aunt Thirza. She knew all about Plant. She sent those men to kill him. And she told Cathy that lie," her voice grew stronger and stronger, "so that Cathy should be angry with him too. And she sent me here in case I guessed. And it all happened because of what you just told me. She was scared of you and Plant after that night. D'you see? *You* killed Plant, just as if you'd shot him yourself. Don't stand there like that, looking as if you minded. Yapping and fussing and poking your nose into something that wasn't a mite to do with you, you've got Plant killed." She stood up and the cloak dropped to the floor again. In her long white nightdress, with her white, distorted face and venomous eyes she looked like a malignant little ghost. "I hate you," she said. "I'll hate and loathe you till the day I die. I hope they'll catch you and hang you." Long shuddering rigours began to shake her body, she put her hands to her face and burst into wild crying.

Too shocked to consider his words, or even to know that he was speaking, he said, "You were in love with Plant, Letty."

She moved her hands to the sides of her face so that the thin fingers were lost in the tumbling brown hair and her hands held her quivering chin. Framed thus, as in a calyx, her face looked like some strange dead flower beaten down by the rain.

"Of course I was. All the time. From the moment I saw him. And now he's dead and I've got to go on living all my life knowing it was on account of me. I can't bear it. I just lived on day after day hoping he'd come in so I could just see him and hear him, hoping perhaps one day he'd notice me. I messed about with you so's he'd notice and see I wasn't a child any more. Now he's gone, and you come here and think I'll go off with you. I'd rather cut my throat."

She began to cry again, bitterly, hopelessly, and he stood there looking at her and feeling each of her sobs tear through his entrails. The last of the fragile coloured dreams which he had reared around her had been dashed to the ground by her words, but he felt no resentment, only a great and terrible pity. He had loved Letty and she had loved Plant. It was all too easy to imagine how he would be feeling if she were dead and he, even in the most indirect way, responsible for her death. And he knew how savagely and completely he would hate the person who had, by one empty, loud-voiced threat brought such tragedy about. He could understand and almost share her loathing for himself.

But there wasn't time in this pressed and harassed moment to think of such things. There had always been, since the first moment, two sides to his relationship with Letty, the emotional and the practical. One had made him kiss her; the other had in its far reaches, made him a murderer and a fugitive. One was finished now, it was dead and must be buried with Plant's name over it as an epitaph; but the other was still alive and urgent. Tonight, in a very few minutes, he must go away — and how could he leave Letty in the very position from which he had striven to rescue her?

If only, he thought desperately, there were more time. Time for the shedding of tears and the slow inevitable return of reason; time for wounds to heal and loyalty to prove itself. But there was no time. And he was driven to insult heartbreak by practical talk. He did it as delicately as he could.

"Letty, just listen to me one more moment. I understand how you feel; I see why you hate me. I can bear that, if you'll just let me help you now. Plant is dead, but you still have your life to live, and you can't go back to Mrs. Rowan's house. You do see that now, don't you, Letty. So come with me and let me find you a home. I have fifty pounds. You can have that to start with and I'll see that you never lack money. I don't expect you to forgive me, or to like me, or to want to see me again, but please, let me look after you."

She made some reply, but the words were swallowed by a gulping sob. He waited. Behind her hands she was fighting for some control, and having gained it she lifted her face and shook back her hair.

"What does it matter what happens to me now? I don't want your rotten money and I don't want looking after. A fine job you've done, looking after me. I was fond of my aunt and I loved Plant Driscoll. Now he's dead and you've made it so I never want to see her again. And all on account of your interference. I was all right at the Coffee House; I had a roof over my head and food in my belly, and I'd have come round to their way of thinking in time. I was happy there, but for you pestering me." Her voice was no longer redeemed by its gentleness. Coarsened by crying, it had a rough nasal quality which made the simple, matter-of-fact statements sound like abusive railing.

It affected him physically. He felt sick again, and the wound in his back became the centre of intolerable pain. But he said doggedly:

"All right, Letty. Granted that I've done badly, won't you give me the chance to put things right, to make amends?" He stopped, not daring to mention money, or looking after her. "Letty, what will you *do?* You say yourself you don't want to see your aunt again. Plant's dead and I shall be far away. You'll be all alone."

"I shall manage," she said. "I managed before. I shan't go back to her and I shan't come with you, not if you stand there and ask me all night."

She turned and took some wavering steps towards the door. The lines of her body, the droop of her head, all spoke of abject misery. He looked at her and felt something of himself, not heart or mind, something more vital, something of his very essence, move out towards her. He stepped forward quickly and took her by the arm, and was, even then, sensuously aware of smallness, the brittle, stick-like fragility within the grasp of his big hand.

"Letty, at least you must remember, even when you hate me, that everything I did, every single thing, I did because I loved you. And I love you still. God help me, I'll love you as long as I live."

She wrenched her arm free and lifted her head and looked at him for an instant that seemed a timeless eternity. There was such hatred and contempt — and at the same time such despair in her eyes that he stepped backward, shrinking from her stare.

"Love!" she said. "You don't know what you're talking about."

CHAPTER
TWENTY-THREE

He had no recollection of leaving the cottage or moving along the path, but after some time, long time, short time, there he was leaning helplessly against the shaft of the gig, knowing that he could never muster strength enough to climb into the seat, and that it didn't matter. There was no point in going to London or anywhere, he was going to die, and he might as well die here as anywhere else.

Old Doctor Coppard climbed stiffly down.

"What's the matter, Humphrey? Are you worse?"

"I can't even . . . get into . . . the gig, sir," said Humphrey feebly.

"Nonsense, nonsense," said the old man briskly, wondering, within himself, for the thousandth time, at the interdependence of mind and body. Humphrey's collapse meant that the girl had refused to come.

"She wouldn't come," Humphrey said, still leaning against the shaft. "And I'm going to die. You'd better get home, sir, and not bother any more."

"Unless you want me to strain my heart, Humphrey, heaving your great hulk, make an effort and get in the gig." He set his hands under the boy's armpits and pushed. Humphrey clawed at the seat and the dashboard with hands that felt like putty and pulled, desperately. The putty hands held and he found himself leaning back in the seat, panting. Doctor Coppard climbed into his place and took Humphrey's wrist in his hand. He held it for a few seconds and then dropped it, and grunting twisted around to rummage in the space behind the seat.

"Here, take a swig of this," he said, unstoppering a flask. When Humphrey had drunk the old man returned the flask to its place, settled the rug and gathered the reins into one hand. But he did not rouse the horse, and with his other hand he stroked his chin, rhythmically, meditatively. Finally he let his hand fall, and had Humphrey been looking, and had there been light enough to see by, he would have seen that the profile thus bared was set in stubborn, rocky lines, and that the whole of the plump, genial, self-indulgent old face had taken on a grim recklessness.

"Look here, Humphrey ... unless you've the strongest feeling against it I'm going to chance my hand. I've lived in Bury for forty years, paid twenty shillings in the pound and looked on my word as my bond. At a pinch that should mean something ... And this is the pinch. You're not fit to go a-travelling. I'm going to take you home and put you to bed. I shall swear, and stick to it, that you were never out of my company last evening. Even if somebody says he saw you and recognised you I shall say it's a case of mistaken identity and challenge him to prove otherwise. I could kick myself for not taking that line at first. I got in a panic and thought of nothing but running away.

But you aren't fit to run, Humphrey. What d'you think of my scheme?"

"You're putting yourself in a dangerous position, sir. As for me . . . I don't care. I've made such a mess of things . . . I'd be better dead. But before you decide on any action you ought to know . . ."

He fumbled around in his reeling, tortured mind for the thing which Doctor Coppard should be told, found it, and produced it. It involved speaking a name, and he spoke it, with difficulty, as some people speak the names of the dead. "Letty said, sir, that Mrs. Rowan betrayed Driscoll. She may, very easily, have included me."

"Did she know that you worked with him?" It was the same calm dispassionate voice in which he had heard the old man ask, "Does it hurt when I press *here*? or *here*?"

"I don't know. I never told her. Driscoll may have done."

"We must risk that. It's her word against mine. And which d'you think would be more acceptable to any reasonable body? To any magistrate?"

"Who can tell? I'm sorry, sir, but I can't mind either way. I'd rather you didn't risk your reputation. I'm not worth it. I'm likely to die. And I've nothing to live for."

Doctor Coppard slapped the reins and spoke to the horse. The gig moved on, headed for Bury. The old man drove more slowly, trying to ease his passenger from the worst of the bumping now that time was no longer of paramount importance. As he drove he turned things over in his mind, now trying to find some profound, enlightening philosophic statement which would in the moment of its utterance restore Humphrey's broken spirit, and now imagining and meeting the dangers of the immediate future. The miraculous, healing utterance eluded him, and he was tactful enough to refrain from offering trite comfort. The plan for the future did emerge with some sort of clarity and firmness, and he would have liked to talk it over with Humphrey. But the tone of voice in which the boy had said, "I've nothing to live for," had by its utter desolation made discussion of precautions for his physical safety seem somehow insulting. So for a long time the old man drove in silence. It was still pitch dark, but there was a subtle change in the quality of the darkness. The night had turned and was moving now towards lightness. Here and there in isolated places there were signs of early rising, a light in a window, a cock crowing, a pump handle thumping.

Humphrey lay flaccidly, his good shoulder taking his weight against the back of the seat, his limbs locked in a weakness which was a positive, rhythmic, throbbing thing. Through his mind went stringing the whole story of himself and Letty, an endless circle which began with the scene in the inn yard at Newmarket and ended with Letty turning upon him with that bitter stare, that unforgettable cry; and then began again. Painstakingly, as he surveyed each scene, he sought for the place where he had been mistaken, blind, self-deluded, stupid. But until that final scene with Mrs. Rowan he could not find himself at fault. And even then the reckless threat had seemed necessary to ensure Letty's well-being. It seemed as though, at each turn, he had acted under some compulsion, as though it had been, since November, his destiny to fight Mrs. Rowan and to be defeated by her. And the simile of two dogs fighting over a bone which had occurred to him once before returned, completely justified. For they had utterly destroyed Letty between them. Mrs. Rowan had ruined her chances of ordinary happiness and he had held her back from the disreputable, but potentially happy life of the Coffee House. And they had been so busy fighting one another that they had never seen that Letty was not to be possessed by either of them; Letty had given herself and her allegiance to Plant, who had never noticed her existence except as a kind of joke. So now she was left without love and without a pattern of life. In fact she was like himself. They were one at last in bitter desolation.

Suddenly, as though continuing aloud a train of thought previously pursued in silence, Doctor Coppard spoke.

"I suppose we all think our own experiences unique in their unhappiness. I was in love once, if you can believe that. She had a riding accident and broke her wrist, and I set it and lost my heart. Her people were very high and mighty and set on her making a good match. And she was like putty, took the shape of whichever hand touched her last. They dragged her off to London and married her to a titled nincompoop. I never saw her again. I'd have committed suicide but I hadn't the temperament, I suppose. I knew enough about the ways and means to know that none of them was very nice. And I was so damned busy. Men kept coming back from the French war — the old French war I mean — with all sorts of bits and pieces needing attention. And women *kept* having babies. I used to wonder what was the good of helping a baby into the world where people could be as damned miserable as I was. But I used to go on doing it and looking sourly into the cradles. The proud parents must have hated me." He gave vent to a sound that was half a laugh, half a sigh, and the sound did more than his wordiness to evoke the vision of him as a young man, in old-fashioned clothes, going about his business with a sorrowful heart. "Odd, you know, Humphrey, if I had given up then, about a couple of hundred babies, a dozen stones and five or six cataracts would have gone to somebody else's credit. Now, when I die, I shall go to my God as a craftsman. I'll have a right to look Him in the face and say, 'Several things you botched I set right.' Whereas if I'd died of love I'd have had to say, 'One of your works was so perfect that the mere sight of it killed me.' I suppose you think I'm being blasphemous."

Humphrey roused himself. "I think you're trying to cheer me up, sir. But there is no comparison between the cases. I am the one who has botched everything. And I know it."

"You've never botched a job of work, Humphrey. And heartless as it may sound at this minute, it's what we do with our hands and our heads that matter in this world. Ah, well, here's the turnpike, thank God. I'm anxious to have you home and in bed." He shook the

278

reins and called to the horse. "You're running a slight fever, you know, my boy. You must take that into account when you consider your feelings. Things'll look better in twenty-four hours."

As though a slight drop in one's temperature could erase the memory of Letty's face, alter one aspect of the story which began in the inn yard at Newmarket and pursued its doomed inevitable way to its bitter end.

The tired horse seemed to sense that the journey was ending, and took heart as they neared the town. They rattled along the Westgate at a brisk pace. Nevertheless the sky ahead of them was touched by the faintest, almost imperceptible lifting of darkness as they turned on to Abbey Hill and made for the stable yard.

"Now I want you to leave everything to me," said Doctor Coppard. "You're sick, you're exhausted. Just relax and leave it to me. Only remember, we've been together the whole time. That's all you need bother about."

He climbed down, even more stiffly, and helped Humphrey to alight.

"Sit on the block, Humphrey. I'll just let the horse in." He unhitched the gig and opened the stable door. "There now. D'you think you can manage, leaning on me? It isn't far."

Humphrey remembered that he had walked up the cottage path and stood through some part of that interview, and made his way out to the gig again, and conscience spurred him to effort.

"You needn't hold me, sir. Let me take your arm. That'll do."

A few steps brought them to within view of the back of the house, and Humphrey felt the old man's arm stiffen. He raised his eyes and saw that there was candlelight behind the kitchen window.

"Mrs. Gamble's about. That might mean that something is afoot," said Doctor Coppard quietly. "Make the best of yourself. Humphrey. And bear in mind that it is not entirely your affair. You may not care what happens. But I care. Keep your mouth shut and do exactly as I tell you."

Humphrey said, "All right, sir," in a voice that seemed to come from very far away, and they stumbled on to the kitchen door where Mrs. Gamble met them.

"There's a man here, sir. He came hours ago and asked for Doctor Shadbolt and then for you. He would wait, and he seemed a decent sort of person, so I put him in the surgery. But I thought it best to stay up myself."

She had begun making her report before it dawned upon her sleepy mind that Doctor Shadbolt should at this moment be in Cambridge, and as she was speaking to her master her eyes were fixed upon his assistant with amazement and curiosity. But as soon as her pre-arranged speech ended Doctor Coppard forestalled her comment and said in a loud, jovial voice:

"I had to get Doctor Shadbolt home to help me. And now he's worn out. Come on, Humphrey, no nonsense. Up to bed you go. Doctor's orders."

"The bed is all ready, sir. And I've a pot of tea on the go if you care for a cup."

280

"I would. Bring me one along to the surgery. And plenty of sugar, mind."

They had moved to the foot of the stairs, and were both aware that just beyond them the surgery door was open and that a man's figure was standing square in the aperture. Doctor Coppard's hand closed upon Humphrey's arm and then fell away as the man stepped out and said:

"Doctor Shadbolt. Doctor Coppard," in a tone which was not quite a question and not quite a statement of recognition.

The old man moved so that he interposed his bulk between the man and Humphrey, who had obediently begun to mount the stairs.

"Yes, yes," he said with testy good humour, "I'll attend to you in just one moment. I know you've been waiting, but these things will happen. Let me hang up my coat, will you?"

"It was Doctor Shadbolt I wanted to see," the man said, coming forward so that his whole body came into collision with that of Doctor Coppard who, having started Humphrey up the stairs with a gentle push, was going towards the row of pegs on the wall at the back of the stairs. The old man seemed to lose his balance, side-stepped without nimbleness, caught at the man's shoulder, and then at the newel-post of the stairs, and there, recovering himself, said very firmly, "I can't have him bothered at this moment. He's dead on his feet. He's ridden all the way from Cambridge at my special request and worked like a black most of the night. It's no good," he said, looking up the stairs at Humphrey's retreating back, "I'm still your master, my boy, and when I send you to bed, you go! Now sir, Doctor Shadbolt is definitely off duty for twelve hours, but I'm ready to attend you. But I'll sit down, with your permission, and take a cup of tea while you tell me all about it. I've been on my feet most of the night, too."

"I don't want to trouble you, sir," said the man with a stony intransigence in his voice. "My business concerns Doctor Shadbolt."

"Then it must wait. I'm sorry. He's exhausted and he's had a nasty knock on the head. He's gone to bed by my orders — you saw him yourself. If you want a doctor I'm afraid you'll have to make out with me. I'm considered quite competent, you know." He glanced at the man with dry humour, and then, seeing that he was about to speak, forestalled him. "Only you must wait while I drink this tea. Thank you, Mrs. Gamble. You remembered the sugar? Now sir, if you'll tell me your business while I sip this I'll be ready by the time you've finished." He reached out and took from the stand under the clothes pegs the thick gold-headed stick without which he never left the house, and which was so much a part of his personal equipment that anyone knowing him better would have realised that for him to go out without it implied a state of haste and urgency unprecedented in forty years of practice. With the stick in one hand and the cup of steaming black tea in the other, he turned towards the surgery door.

The man stood in his path. He was short and stockily built, his thickness emphasised by the heavy riding coat he was wearing. He had an air of confidence and authority, but it was overlaid at this moment by a kind of exasperated indecision. He was a sensible and experienced man, and he had sensed from the first a trace of something almost fantastic in the story which had brought him here. The old servant's stubborn and circumstantial evidence of young Doctor Shadbolt being in Cambridge and not expected back until tomorrow, and his long wait in the cold, ordinary little surgery had quickened his sense of fantasy; and then the young man's arrival and his deathlike appearance had quenched it and he had thought, Ah . . . something in it after all! And now here he was faced by this ponderous, calm-spoken, slow-moving old man with a cup of tea in his hand and both sense and experience failed him. For a moment he entertained the idea of darting up the stairs and accosting his quarry. But if there had been a mistake such extreme measures would make him look very foolish. And he had seen the young man go upstairs, he had seen that he was in no state for running away; and the house was being watched. He could afford to take one chance. So after a final dubious glance up the stairs he stood aside and let the old doctor shuffle into the surgery and then followed him and took up a stand just within the door, which he left open. From there he could watch the stairs and the front door.

"Now," said Doctor Coppard, "what is your business? Pretty serious to bring you out at this time of night, I'm afraid."

The man brought his stare to bear upon the old man's face. His eyes were rather prominent and very blue.

"I wasn't in need of a doctor, sir. My name is Fulford, I'm Riding Officer for this area." He watched to see the effect of his words.

"Oh yes, Mr. Fulford. And if you didn't want a doctor, why did you come here?"

"I told you. I wanted to see Doctor Shadbolt. I am making some inquiries concerning an affair . . ." Once again the whole thing seemed fantastic. "Look here, sir, I think it would be better if I talked to Doctor Shadbolt himself. You are in no way concerned with this matter. I'd rather you kept out of it entirely."

"As you wish, of course. But as I explained, it means waiting. You see, I feel very much responsible for my apprentice. I got him back in a hurry to help me with an emergency operation on a most difficult patient. Operating isn't easy, you know, even when you have the patient's co-operation. This poor woman is mentally afflicted, and I can tell you that Humphrey had a very gruelling time. I don't know whether you noticed his head. At one point she hammered him with the heel of her shoe. She also dug a scalpel into his shoulder. I blame myself for that. I didn't expect her to be active so soon, and I hadn't got all my tools out of the way. But the crack on the head concerns me most, he may have a mild concussion . . . so you see, if there's anything I can do to save him being bothered, it's my duty as well as my pleasure to do it." He drained off the last of the tea and set the cup aside.

Mr. Fulford did not speak for a moment. Then he said in a slow, cautious way, "I am to understand, sir, that you and Doctor Shadbolt were performing this operation together during the night just ending . . . the whole night?"

"Not operating. We're not so slow and clumsy as all that! But we've been there since about . . . about eight o'clock. She lives alone, you see, and is really more than a little crazy. We got her ready and then we fought her to a standstill as you might say. Then we performed and she perked up and stabbed Humphrey, and I dealt with that — a nasty little cut. And then we made her comfortable. Humphrey got a fire and made some gruel and we waited until she fell asleep, which with her customary refractoriness she refused to do until just a little while ago."

"And you were there, sir, with Doctor Shadbolt for the whole of that time? From just after eight until a little while ago."

"That is so." He leaned forward, resting his hands on his stick, and said humorously, "Now, may I ask you a question for a change? What is the point in all this catechism? Does it really matter to you, Mr. Fulford, how Doctor Shadbolt and I spend our time."

"It matters very much, sir. At least, I'm not concerned with you. Only in so far . . . Just tell me this. Would you take your oath that Doctor Shadbolt was never out of your sight between say, ten o'clock and eleven?"

"Out of sight, but within hearing. He fetched the stuff for the fire and, as I said, he made the gruel. Look,

I'm trying to keep my temper, but I've had a devilish tiring night on top of a heavy day. I can't make head or tail of what you want or why you're here. Will you be more explicit."

"I'll be very explicit. Tonight three of my men made a raid on a farm where liquor, tobacco and tea, which had not been through the customs, smuggled stuff, was being unloaded. The owner of the premises was killed, and one of my men was killed by the man who was assisting with the unloading. Doctor Coppard, this isn't an easy or pleasant thing to say, but from a source which I have always found reliable I have the information that since the New Year your assistant, Humphrey Shadbolt, has been an active partner in this smuggling business. Now perhaps you see why evidence as to his movements tonight is of the greatest importance to me. And perhaps, sir, in view of the gravity of the charge you would like to withdraw your statement."

"I should like you to moderate your language, Mr. Fulford. What do you imply by 'the gravity of the charge'? What charge? And what do you mean by suggesting that I should withdraw my statement? Are you insinuating that what I have been telling you for the last ten minutes is untrue?" He had every appearance of a reasonable man in whom the sense of insult wars with a sense of justice. Striving for calmness, he said, "I agree that you may have a serious charge to bring against somebody. I admit that you have your duty to perform. But you may not force your way into my house and lay your charges against Doctor Shadbolt, or call me a liar, with impunity. I'm not in the habit of having my word doubted, Mr. Fulford, and if I say that Humphrey and I have been together with Mrs. Naylor since eight o'clock tonight, I expect you to believe me. Well, do you or don't you?"

The Riding Officer stood his ground. "I am not doubting your personal integrity, sir. I am pursuing a difficult and unpleasant inquiry. It would have been easier if I could have interviewed Doctor Shadbolt himself. You forbade that, so please bear with me for a moment more. I have to consider the possibility of my information having been in a measure accurate. You say that Doctor Shadbolt has been in your company the whole evening. But may he, at other times, have aided and abetted this man, Driscoll?"

"The question is hardly *may* he: it's *could* he? I imagine that to engage in this lurid trade one has to be present in person. And I can assure you that except when called to a patient, or for an hour in that Coffee House over the road — and that's within call — the boy has never been out of this house on any evening during the past three years. He's studying hard, and I admit that I like him to be here in the evening. Perhaps I'm selfish, but I'm growing old and if anything arises that is within his scope I prefer not to go out once I'm settled down."

"But he does go to the Coffee House?"

"Yes — but not for long enough to engage in any nefarious undertakings under cover of that absence. Unfortunately he has taken a fancy to one of the girls there — a niece of Mrs. Rowan's, I believe. I say unfortunately, because he's a decent boy with no ideas outside matrimony, if you understand me; and that, just for once, finds me and Mrs. Rowan on the same side of the fence. *I* think he's too young for marriage, and Mrs. Rowan has other plans for the girl. I've tried to talk sense to him, and Mrs. Rowan has threatened him with everything short of murder if he doesn't leave the girl alone — but you know what young men are. Keep away he cannot. But all this is beside the point, which is that I keep my assistant pretty well under supervision."

"It may not be irrelevant. Mrs. Rowan has threatened him, you say. In what terms?"

"Oh, vague, spiteful, female rubbish. That he'd regret interfering in her business. A significant term that — *business* — where a young girl is concerned. I daresay she looks on him with suspicion; he lives with me and Mrs. Rowan knows how I regard her. I was one of those who tried to close her establishment."

"So she wouldn't refrain from injuring your assistant for fear of the reflection upon you."

"Not she. She'd injure us both and take joy in the process." He lifted his stick and brought it down with a thump. "Bless my soul, you're not going to tell me that all this coil is of Mrs. Rowan's making. You don't mean to say, my good fellow, that you've come here with this infamous suggestion on account of information you received from that bawd mistress. What? I'm right. You did! And you've been standing there straining your eyes and ears while you weighed that woman's word against mine. I'll be damned. Tell me . . . how long have you ridden this area, Mr. Fulford?"

288

"Four months. Yes, I know what you're about to say. But I have been in the service for eighteen years, sir; and of every three arrests I have made, two have resulted from information laid by persons of, shall we say, dubious reputation. Driscoll would have been arrested tonight if he hadn't been killed. And whoever was helping him did kill one of my men and did get away . . ."

Doctor Coppard rose slowly and stiffly to his feet and stood leaning on his stick. They faced one another, each aware of his own strength and his own weakness. The old doctor knew that his word carried weight, but that his case was founded upon a lie; the Riding Officer suspected that his charge was valid, but knew that it could be reduced to absurdity.

"Well," said Doctor Coppard, "it's your job to find out who the other man was. It was not Doctor Shadbolt. If you weren't obviously such a good public servant that your sense of duty outruns your sense of what is seemly, I should be very much annoyed by your coming here tonight and keeping me from my bed with such a fandangle of nonsense. I'll give you one word of warning, though. If I hear any more about it I shall take action. Once a rumour like this starts it's difficult to say where it will stop. So if you're the sensible fellow I take you for you'll drop a hint to your informant that if I hear so much as a whisper of this again I'll make the town too hot to hold her. And you — in that case, would be the laughing stock of Suffolk. Because," he brought out the words with slow deliberation, "Doctor

Shadbolt is a clever young man, but even he can't be in two places at once."

The Riding Officer stood and absorbed the full significance of that too-obvious statement. It announced that the old man would fight. And already, in his ponderous, rambling, apparently purposeless way he had outlined his plan of campaign. Mrs. Rowan bore both him and his apprentice a grudge — that accounted for her story; the young man had been beaten over the head and stabbed with a scalpel — that accounted for marks left on him by the excise men.

Oddly enough, though he had entered the house with the feeling that the charge he was bringing was far-fetched and fantastic, now, as he prepared to take his leave, he was convinced of its validity. Why should that be? He answered the question himself in a sudden flash of insight. One believed what one wanted to believe, given evidence equally balanced. And if he carried the thing further and made it public people would believe what they wanted to believe; and which would it be, Doctor Coppard or Mrs. Rowan?

"No," he said thoughtfully, "nobody can be in two places at once. And I believe the Bible says something about no man serving two masters. May I say that your apprentice is very fortunate in his master, sir?"

The old man's face gave no sign of understanding. "I see no reason for saying that, Mr. Fulford. Humphrey has served me faithfully for almost four years. In return I have taught him his trade. But I shall reap the benefit of that. I am looking forward to an easy old age while he takes my place in the community."

That was another artlessly significant sentence. It told what the old man had at stake. The Riding Officer buttoned his coat and reached for his hat. Doctor Coppard, leaning heavily upon his stick, moved into the hall, politely escorting his visitor to the front door, but keeping, unostentatiously, between him and the stairs. Near their foot the man did halt, undecided, frustrated again.

"I'd feel far more satisfied that I'd done my duty thoroughly if I had seen Doctor Shadbolt himself."

"If you care to come back, say at six o'clock this evening, you may do that. I'd like you to feel satisfied. But I can't put your feelings before the risk of your worrying him if he has concussion. By six o'clock I shall know. What you hope to find out from him I really can't see — but of course you must do your duty . . ."

Pointless to insist. Their tale — if it was a tale, and upon that point he would never be utterly sure — had obviously been well prepared beforehand, every detail dovetailed. So, without knowing that he had only to dash up the stairs and burst into Humphrey's room with the question — where were you last evening between ten and eleven o'clock? — to obtain at least a justification for his visit, the Riding Officer went on to the door. Doctor Coppard opened it upon the grey dawn. It was light enough to show a bulky figure waiting a few yards from the steps, and another at the corner.

"Early risers," said the old man cheerfully. "Well, the mornings are getting lighter. I always think of February as the turn of the year. Goodnight, Mr. Fulford, or rather — good morning."

He must have known who they were and why they were there, thought the Riding Officer with unwilling respect. There'd be no shaking him. One would try, of course; look up this Mrs. Naylor and hear what she had to say; keep a sharp ear and eye for anything which might lead to more definite proof of Shadbolt's complicity. But one would know that at the end one would come face to face with the old man's calm and stubborn assertion that nobody could be in two places at once. He soothed himself with the thought that Driscoll was dead and one more distributing centre closed; in its main object their raid had succeeded.

CHAPTER
TWENTY-FOUR

Humphrey had tumbled, fully clothed, on to his bed, pulled the coverlet over him and willed himself to die. For a few minutes he lay in a state of complete exhaustion with nothing between him and a blissful unconsciousness save the recurring vision of Letty's face and the sound of her voice saying cruel, unforgettable things out of her own misery. For a few minutes it seemed as though nothing but death could ever put an end to his torturing thoughts, and at the same time as though only those thoughts were keeping him alive. If he could once forget Letty and the mess he had made of everything he would float, sink, melt away into nothingness.

Five, ten minutes passed, and although he was not aware of it, the restorative effect of lying prone on a good hard bed, with the warmth of covers soothing his shivering body, began to make itself felt. The blind, mindless determination of the flesh to mend itself, to cling to life, set to work within him. All at once the recurring visions of Letty's face became interspersed by those of the two men in the surgery below him. At first he encouraged thoughts and speculations about that interview as a welcome relief from his misery; but as the moments passed an active, almost an anxious, interest, began to stir. The old man, he thought, would bluff bravely, but the stocky fellow must have some evidence — Mrs. Rowan's evidence — or he would not be here, and when it became clear that to pursue his course meant to involve himself in perjury, Doctor Coppard would give in. They'd come up and take him away and hang him.

He saw that he was trapped. He should never have let himself be brought back here. It seemed quite astonishing now to think that he had stumbled out of that cottage in such a state of mind and body that he had let himself be brought back and handed over to the hangman. He didn't mind dying, life was finished for him, but he did not want to hang. He had said — and meant it — that he didn't care what happened to him, but that was quite untrue. He had let Doctor Coppard heave him into the gig and outline his plan, but at that moment he was sure that he was going to die. He'd been wounded and bled a lot, and had that dreadful interview with Letty, and he had felt like dying. But now he knew differently. His wounds were superficial, the only serious one had been expertly dealt with, and men didn't die because their hearts were broken. He knew that, now, when it was too late. If he'd been going to die he'd have died just outside that cottage door, or at Letty's feet when she said that she hated him. Fool, fool, fool that he was.

But he wasn't finished yet. He reminded himself of how he had crawled in the ditch and then staggered, bleeding, along the road. And he'd sat through that jolting journey and still had strength enough to get into the cottage and talk and argue with Letty. He was no more ill now than he was when he was planning to take her to London. And if he lay here now, like a clubbed bullock awaiting the butcher's knife, and let them take him away and hang him, it would be because he loved a girl who preferred Plant Driscoll. A fine end . . .

He began to struggle up from the bed. The body, wise with its own wisdom, unwilling yet to share the mind's anxiety, protested, clinging with invisible tentacles to the healing bed, protesting with pain as its grip was broken, but he got to his feet and reached the door.

As he did so he heard the voices in the hall and, without waiting to try to hear what they were saying, judged that the way by the stairs was closed, and staggered back into his room and went to the window. The drop, he realised immediately, was suicidal and there was no time to improvise a rope. But he wouldn't be taken like a rat in a trap. He looked round wildly for some weapon, heavy and lethal enough to do damage even when lifted and directed by a hand as moist and limp and quivering as his. The only likely thing that offered itself was the stout wooden boot-tree, one of a pair laid away in the corner when he put on his best boots to go to Cambridge, aeons ago. He stooped for it, turned dizzy, and rose, clutching the wall. There was the sound of feet on the stairs. He took up his stand behind the door. He'd bring the boot-tree down with all his force on the back of the fellow's head as he entered; then he'd run down-stairs and out by the back. He got ready.

Fortunately for himself Doctor Coppard halted on the threshold and asked softly, "Humphrey, are you asleep?" Then he saw the empty bed and came quickly into the room and looked round and saw Humphrey white-faced and wild-eyed behind the door with the boot-tree in his hand.

"It's all right," he said placidly. "He's gone. You get back to bed." He took the boot-tree and laid it on a chair. "I'm glad he didn't insist on coming up, Humphrey. I take it you intended to clout his head. Then we should have been in a mess!"

"I didn't think you'd get rid of him, sir. And I couldn't just let myself be taken. I don't want to be hanged," said Humphrey, feeling foolish, and relieved, and perilously near hysterical tears and laughter.

"A very healthy symptom," said the old man. "Come on. You lie down and I'll tell you all about it. I'll help you out of your clothes presently, but first I'll sit down and tell you. I'm getting a bit old for this play-acting. But I fooled him." He had decided on the way upstairs that that was the best thing to say to Humphrey. He knew better. He was shrewd enough to know that the man had not been fooled; out of it all he had only thoroughly believed one thing, but that was enough. It would deter him from taking any definite steps until he had something more than Mrs. Rowan's word to go upon; and that might be hard to find. And by the time he had found it — or failed to find it — he would be beginning to believe the whole of Doctor Coppard's story, because men believed what they wanted to believe, and when Mr. Fulford found that he couldn't bring a case he would want to believe that there wasn't a case to bring. In fact, thought the old man, beginning his account of the conversation, the day had been won at the moment when he had pushed himself between the Riding Officer and Humphrey. Accosted then Humphrey would have neither the knowledge, nor the wit, nor the will to tell a good lie. Accosted then Humphrey would have said, "My life is over, take me away and hang me," or words to that effect. Time was wonderful. Such a small dose of it had brought the boy to the realisation that he didn't want to hang, brought him to the point where he was prepared to resist violently. Doctor Coppard had seen some miraculous recoveries, but he had never seen a prettier sight than Humphrey, behind the door, armed with a boot-tree. For there had been a moment, after he had helped Humphrey into the gig, when he had thought — he's done for, a bullet and a bitch have finished off the best boy I ever knew.

He ended his account of the interview. "Now all you have to do is to get well. I'll mix you a draught and a good sleep will do the rest. I think I shall nip along to Mrs. Naylor's now and just whip that damn great cyst off her neck. It's very unsightly. And she'll never know whether you helped or not, or whether it happened at Christmas or Easter. And then if that nosey-parker starts prying about there'll be something for him to see. Perhaps after all we've been coddling her up to good purpose."

His tired old eyes twinkled and he looked at Humphrey with such a conspiratorial and at the same time pleading air, come along, smile at me, I've done my best for you, let's see a cheerful face, that Humphrey was obliged to smile.

"You've been wonderful, sir. All along. I can't tell you . . ."

"Don't try," said the old man hastily. "And I don't want you to feel that you've got to go about for the rest of your days with a yoke of gratitude on your neck, Humphrey. I tell you frankly I did what I did deliberately, from the most selfish motives. I'm an old man, my useful time is nearly over. You're young and you're going to be a good doctor. By Midsummer you'll be able to take my place. That's been in my mind all along, you know. And I'm a very pig-headed chap. I should have hated a little thing like this to upset all my plans."

"I promise you, sir . . ."

"And if I may say so," Doctor Coppard interrupted again, "if I may just say one thing — don't fret about the girl. That sort can always look out for themselves, really, you know."

Kindly meant, of course.

"I suppose so. I'll try not to, sir."

But when at last he was alone, undressed and at ease between the smooth sheets, Letty made one more of her attempts to reclaim him. Once more he went through it all again; Letty on the coach; Letty in the blue dress; Letty slipping her hand into his and calling

298

him by his name for the first time; Letty crying that his pestering had ruined her life; Letty saying that he did not know the meaning of love.

But somewhere a subtle adjustment had been made. For some reason he no longer felt responsible for her, and instead of wondering what more he could have done, or how differently he might have done it, he thought that he had done what he could and that his failure was, finally, Letty's own.

So he mustn't go on destroying himself over Letty. He must get back to work and repay what he owed to two people whose claim on him Letty had usurped and then thrown aside — his mother and the old man. Now, before he went to sleep, he must get back to the moment when the coach stopped at Newmarket, and he must regard everything that had happened since as a brief, unimportant episode. As though, travelling, he had taken the wrong turning and wandered for a time in a strange country, full of danger and darkness, and then found himself, by the mercy of Providence, back on the right road again.

He fell asleep.

As he did so a woman, going to dip water from the pond on Depden Green, threw down her bucket and screamed. And men came and took up Letty's body, dead and dripping, and wondered how long it would be before people fancied drinking from that pond again.

And it was spring on Olympus, but the Lady Venus wore a face of discontent. Jupiter said, "How now? Did I not send you a calf?" "There were two," she said, "and the one that escaped was the better."

"Ah yes," said Jupiter, "but remember, when wise men are old they become as gods and often defeat us. Do you not remember that on a certain occasion the God of the Jews, the one they called Jehovah, was ready to receive just such an oblation and was put off with a ram from a thicket? There was an old man concerned in that story too!"

Also available in ISIS Large Print:

Gad's Hall

Norah Lofts

There were no screams in the night, no objects flying through the air, no murderous, disembodied voices — but Gad's Hall was haunted just the same.

For the Spender family, the ancient, beautifully kept house had seemed a godsend, an incredible bargain, almost a gift from its owner — a kindly man who merely wanted someone to protect the family homestead, to make Gad's come alive again.

And it did. Soon a strong-willed, sensible woman would be overtaken by irrational feelings she could not control, all because of the unspeakable secret kept by the women who had lived at Gad's Hall more than a century ago . . .

Rich in historical detail, suspense and romance, Gad's Hall subtly entices us into the realm of the supernatural with the tale of a house forever doomed by a young girl's powerful obsession.

ISBN 978-0-7531-7942-0 (hb)
ISBN 978-0-7531-7943-7 (pb)

Out of this Nettle

Norah Lofts

And when the clans were broken — massacred in a brutal revenge at Culloden Field — Colin Lowrie was forced to take flight on a journey half-way round the world. A journey to a barbaric slave plantation in the West Indies, then on to New Orleans and a life of lust and debauchery — and to a strange eerie love affair with an eccentric heiress . . .

And always, wherever destiny or chance took the young Scottish rebel, he carried with him the dream of Braidlowrie — Braidlowrie, the home of the Lowries — the home from which he was forever exiled . . .

ISBN 978-0-7531-7940-6 (hb)
ISBN 978-0-7531-7941-3 (pb)

Charlotte

Norah Lofts

When young John Vincent died, the outward respectability of the Cornwall household was undermined. Strangers pried, asked too many questions and pointed accusing fingers at Charlotte — herself eager to escape from the oppressive atmosphere of her father's home.

She fled deep into the countryside and there taught at a school run by the untrusting and untrustworthy Mrs Armitage, who was prepared to keep quiet about Charlotte's past — but only up to a point. When the events come to be recreated, some questions naturally arise. Had Charlotte been responsible for the death of the little pupil she loved? And has that crime been repeated?

In darker moments, even Charlotte herself cannot be sure.

ISBN 978-0-7531-7880-5 (hb)
ISBN 978-0-7531-7881-2 (pb)

Peter West

D. E. Stevenson

Beth Kerr is the daughter of the boatman in the small village of Kintoul. Her mother died at an early age, after an unhappy marriage that caused her family to cast her aside. As the years pass, Beth grows into a beautiful young woman, watched over by the quiet Peter West. The owner of Kintoul House, Peter is a lonely man with a weak heart and few family members and friends. They both struggle with their feelings for one another, before being forced to embark on marriages decided upon by their families. But will their lives follow the paths set for them, or will they find their own way?

ISBN 978-0-7531-7824-9 (hb)
ISBN 978-0-7531-7825-6 (pb)

Hester Roon

Norah Lofts

The Fleece Inn stood where the three roads joined — the roads to London, to Norwich and to the sea. Its trade was prosperous, its hospitality famous and the host was jolly and generous.

To his servants he was cruel and menacing, and to Ellie Roon, the most menial servant at the Fleece, he was a figure of terror. Ellie was used to being bullied, but when her illegitimate daughter was born — in a rat-ridden attic of the Fleece — she decided that Hester must have a different kind of life.

And so, Hester Roon began her eventful progress in the harsh world of 18th century England. After fleeing from the inn, and the attentions of the owner, she became involved in the London underworld. From there she found herself in a world far beyond her imaginings . . .

ISBN 978-0-7531-7734-1 (hb)
ISBN 978-0-7531-7735-8 (pb)

ISIS publish a wide range of books in large print, from fiction to biography. Any suggestions for books you would like to see in large print or audio are always welcome. Please send to the Editorial Department at:

ISIS Publishing Limited
7 Centremead
Osney Mead
Oxford OX2 0ES

A full list of titles is available free of charge from:

Ulverscroft Large Print Books Limited

(UK)
The Green
Bradgate Road, Anstey
Leicester LE7 7FU
Tel: (0116) 236 4325

(Australia)
P.O. Box 314
St Leonards
NSW 1590
Tel: (02) 9436 2622

(USA)
P.O. Box 1230
West Seneca
N.Y. 14224-1230
Tel: (716) 674 4270

(Canada)
P.O. Box 80038
Burlington
Ontario L7L 6B1
Tel: (905) 637 8734

(New Zealand)
P.O. Box 456
Feilding
Tel: (06) 323 6828

Details of **ISIS** complete and unabridged audio books are also available from these offices. Alternatively, contact your local library for details of their collection of **ISIS** large print and unabridged audio books.